KILLER, PAPER, CUT

BOOK #9 IN THE KIKI LOWENSTEIN MYSTERY SERIES

JOANNA CAMPBELL SLAN

spot on publishing

Joanna Campbell Sean **Spot On Publishing** 9307 SE Olympus Street

Hobe Sound FL 33455 / USA http://www.SpotOnPublishing.org
http://www.JoannaSlan.com

Zentangle® — The Zentangle® Method is an easy-to-learn, relaxing, and fun way to create beautiful images by drawing structured patterns. It was created by Rick Roberts and Maria Thomas. "Zentangle" is a registered trademark of Zentangle, Inc. Learn more at zentangle.com.

Revised 01/19/2021

Covers: http://www.WickedSmartDesigns.com

Killer, Paper, Cut: Book #9 in the Kiki Lowenstein Mystery Series by Joanna Campbell Slan. – 2nd ed.

CONTENTS

1

A Friday evening, ten days before Halloween... The Old Social Hall, St. Louis, Missouri

*B*lood spurted all over my hands and plopped onto my Keds.

I've seen some pretty clumsy crafters in my day, but Mary Martha Delaney took the cake and iced it, too. She had managed to cut through the paper, her mat, the table, and her palm—and we were only five minutes into our project.

Worse yet, the silly thing watched the blood run down her arm before smearing it on her blouse. At first glance, Mary Martha looked like a kindergartener covered in poster paint. There was red stuff on her sleeve, wiped across her bosoms, and dripping on her white stretch pants.

Did I mention the sight of blood makes me woozy?

It does. Especially now that I'm seven months pregnant.

But I was the C.I.C.C. or Crafter In Charge of the Crop, "crop" being the accepted term for a scrapbooking party.

My name's Kiki Lowenstein, and I'm a scrapbooker. I was also hostess of this little soiree because I own Time in a Bottle, the scrapbook and craft store that sponsored this event, a fundraiser that we'd named the "Halloween Crafting Spook-tacular."

In my private life, I'm the mother of Anya, who is thirteen going on thirty, and five-year-old Erik. Rounding out our household is my sweetheart and the father of my baby, Detective Chad Detweiler, and Bronwyn Macavity, otherwise known as "Brawny," our live-in nanny.

Yep, a lot of people depend on me. I'd promised my family that I could handle this crop, even though I was so tired that passing out sounded, sort of, heavenly. Like a brief unscheduled nap. But I couldn't relinquish my responsibilities that easily. Nope, I'm too much of a trooper.

While I struggled to keep from fainting, Mary Martha's friend Dolores Peabody reached over and pressed a tissue into Mary Martha's cut. That proved largely ineffective. In fact, it increased the flow. Now Dolores sported a bright red smear of blood across the front of her tee-shirt. Mary Martha turned and managed to wipe blood on me, explaining, "Your belly was in the way."

The sour look she cast at my tummy told me that she knew I wasn't married. I'd run into that response before, so I wasn't unprepared. Irked yes, but not totally taken off guard.

"Maybe this will help." Patricia Wojozynski was another friend of Mary Martha's. Patricia pressed her cotton hanky into Mary Martha's hand. But Patricia underestimated the amount of blood we were dealing with. Soon she too was wiping blood all over her own clothes.

Time to pull up my big girl maternity panties and take control.

"Mary Martha, we need to get you to the emergency room." I

reached down to put steady pressure on the wound. My free hand cupped her elbow and urged her to stand. This produced no result because Mary Martha was big enough to be both a Mary and a Martha.

"Heavens no. Thank the good Lord, it's just a scratch. I'll offer it up to Jesus."

Something told me he'd rather have flowers on the altar, but who am I to judge?

"Gee, I don't know. This is bleeding pretty good." The smell of copper in the air encouraged me to heave.

"Pretty well," said Clancy, from her spot ten feet away. Nothing made her madder than misuse of English grammar. Clancy was conducting this portion of our event. Although she's new to crafting, she's learning fast.

"Uh, pretty well," I repeated after my friend. "Clancy, we've got a problem here."

"Good luck," she said, without turning a hair of her perfectly shaped auburn bob. "Let's continue with our project. The next step is to rub your chalk applicator across the brown chalk and use it to edge your pumpkin."

Edge their pumpkins, my left foot. Clancy was purposely ignoring my crisis. Given a taste of teaching cardmaking, Clancy had become quite the expert. She loved seeing novice stampers turn out brilliant results. I have to admit that I'm impressed by her newfound ability. Funny how when a person finds her crafting niche, she can really shine—and that's exactly what Clancy has done.

"Laurel? Can you help Kiki?" Clancy called out to our other co-worker.

"I'm on it." Laurel Wilkins trotted over. In one hand was the first aid kit we brought to every crop. But she was stopped in her progress because of all the junk Mary Martha and friend had spread all over the floor.

"I think Kiki is making this worse!" said Mary Martha.

Nice. Really nice. I fought the urge to give Mary Martha a kick in the shins. Suffice it to say, I haven't been in a good mood lately.

"Oh, my," said Laurel. "Does it hurt much, Mary Martha? Are you okay? You poor baby. How about if we go to the ladies room and see how much of this we can get wiped off? Then I'll dress the wound."

"It's God's plan that you'd be here to help, Laurel," said Mary Martha.

"Kiki, could you help her get over to me? I'll take it from there," said Laurel, tossing that fabulous mane of blond hair out of her face. As usual, she looked as if she'd just stepped from the pages of a Boston Proper catalog. I, on the other hand, looked as if I'd swallowed a beach ball and forgotten to burp.

I could do this. I've done harder things. Taking Mary Martha's elbow, I walked her around the end of the table and pointed her toward Laurel.

My stomach heaved as I stood in the middle of a room full of crafters, soaked in Mary Martha's blood, surrounded by bloody pieces of facial tissue.

Why, oh, why had I agreed to hold an offsite crop?

Was it because the idea of helping people with diabetes had proved irresistible?

Or because I was a fool?

2

---

*I*t seemed like a good idea at the time.

If I wasn't so squeamish about getting a tattoo, I'd have that phrase inked to my upper thigh. When our friend Laurel Wilkins asked that we help her with a charity crop to raise money for the Diabetes Research Foundation, I said, "Sure! Easy-peasy. We R Crops."

I underestimated the amount of blood, sweat, and tears necessary to pull off a really stunning, over-the-top, mega-successful event. Actually two events worth of its title—the Halloween Crafting Spooktacular—to be held on two consecutive nights before the actual holiday.

So sue me.

When I bought Time in a Bottle, I thought I had a pretty good understanding of what the store's founder, Dodie Goldfader, did to make everything hunky-dory. Boy, was I ever wrong. There were tons of behind the scenes details that I never expected. Instead of a learning curve, I was climbing Mount Everest without benefit of a Sherpa. In a snow storm. While pregnant. In high heels.

Sigh.

In order for any off-site crop to be successful, there were a myriad moving parts that had to be coaxed into alignment. Since this crop was a fundraiser, every tiny detail had to be considered carefully so that we didn't waste a cent of the money coming in. The event had to make a splash, or people wouldn't shell out their hard-earned coins to come. The party had to appeal to scrapbookers, cardmarkers, and papercrafters of all ilk. The make-and-take portion—the actual crafts we'd be teaching our guests—had to be unique, simple to do, but cool enough that they wouldn't bore our regular store clientele to tears. The entertainment had to be exceptional, and the location had to offer a high "wow" factor. And last, but definitely not least, we had to have food. Really, really good food.

After considering all our options, I had concluded that there was really only one place worthy of such a big Halloween event, the Lemp Mansion on DeMenil Place. The mansion has a history of misery second to none.

In 1876, beer baron William J. Lemp and his wife Julia moved in, turning the thirty-three room house into a showplace. Lemp also decided to use his home as his office, taking advantage of a tunnel extending from the house to the caves under St. Louis. These naturally occurring storage shelters provided the refrigeration so vitally important to the brewing process.

Thanks to a series of shrewd business decisions made by William, the Falstaff brand expanded from a local brew to a label enjoyed around the world. Although the Lemps were thriving financially, unbeknownst to William and Julia, their fourth son, Frederick, had significant health problems. When Frederick died from complications, William shot himself in despair.

William J. Lemp, Jr. ("Billy") took over the family business. He and his wife Lillian, nicknamed the "Lavender Lady," moved into the Lemp Mansion. An acrimonious divorce followed. Billy was granted only visitation rights to see his son, William III. Two years later, Prohibition dealt a harsh blow to the business, and Billy was forced to sell first the trademark name and then the brewery.

Meanwhile, after suffering her own marital problems, Billy's sister shot herself. Two years later, later, Billy shot himself in his office in the mansion. And two decades later, the last Lemp to live in the mansion, Charles shot first his dog and then himself in the head.

In 1980, *Life* magazine named the Lemp Mansion one of the nine most haunted houses in the country. Supposedly, the Lavender Lady walks the halls at night. Both the Discovery and the Travel Channel have given the Lemp Mansion a nod for being terrifying.

Since I'm such a Chicken Little, I decided that we'd tour the Lemp Mansion while it was still daylight, walk one block over to The Old Social Hall, where we'd have our crop. While we worked on our projects and ate, we'd have an actress, Faye Edorra, entertain us with ghost stories. Faye billed herself as a "historical re-enactor," so I hired her to put on a one-woman show, complete with visuals that would give my attendees a reason to whip out their cameras and take copious photos. Faye had proposed dressing as the Lavender Lady herself. As a way of memorializing the tragedies that had occurred in the Lemp Mansion, Faye would wear ripped and bloodied clothes in shades of purple. While our guests worked on their projects, she would stroll around the room offering to stop and pose so our guests could have their pictures taken with her as "Lillian Lemp."

Once I had the big entertainment (the Lemp Mansion), the ongoing entertainment (Faye Edorra) and the actual crop location (The Old Social Hall) taken care of, I moved on to procuring our food.

You can't have a crop without food. It's simply not done. Although my friend Cara Mia Delgatto had moved to Florida, I still relied on her family restaurant for most of our catering needs. A young woman named Angela Orsini had recently been promoted to the post of catering manager. Angela and I had worked up a fun menu for the charity crop. The Old Social Hall had a kitchen, so we were good to go. There were two large meeting rooms. I figured that we would crop in Room A, and then adjourn to Room B to eat. That would keep food and drink away from paper products, preventing the predictable disasters caused by spillage.

When all those moving parts were in place, I turned my attention to our *raison d'être* (in high school French class, I learned that meant "reason for existence"), the crafting portions of our crop. Time in a Bottle is famous for having the coolest make-and-take events in town. Not only are our projects creative, we also strive to teach crafters a new skill. Yes, we've set the bar high, and pregnant or not, it's my job to keep jumping over it.

Except that right now, thanks to the fact I was wearing Mary Martha's blood all over me, I wasn't jumping. I was gathering bloody tissues and tossing them into the trash. I couldn't decide whether I wanted to puke or faint or both. I settled on heading for the bathroom so I could be prepared for either possibility. As I started through the doorway, who should pass me but Mary Martha!

While I'd turned pea green, she looked positively radiant.

3

——————

*a*fter being sick as a dog, I splashed my face with cold water, rinsed my mouth, and struggled to wipe blood off my maternity top. That proved futile, but it did help dilute the smell. Even though my lovely blouse was soaked through, I felt a lot better. I headed out of the bathroom, planning to find a quiet spot where I could sit down for a minute while my head cleared and my tummy settled. The only empty chair was over by Mary Martha and friends.

"The food will be ready when you are. Is this what you expected? Crowd-wise?" asked Angela, after I'd plopped down gracelessly into the chair. "With this much activity? Usually we plan for ten percent of the people not to show up, but every place here is filled!"

What had started as a modest idea to happen on one night only quickly became an overnight sensation. The media loved the irony. Here we were pairing a candy-centric holiday with a diabetes research fundraiser. Almost as soon as we sent out our email newsletter, I began fielding calls from the media. Two days after we announced the event, we had sold out all our seating at our Halloween Crafting Spook-tacular and had two-thirds as many names on a waiting list.

It wasn't just the media exposure that brought people in. Father Joe Riley was a friend of Laurel's and a former student of Clancy's. The young Episcopal priest had given our event his whole-hearted endorsement from the pulpit.

"There are those who think celebrating Halloween is wrong," he told his audience. "But that totally depends on your intent. Is it to glorify death? Then, it's wrong. Is it to appreciate life and honor the memories of the departed? That's worthy. And I can think of no effort more worthy than to support research into the cure of diabetes."

Once word got around that Father Joe endorsed our crop, the waiting list had grown dramatically. Since the crop was for an important cause, I called Angela and asked if there was any way we could schedule a second event for the following night.

"We'll make it happen. My stepson has diabetes, so I'm totally onboard," she said.

After she said yes, the other pieces fell into place. Here I was, fresh from hosing myself down in the bathroom, staring at thirty-five women and their scrapbook supplies. Make that thirty-four. Mary Martha was still being coddled by Laurel. I glanced at the accident-prone crafter and tried not to let the sight of her blood really register on my senses.

"Oh no," said Mary Martha, "I don't know how I'll ever finish my Halloween card."

"I can help you," Laurel said, glancing around for a place to sit.

"There's an extra chair right here," said Dolores. "Or there was. Kiki took it."

I can take a hint. For whatever reason, these ladies were not interested in my company. I stood up and whispered in Laurel's ear. "Keep an eye on Mary Martha. She's the most accident-prone crafter I've ever met."

I wobbled my way to the front of the room where Clancy was prepping for the next make-and-take session. When I couldn't find a chair, I sank down gratefully on the four-wheeled cart we'd used to haul supplies into the building.

The crafters all worked on their projects for another twenty minutes without incident. Clancy kept an eye on her watch and the door. A young man in black slacks and white shirt stepped into the room and rang a small copper bell. "Dinner is served!"

Laurel helped Mary Martha step over the mess she'd made. I heard the injured crafter say to Laurel, "You will sit next to us, won't you? I want you to see the pictures I took inside the Lemp Mansion."

"I'd be delighted," said my co-worker. What a study in contrasts they made. Laurel has an enviable figure, and she dresses with a hint of sexuality. Mary Martha, on the other hand, was wearing a bloody tee shirt paired with sweatpants. While Laurel is always perfectly groomed, Mary Martha needed to take a trip through a car wash in a convertible with the top down.

I told myself that I was being needlessly judgmental and unkind. And I was. But I was also really, really tired. Just a few nights ago we'd had a Halloween party in Illinois, at the farm owned by my sweetie Detective Chad Detweiler's parents. It had been a wonderful evening, but all the festivities had taken a lot out of me. Detweiler's parents and I were getting to know each other, but with a baby on the way, we did a lot of dancing around each other emotionally. I was drained from my visit.

After our guests took their seats in Room B, the room reserved for eating, Angela's catering staff served ghoulish treats —spooky punch with frozen "eyeballs" and appetizers with spiders on them. This was prime time for me and my co-workers to circulate with coupons designed to bring the crafters back to Time in a Bottle. While I passed out my coupons, Laurel hovered over the hapless crafter and her friends, making them feel welcome. Faye Edorra also made the rounds, stopping long enough for our croppers to have their pictures taken with the Lavender Lady. Mary Martha and friends asked Laurel to snap their photos.

I stayed as far away from Faye as possible because the fake blood smeared all over her looked all too real for me. Our crafters were absolutely thrilled at the chance to pose next to Faye in all her ghoulish gore. A couple of them even dipped their hands into her vat of fake blood.

Angela's dinner was well-received. Guests had their choice of mini barbequed chicken sandwiches or Asian lettuce wraps with spicy sweet potato fries. For vegetarians, there were Boca Burgers. Many croppers brought a favorite dish to share. The assortment of casseroles, salads, and veggies was astonishing. People ate and ate and ate, a sure sign of a good time. In between mouthfuls, they talked about what they'd seen at the Lemp Mansion. That, too, had been a big hit.

The wait staff bustled about clearing dishes. A few of the women lingered over coffee and tea, but most had headed to Room A where their crafting supplies were.

"Be right back," said Laurel, as she walked toward the ladies room carrying her purse.

"Remember, we'll be coming back to this room later for desserts and a presentation by the Lavender Lady. Now we'll move to Room A for our door prizes," said Clancy. It took a while to get everyone herded from one room to the other. But the promise of winning door prizes finally hurried people along. Clancy began drawing and calling out numbers we'd assigned to the crafters when they first arrived. The excitement grew as she called one number right after another. Since we were on a tight schedule, she made the announcements, while I distributed the gifts to an endless stream of squealing crafters.

I was handing Dolores Peabody a shopping bag done up with ribbons when I heard the scream.

4

*A*t first, our crafters and I thought it was a prank. I knew it came from the restroom, but I didn't race toward the sound. Instead, I stood and went over to the hallway.

"Call out the next number!" yelled a woman in the back. Clancy shrugged and said, "Probably a joke. Four-six-six-seven eight!"

"Woo-hoo!" yelled a cropper. "That's me!"

But as our guest trotted to the front of Room B a voice hollered, "Call 911. We need a cloth! Something to staunch the blood!"

I took off as fast as my burgeoning belly would allow. "I'll call 911," yelled Clancy from behind me.

Angela and I converged in the hallway. We hit the bathroom door together, throwing it open, and rounding the corner. There we skidded to a halt. One of our longtime crafters Bonnie Gossage was on her knees, pressing her hand to the side of Laurel's neck. With each pump of the girl's heart, a little blood spurted between the attorney's fingers. Another spot between Laurel's ribs was also leaking blood. More blood was flowing from her forearm.

"Angela," I said, "tell a server to stand outside with a white tablecloth? Clancy's already called 911."

"Will do," said the caterer. I dropped to my knees offering Bonnie my help.

"What happened?" I asked.

"Laurel was like this when I walked in," said Bonnie. She's an attorney by trade, a fine one, and I doubt she ever gets very rattled, but this had her quivering in shock. Me, too.

"I'll clamp my hands over yours," I said. That gave us a better purchase on Laurel's throat. However, Laurel started sliding along the tile. At the rate she was moving, she'd soon slip away from us.

"I'll keep my hands on the cut. You prop her up so she can breathe," Bonnie said. She was right; Laurel's airway would fill with blood, and she might drown if we didn't get her into a different position. Unfortunately, I would have to reach over my belly and twist to lift Laurel. Moving her wouldn't be easy.

"On the count of three," I said. "One, two, three."

My kneecaps ached as they pressed against the hard bathroom tiles. Blood squished between my fingers. The smell of Bonnie's strawberry scented hair mingled with the coppery tang of blood. If I'm ever asked to do a life review, those minutes will surely count as the longest of my life.

Amazing how many prayers you can cram into such a short space of time.

Either God was listening, or we were lucky. Incredibly so.

The emergency dispatcher located an ambulance around the corner from us. The emergency techs inside had just returned from a hospital run. The bus was empty.

The next few minutes were a blur. Later I'd realize that I'd gone into shock, but I didn't understand that at the time. Everything seemed to slow down, and I could only remember bits and pieces.

I can't say exactly how they managed to pry our fingers off, or to get the IV started on Laurel, but they did. I don't remember what we told our waiting crafters. I believe Clancy announced there'd been an accident. Sirens drowned out a lot of her words. I remember that my teeth started chattering. Clancy noticed and said something, although I can't recall what.

Uniformed first responders showed up on the heels of the EMTs. They cordoned off the bathroom. Radios crackled. The uniformed police called in detectives and reinforcements.

My hands started shaking. I opened my cell phone. Anyone with a police scanner would soon know there'd been a stabbing at a scrapbook crop in The Old Social Hall. I could think of at least one person who'd be terrified. I called my own law enforcement officer, Detective Chad Deweiler.

5

———

The same time as the crop...
A coffee shop in Webster Groves, MO

I "can't tell her," said Leighton Haversham as he stirred his decaf mocha latte. "Kiki's like a daughter to me, and since she's pregnant, I just can't bring myself to do it." Detective Chad Detweiler resisted the urge to jump up, grab Leighton, and shake him hard. If the older man didn't look so miserable, he might have. But Leighton couldn't meet Detweiler's eyes. He kept stirring that same cup of light brown liquid without actually drinking a drop of it.

By now, Leighton's latte was probably lukewarm. Detweiler had long since downed two cups of black coffee without any cream or milk.

"I'll tell her," said Detweiler, at long last. "Kiki's going to hate me."

"She won't be happy."

Leighton sighed. "I'm sure you'd like to wring my neck."

Coward, thought Detweiler.

Leighton had asked to meet in a public place because he was scared that Detweiler would throw a punch at him. Well, he was right. Detweiler couldn't believe what the man was asking of them. How could he do this to Kiki?

As if reading Detweiler's mind, Leighton mumbled, "I wouldn't do this except that Melissa, and I haven't spoken for years. It's all my fault. I wasn't a good father. I let her down. When her mother and I split..." and then he stopped. "Well, that's just an excuse, I guess. I wasn't there for the girl, and she's never asked anything of me, so I can't very well tell her no, can I? Not when she's begging me for a place to live? A place of her own? So she can start over?"

Detweiler could see his point. But then, he imagined the look on Kiki's face when he told her they'd have to move out of the tiny cottage in Webster Groves, and suddenly, he didn't feel so forgiving of Leighton. He jammed his fists in his jacket pocket so he didn't give in to the urge to slug him.

With a jolt, Detweiler realized how upset he was. And it surprised him. Usually, he took a "live and let live" attitude. He understood that people did the best they could. Sometimes they made good choices. Other times, not so much. Everyone was trying his or her best to get by.

His mother had taught him compassion, explaining that others had their own problems. His father had taught him patience, reminding Detweiler to respect the rhythms of other people.

So he was trying to empathize with Leighton, really he was, but somehow he just couldn't!

Watching Kiki's belly grow had changed everything for him. It had kindled a sense of terror. All of his protective instincts were on high alert. It was up to him to make sure that she and their child was safe. His feelings only intensified as he watched Kiki make dozens of small sacrifices every day. She struggled with morning sickness, dry skin, and heartburn. She'd given up all artificial sweeteners, which meant taking a pass on her beloved Diet Dr Pepper. Of course, she didn't drink alcohol.

Now Leighton was asking him to add a new burden to her life. He was asking that Kiki and Detweiler, their two kids, nanny, and three pets move out of their house. Detweiler couldn't believe how angry he was.

Their waitress refilled his coffee cup one more time. Detweiler muttered, "Thanks," and worked his jaw furiously. He was itching to point out to Leighton that Melissa's sudden interest in her father sounded fishy. Especially when she hadn't communicated with him once in years.

Until now.

Her timing seemed calculated, especially seeing that Leighton's newest book was quickly gaining traction in the bookstores.

"So Melissa wants to move to St. Louis?" asked Detweiler. "Yes," said Leighton, eagerly. "Do you remember when the local paper did that spread on the cottage? About how I remodeled it hoping to make it my writing studio, but that didn't work? So then Kiki moved in? Well, it was in my agent's office and Melissa saw it."

"Your agent. In New York."

"Right," said Leighton. "Isn't that something?" Indeed.

Didn't that just knock over the milking pail? Detweiler remembered the article. The place wouldn't have looked near so darling had it not been for all the work that Kiki had put into it. She'd set down roots in more ways than one, claiming the place and adding homey touches.

"Kiki doesn't have a lease?" he asked.

"Correct." Leighton spoke with a certain reluctance. Straightening slightly in his seat, he added, "Legally I'm within my rights."

"Of course," Detweiler said. "I'm just searching for an excuse you could give your daughter. A reasonable way to avoid having to move Kiki, Anya, Erik, Brawny, and me out of the house."

He'd listed everyone on purpose. Yes, the house was crowded. Right, they needed a bigger place. But Anya loved Webster Groves, and in particular, she was attached to this house because of Leighton's donkey Monroe, and the beautiful, spacious yard. As hard as it would be to tell Kiki that Leighton wanted them out by the end of the coming week, it would be ten times harder to tell Anya. As for Erik? The boy was only beginning to adjust to his new life in St. Louis. He'd had a few setbacks, but the last ten days had been great. Uprooting the child again was the last thing that Detweiler wanted to do.

Furthermore, there was the problem of where they were going to live. He'd given up his small apartment last month. It made no sense to pay rent there while he was living with Kiki. Instead, they planned to save that amount and put it aside to help pay for the hospital expenses that would happen in January. Coming up with first month, last month, and a deposit would strip their bank account.

Of course, there might be an upside to all this. Maybe the added expenses would encourage Kiki to agree to getting married sooner rather than later. Initially, Anya had been a stumbling block. She hadn't wanted to be the only Lowenstein in the family. But given time, the teen had changed her mind. They had discussed the possibly of her having a hyphenated last name.

Yes, plans were in the works for the wedding, definitely things were moving in the right direction. But this was Kiki's busiest time of year at the store. So far, every time they'd sat down to set a date, something or someone interfered.

Meanwhile, he'd ordered a beautiful diamond engagement ring for her from Mary Pillsbury. He hadn't decided when he'd give it to her. Life had become incredibly hectic, what with two kids, the store, and his full-time job.

And yet, he'd never been happier.

"So, you'll tell her?" Leighton asked for the third time.

"Yes," said Detweiler through clenched teeth. He was still seriously hacked off with Leighton when Kiki text-messaged him: There's been a stabbing at our crop. Please come quickly. I'm okay. Laurel is not.

6

Back at The Old Social Hall

$\mathcal{I}$t seemed like forever before Detweiler arrived. Flashing his badge at the other law enforcement officials who'd gathered, he broke through the crowd, crossed the dining room in two seconds flat, and grabbed my shoulders. "You okay?"

"I am. Laurel's not." I told him what happened. "Hadcho's here."

Detective Stan Hadcho is Detweiler's partner. When he heard the address from the dispatcher, he'd raced to The Old Social Hall, because he knew that I might need help. Once he'd seen that I was all right, he hurried over to assist the other officers.

"Good," said Detweiler. "I'll let him deal with the others. You sure you're okay? The baby all right?"

I did my best to smile. It was wonderful to be so cherished. "I'm just a little shaky, that's all."

"None of this blood on you is yours?"

"No," and I explained about Mary Martha. "The rest happened when I helped Bonnie Gossage put pressure on Laurel's wounds."

I glanced down at my cotton maternity top. Detweiler's mother, Thelma, had made it for me. To underscore the peasant blouse styling, she'd chosen a lovely paisley on a periwinkle background. The neckline featured a drawstring tassel. "I sure hope these stains come out."

"Mom'll gladly make you another," he said. "If you're sure that you're okay, I'll see how I can help."

"Go," I said.

For the next thirty minutes, first responders raced around, securing the scene. Bonnie didn't come back to the craft room for a long time, and then she reached into her supplies and grabbed a plastic grocery bag full of clothes. Since she has little kids, she always travels with extra duds. In short order, she came back dressed in things that were clean and dry. As I watched from across the room, she handed her blood-soaked clothes to one of detectives. He bagged them up and offered her a receipt for the evidence. Next a uniformed officer asked me for my things. Wendy Green, one of my scrappers, had an extra sweatshirt in her bag, so she loaned it to me. I handed over my blouse, thinking sadly of how much I'd loved it. The crime scene investigation techs swarmed the bathroom and hall, dusting for fingerprints and collecting whatever they could.

An officer took Bonnie aside, presumably to interview her in one of the small rooms off the hallway. As I watched her leave, I caught a glimpse of the gurney rolling down the hall with an IV attached on a pole. That told me what I wanted to know.

Laurel was still alive.

As for what sort of shape she was in, I couldn't hazard a guess.

Clancy walked a plain-clothed detective over to me. "This is Kiki Lowenstein."

"You're Detective Detweiler's fiancée? The daughter-in-law of Police Chief Robbie Holmes?" he asked me.

"Right," I said, even though my relationship to Robbie wasn't exactly so straight-forward. He had recently married Sheila, the mother of my late husband George.

"Then I suppose you know what happens next. We need to interview everyone. There doesn't seem to be a way to separate all your croppers from each other," said Detective Murray. Detweiler and Hadcho walked over to join us. It seems that Murray and Hadcho were old friends. Murray and Detweiler knew each other by reputation only.

"My officers will have to get all your guests' contact information and take statements while the crime scene investigators finish their jobs," said Detective Murray. "Of course, we'll also need to talk to everyone on the catering staff."

"I can help," said Hadcho, "since I was a first responder." "We can help, too, by keeping everyone busy," I said.

I told Detective Murray about the make-and-take project we had already prepared. Since we had to stay right where we were, and we couldn't go into the next room to eat our desserts, doing our crafts would provide a welcome distraction. With his permission, we got started. The group reacted sluggishly, as if someone had poured molasses on all their limbs, but with a bit of encouragement from Clancy and me, they got down to the business of crafting tiny monsters to be glued to empty toilet paper rolls and used as décor items or game pieces.

Twenty minutes later, Detweiler came over to see how I was doing. A glance at the wall clock told me that it was almost nine thirty.

"They're almost done gathering statements," he said. "What are you planning to do? Break it up and call it a night?"

"I don't think I have any choice but to continue with the crop," I told Detweiler. "We're scheduled to be here until two. It's for charity, and I can't give all these people their money back. There's nothing I can do for Laurel. Not right now."

I'd been holding everything inside, but suddenly, I couldn't contain the tears.

Detweiler pulled me close and held me in his arms. "It's okay," he stroked my hair. "She's going to make it. You and Mrs. Gossage did a wonderful job of keeping her alive. If you two hadn't slowed the blood loss, she wouldn't have survived."

He went on to tell me that the knife wounds weren't as bad as they looked. "I talked with one of the EMTs. Laurel must have instinctively thrown up her arms to protect herself. The blade moved off course. Instead of opening up her throat, it nicked her collarbone. Cut her arm, and there was the jab to her ribs."

I couldn't believe the amount of damage that had been inflicted.

"Knives will do that," he said with a sigh. "Has anyone thought to contact Mert?"

Mert Chambers was my former cleaning lady and also my former best friend. When her brother Johnny was hurt helping me foil my husband's killer, she decided I was to blame. Since then, she had avoided me. It had been Mert who suggested that her friend Laurel Wilkins could come help us at the store.

Detweiler was right. I hadn't thought about telling Mert.

"I'll text-message her," I said. "What hospital did they take her to?"

"South County," he said.

I carefully drafted my message. I didn't say there'd been a knife incident. Only that Laurel had been hurt and the EMTs had her in the bus.

My phone rang immediately.

"What the blue blazes? Is she okay?" Mert didn't bother to say hello.

"She was stabbed." "What!" Mert yelled. "But she'll make it." Mert hung up on me.

"Someone here must have seen what happened to Laurel," I said. "There were so many people. The croppers and the catering staff."

"The local force will get to the bottom of it."

"The locals? Why won't you get to the bottom of it?" I could hear the high pitch of my voice. The metro St. Louis area has ninety-one separate municipalities. Most have their own policing force. Detweiler worked for St. Louis County. As I stood there, hyperventilating, it dawned on me that he couldn't work the case because this wasn't in his jurisdiction. He could only intervene as part of the Major Case Squad. A Major Case Squad was only convened when the crime was homicide.

"Oh," I said.

"Any idea why someone would have wanted to attack her?" he asked.

"No. You know Laurel. She's an absolute sweetheart. It sounds like a lame cliché, but why on earth would anyone want to hurt her?" I paused. "Why do it here? Now? Is it possible this was somebody's idea of an ugly Halloween prank? Could it be that she was in the wrong place at the wrong time?"

"Anything is possible. Hadcho says someone in the kitchen thinks she saw somebody running around behind the building. Of course, Detective Murray will check into that. Could this have to do with her personal life? Is she done with school?" Detweiler pulled me to his chest again. All around us, crafters were working on their projects, only to be interrupted and pulled away from their hobbies by officers taking statements.

"Not exactly. She worked on a research project over the

summer. I don't know much about it except that it's finished. That's why she's been available to help at the store."

I didn't say, "I know next to nothing about Laurel's personal life."

That was true, but I hated admitting it.

Later, I told myself. Later, when things settle down, I'd tell him that Laurel managed to be both a friend and a mystery to me. A mystery to all of us at Time in a Bottle.

7

———————

*D*etweiler gave me a quick kiss. "I'll see you at home, later. You're in good hands now. Hadcho's going to hang around."

Angela came to Clancy and me and asked about serving dessert. "We could set tables in the far back of the room and let your crafters rotate through. What do you say?"

"Why not have Faye do her thing, too?" asked Clancy. "That should also help people feel a little better about the evening."

"Where is she?" I asked. "Over there," Clancy pointed.

Faye wasn't a crafter, so she'd opened her e-reader and made herself comfortable when the interviews began. The purple ostrich feathers that rose from the top of Faye's Victorian chapeau fluttered slightly as people walked past her. She was still wearing her blood-soaked costume.

"Detective Murray?" I flagged the officer down. "Would it be possible to have our actress do her thing? I'm paying her either way. Of course, I don't want to interfere with your questioning, but if she's telling her stories, the croppers won't be talking to each other."

He stroked his chin. "Sure. Why not? She's the one dressed like the Lavender Lady? But more ghoulish?"

"Right."

I walked over to Faye and tapped her on the shoulder. "You're on," I said, and I did my best to smile. I just hoped her ghost stories weren't too gruesome.

As if reading my mind, Clancy came over and leaned close to me. "While we were talking to Detective Murray, I told Faye to keep it low key."

"Good." I breathed a sigh of relief.

"She said it won't be a problem. She has plenty of material. Her husband used to work as a history prof at one of the community colleges." Clancy smiled. "I do think you better make a statement though. From here on in, it's damage control."

Clancy has good instincts. I stood up and rang the small bell we'd brought.

"Everyone? Could I have your attention? Please? I know you are all worried about Laurel. Um, the good news is that the emergency techs got here quickly," I started slowly, choosing my words with care. "The bad news is, of course, that Laurel was seriously injured by her assailant. As most of you already know, none of us can leave, at least not until the authorities take your statements. If any of you saw anything, please speak up. The ladies' restroom here on this floor is off-limits. If you need to use the facilities, please talk to Clancy or me, and we'll get permission from an officer to take you to the men's room."

Now what? The faces in the audience stared at me expectantly.

"Angela's staff will be serving dessert. You'll rotate through, using the tables in the back of the room so that nothing gets spilled on your work."

I paused, trying to collect my thoughts. "If you don't mind,

I'd like us to have a moment of silence. I'm sure that Laurel would appreciate your prayers."

I bowed my head. I didn't look to see if others followed. I assume they did. After what seemed like an eternity, I opened my eyes and said, "Thank you. Without further ado, let's hear it for Faye Edorra!"

8

————

$\mathcal{I}$ couldn't concentrate on anything that Faye said, but her audience sure seemed spell-bound. Instead of listening, I stared off into space and worried about Laurel. The police finished up their interviews with surprising swiftness. The crime scene investigators would probably work until the wee hours of the morning. A yellow "Do Not Cross" tape cordoned off the ladies room. The croppers adjusted. After a while, no escort to the men's john was necessary.

Hadcho walked in and out of our room, asking our guests to come with him to the interview area. More than one of our croppers seemed happy to follow him. Hadcho is part Native American, and he reminds me of Daniel Day-Lewis when he starred in *The Last of the Mohicans*. From the blushes spreading over our croppers' faces, I could tell he contributed to global warming.

"I've been meaning to get caught up with you, Kiki," said Clancy, keeping an eye on Hadcho's backside and taking the folding chair next to mine. "How's everything going at your house? We haven't talked since that pre-Halloween party at the Detweilers' farm. That sure was a lot of fun."

I knew she was aiming to distract me. I couldn't blame her.

We both needed distracting. I couldn't believe that we'd be coming back here tomorrow night. The thought of returning to this crime scene made me want to run screaming out of the room. But that wasn't the half of it. I had a hunch that everywhere I'd turn, I'd see Laurel with blood spurting out of her.

"Everything is going fine. Just fine," I said, trying to turn my attention to my friend, the Jackie Kennedy look-alike. Clancy was dressed in tailored slacks and a twinset. The outfit rarely varied. Only the colors changed from day to day. Because this was a Halloween crop, she wore black pants and a bright purple sweater set. I'd worn black maternity slacks and the multicolored peasant blouse that was now ruined.

"Define 'fine' for me," said Clancy.

"Really good. Brawny is tremendous. She gets up before everyone else in the house. Runs, lifts weights, comes back, meditates, showers, and makes breakfast for the whole family. After she drops the kids off at school, she goes back to the house and cleans. Does laundry. Makes dinner."

"She's been a big help in the yarn room at the store, too" said Clancy.

"Don't I know it. I saw her working with Amy Gill on a sweater the other day. Margit would have helped the customer, but her mother was having some problems. So I called Brawny at the last minute, and of course, she came right over."

"It's hard to believe that you, of all people, have a nanny. I mean, I've watched you pinch pennies ever since we met. That's pretty highfaluting stuff." Clancy gave me a little bop on the shoulder.

"It wasn't my idea," I said. "Detweiler brought Brawny back from California. She insisted on accompanying Erik. And his Aunt Lori is paying her wages. But I have to admit, I don't know how we would have managed without her. She's my new best friend. In fact, she's with the kids right now. Thank goodness."

"I bet having a chauffeur is a boon by itself." Clancy linked her fingers and stretched her arms. She yawned and I did, too. We'd pulled up chairs to the edge of the room, obvious enough that anyone could get our attention if needed, but out of the way of the general traffic. Despite the horrible situation in the next room, we were both getting relaxed.

This was the first chance we'd had in days to really talk. I always enjoyed sharing with Clancy. She was such a practical, no-nonsense sort of person. I'd been meaning to update her on our newest family members.

"The Detweilers bought us a Toyota for Brawny to drive. They called it a 'pre-wedding gift.' It's used, of course, but I don't care. I was never so grateful for a car in my life. Of course, Anya has her eye on it. She can't wait to get a driver's permit, but that's two years away. Things wouldn't work so well if the house wasn't so centrally located. Close to the store and to the school."

"It was critical that CALA accepted Erik as a legacy, wasn't it?" Clancy was referencing the Charles and Anne Lindbergh Academy, known locally as CALA, the swanky private school that generations of Lowensteins had attended.

"They weren't going to."

"You have to be kidding," said Clancy. "No, I'm not."

"What changed their minds?"

"I think the tantrum that Sheila threw made a difference." I couldn't help but laugh.

"She and Robbie Holmes got back from their honeymoon cruise just in time, right?" Clancy cocked an eyebrow at me.

"Yup. They left late, after all the problems during the wedding reception, but they managed to fly to one of the early ports of call and get on the ship. I was glad for them. Sheila had really looked forward to going on that cruise."

"Sheila holds a lot of clout at CALA, doesn't she?" The twinkle in Clancy's eye suggested this was an understatement.

"You've got that right. At first CALA told me that because Detweiler and I weren't married, Erik wasn't really my son. Therefore, he couldn't be considered as a legacy. According to them, he isn't part of the Lowenstein family. Of course, if CALA didn't accept him, Erik would have had to attend a public school. I wouldn't have minded that. Detweiler and I are both proud products of public school. But then, Erik and Anya would have different holiday schedules, different drop-off schedules, different pick up schedules and snow days, plus a host of other small problems."

"But Sheila came to the rescue."

"Remember my friend Maggie Earhart? She used to be a substitute kindergarten teacher and now she's full time. Well, Maggie's classroom is just down the hall from the admin office. I have no idea what Sheila said to the headmaster, but Maggie heard her screaming all the way down the hall. Something about all the money that Sheila had dumped into that place. All the fundraising she'd personally done. How her friends wouldn't stand for this, and she intended to tell every one of them what a fool he, the headmaster, was. And that was just her opening act."

"You have to admire her efficiency. She swoops in, attacks, and takes no prisoners. Sort of like a one-woman drone strike." Clancy ran a trembling hand through her bob.

"Yup, she's deadly but effective," I said with a shudder. "Which leads me to this: How could someone have hurt Laurel?" asked Clancy in a voice barely above a whisper. "She never hurt a fly! I can't believe that there's an attacker among us, yet it must be true."

"Not necessarily," I said. "Hadcho told Detweiler that someone in the kitchen saw a person running down the alley. The police will check out the report. It could have been a random stabbing. Maybe someone on drugs, hallucinating."

"But why Laurel?"

"I have no idea. None." I hesitated. "It's weird. I text-messaged Mert. She must have raced to the hospital, but I haven't heard back from her. Since she isn't family, I figured they'd give her the heave-ho once she arrived. I hoped that she'd report back to us. I sure would like to know how Laurel is doing."

"Is Mert talking to you?"

"She spoke to me at Dodie's memorial service. She couldn't avoid it. Everyone was standing around, remember?"

"That was the first time, huh?" asked Clancy. "I hadn't realized you two hadn't spoken before then. Boy, that woman can stay mad a long, long time. I wonder why she spoke to you at the service."

"Maybe hearing Rabbi Sarah talk about the meaning of friendship got to Mert. Warmed her heart. I hope it did. Life's too short to carry grudges, and she has a whopper of a grudge towards me."

She nodded. "Yes, Johnny told me as much when we were driving to the Detweilers' farm. He says he's been on her to mend her fences. What happened wasn't your fault, but she's having trouble backing down. Johnny says Mert reminds him of a cat that's climbed a tree and can't figure out how to get back to solid ground."

"I knew she had a temper, but I never realized she is so stiff-necked. Unforgiving of others."

"Usually when people don't forgive others, they can't forgive themselves," said Clancy.

Boy, she had that right.

9

Later that same evening...

At half past eleven, Detective Murray stepped to the front of the room and asked for our attention. He said that the interviews were over, but he reminded my guests that their statements might need to be revisited. The ladies' restroom was still off limits. The crime scene investigators were combing it for clues.

"However, you are all free to go," he said. Nobody moved.

"You can leave," he repeated.

"This crop is scheduled to continue until two in the morning," I said.

"Really?" He looked at me as if I were nuts. And I am. He sighed. "I can't leave anyway. Not until the crime scene guys are done."

The next two and a half hours dragged on and on.

Promptly at the stroke of two, everyone started packing up.

Usually there's a great atmosphere after a crop. Crafters feel revitalized. Happy. Productive.

But not tonight.

There was a real sense of incompleteness. While they'd been busy with their projects, our guests had been distracted. Now that they were getting ready to go home, their thoughts returned to the tragedy that had befallen us.

They stared at me, waiting for me to make it all better. And I felt totally helpless. I had no idea what to do or say. My energy level was at an all-time low. I was already scraping the bottom of the barrel. But now, I felt totally depleted. All done in.

Clancy looked to me, I looked to her and shrugged. Hadcho stood across the room, leaning against a wall, studying the crowd. His mind was already turning over everything he had learned. But what would he discover? Would Murray be up to the task of finding Laurel's assailant? Would she live? And if she died, should I feel guilty? It was my fault that she'd been here.

I got up to make some sort of goodbye speech. My mouth was so dry that my lips stuck to my teeth.

"Everyone? Uh, I wanted to say, uh...this evening...uh..." I couldn't spit the words out.

Bonnie Gossage was sitting two feet away from me. I felt her eyes on me as I tried to put a good spin on the evening. We're good enough friends that she could tell I was flailing around, badly. Suddenly, she jumped to her feet.

"Hey, Hadcho? Can I have my photo taken with you? I want to make my husband jealous. If you have any extra business cards, I'll use them to make a scrapbook page."

Of course, Bonnie knows Hadcho. She's worked with him before on cases. And he knows her. So he knew she was teasing him. See, he has a bit of a rep because he's sort of a clotheshorse. He's more than a little vain. A broad grin split his face. He didn't really mind being objectified.

Not by Bonnie.

He glanced my way.

I saw them exchange pointed looks. They both knew how upset I was.

Bless them. They'd rushed to my rescue.

"Come here, you hunk you," Bonnie said as she slipped her arm around Hadcho's waist.

Her comment brought a twitter of laughter from the other women. After turning beet red, Hadcho agreed to pass out his business cards and let the other croppers take photos. A few of the women hammed it up, pinching his bicep and hanging on his arm.

"You are a doll," I whispered to Bonnie. "You've got them thinking this was some sort of totally bizarre special event that they can scrapbook. Something different from the usual pages of trick-or-treaters."

"Hey, that's what friends are for," said Bonnie. "Besides, we pregnant ladies have to stick together."

"You're expecting again? That's fantastic!" I said.

"Shhh. I don't want everyone at work to know. I'm just a month behind you, so I won't be able to keep my condition secret for long."

I mimed the action of zipping my lip and gave Bonnie a long hug. "I owe you one. You've been such a good friend to me."

"Since you have a nanny and I don't, you've been bumped to the top of my best friend list," she giggled.

"If you need help, my nanny is your nanny. We working moms have to stick together." To seal the promise, we did a fist-bump.

Murray and Hadcho escorted the women to their cars. Since most had come with friends, the groups moved along quickly. Angela and her staff stood in line, thanking croppers as they left.

"We're still on to do this again tomorrow," Angela said to me. "But no stabbings, right?"

"Right," I said. "Thanks again for being so helpful."

"It'll be okay, Kiki," Angela gave me a tiny hug. "The cops will track down the person who did this. We'll be on our guard."

"I'm under strict orders to get you home so you can put your feet up and get some rest." Hadcho walked up to me. "Chad and I plan to be here tomorrow night. As your guests, not as officers on duty, since this isn't our turf. That way we won't have to worry if this doesn't get solved overnight."

"But you think it will be, right? You'll get the person who did this?"

"I should think. Laurel will probably point the finger at her assailant as soon as she's able." He put a brotherly arm around my shoulder and pointed me toward my car.

"Is she all right?" I asked him. "Have you heard what her condition is?"

"She's stable. Bad as it was, a lot of factors worked in her favor. Mrs. Gossage's quick thinking, your quick response, the staff flagging down the bus, all of it. Of course, we'll know more tomorrow."

I climbed into my old BMW, and he slammed the door for me. The key turned in the ignition, and the engine on my ancient convertible fired right up. Clancy flickered her lights at me, a sign that she'd seen me climb safely into my car. We were both ready to hit the road. I flicked mine back. Hadcho waved to us both and turned back toward the building. I couldn't believe how tired I was, and how heavy my belly felt.

As if he knew I was thinking about him, my baby responded with a flutter kick of his own, telling me that he, too, was ready for a good night's rest.

"Not your fault, little man," I said, to the boy I was carrying. "Don't you worry about a thing, hear me? Time to count our blessings. I'm welcoming you, Baby Boy, into our lives. You have a big sister named Anya. And a wonderful daddy named Detweiler. And grandparents who live on a farm in Illinois. And a cranky grandmother that lives here in Missouri, and the list of people who will love you goes on and on."

I paused and then added, "You also have a five-year-old brother named Erik."

But as I drove, a shadow passed over the moon—and over my heart.

It wasn't a cloud. It was worry about Erik's safety.

10

The night Detweiler returned from Los Angeles

*O*f course, I'd known that Detweiler was bringing Erik home with him. I also knew that the boy was not his biological son. And I was fine with that. Really, I was.

I hadn't expected Brawny to come with. Her garb surprised me, although I've since learned that she always dresses in a tartan skirt, white blouse, and knee socks held by garters. That's who she is.

I didn't know that at the time. Her outfit is definitely unusual, and I was surprised by it when she first stepped off the Gulfstream plane. I was also thrown by the wild look on Detweiler's face. He had been gone for longer than we'd expected. In fact, nothing about Erik's arrival was as we'd expected, and the little boy was understandably worried about the changes coming up in his life. There'd been complications on my end, too. My car had been vandalized, so I had to borrow my mother-in-law Sheila's car. I'd been forced to pick up my mother at the last minute. We were all off-balance when we met. But the fact that Brawny was coming home with us was the real shocker. Especially given that a.) Detweiler and I hadn't discussed it and b.) our house is tiny. Really small. The place began as a garage, and then Leighton Haversham, the author, decided to make it into his studio. He turned the garage into a small house, but he actually did too good of a job. The windows that made the place lovely proved a distraction to his ability to write. That's why he rented it to me. When I moved in, it was just Anya and I and Gracie and two cats. Now we've added

Detweiler, Erik, and Brawny, and I'm pregnant.

That said, I pride myself on my flexibility. As I shook Brawny's hand in greeting, I glanced over her shoulder to see Detweiler mouth the words, "Not now."

Not surprisingly, Erik's arrival from Los Angeles was wild. The little boy went from shy to exuberant when he met my harlequin Great Dane, Gracie. Anya was thrilled to meet her new brother, and he was immediately taken with her. Monroe, our donkey, was a big hit. So were both of the cats. Fortunately, Brawny turned out to be a cat lover of the highest order.

Yes, Erik was all smiles and giggles until it came time for bed, and then he refused to turn loose of his nanny. "He'll be fine," said Brawny. "My wee lad needs time for adjusting."

Because we didn't have a guest bedroom, Brawny was more than willing to sleep on our sofa. When Detweiler and I retired to our bedroom, we left her sitting on the couch and reading a book to Erik.

I turned on a box fan to create white noise and give us a little privacy. Detweiler spoke to me in low whispers. "Sorry about springing this on you! We were there at the airport when she insisted on coming. Erik overheard her pleading with me. It was all downhill from there. He threw his arms around her neck and started wailing. I didn't expect her to come, but Erik was sobbing. Brawny started sniffling. The plane was ready to take off. Lorraine Lauber said that she'd pay Brawny's wages as a gift to us—and I caved." He threw himself backwards on our bed and stared up at the ceiling. "I've faced down creeps with guns in their hands, but I've never felt so out of control in my entire life!" I couldn't help myself. I started to laugh. In fact, I laughed so hard that I nearly peed my pants. I would have, too, if I hadn't raced into the bathroom. When I came out, I started laughing again, so heartily that I could barely stand up. My face hurt from laughing so hard as I wobbled over to our bed and flopped down next to Detweiler.

"What?" he asked. "What's so funny?"

Here was this big, strong cop. An excellent marksman. A gym rat who bench presses 152 lbs. A fine physical specimen who can run an eight-and-a-half-minute mile. A man's man. A homicide detective of the first order.

But when confronted by a crying five-year-old boy and two crafty middle-aged women, he'd been outflanked, outranked, and outmaneuvered.

"Honestly, babe," he said, "I had no idea what to do. All I could think about was getting home to you."

I quit laughing long enough to kiss him.

"You aren't too mad at me, are you?" he asked.

I could tell by the way the words rushed out of him that he'd been panicked about my response.

"Hmmm. Let me get this straight. You went to Los Angeles to pick up the son you'd never met. You agree to bring home a boy who's not your biological child. You pick up a Scottish nanny along the way and drag her home, too. Complete with a kilt and sporran."

"It's not really a kilt when a lady wears it," he explained. "More of a plaid skirt, I guess. I don't know the details. Sporran? That's the dead badger pelt that hangs from her belt, right? Uh, yeah, something like that. What on earth happened to me? Was it something in the air? I got to California and acted like a dope!"

"I'd say you got hornswoggled, my darling Detweiler." "I got what?"

"Bamboozled. Tricked. Deceived."

"I'm a fool, aren't I?" His amazing green eyes clouded with doubt.

"No, my love. You're a wonderful, compassionate guy, and I adore you."

11

Three weeks earlier/ Very early in the morning The day after Detweiler returned from Los Angeles

I awakened to the smell of bacon and coffee. But Detweiler's arm was still thrown around me. Anya isn't a morning person. So what? Who?

Someone was in my kitchen.

It had to be Bronwyn. Our new nanny.

I crawled out from under Detweiler's arm. He seemed sound asleep. As quietly as I could, I padded down the hallway and into the living room. Erik was sitting on the sofa, with one cat on each side. He was watching the National Geographic channel and chewing on a piece of toast.

"Hey, sweet boy," I said. "How are you?"

Because he didn't really know me yet, I resisted the urge to grab him and give him a kiss. Instead, I settled for smiling at him. After a minute, he smiled back at me. "Kiki," he said.

"That's right, honey." I wandered into my kitchen.

"Coffee, ma'am? I made you a cup of decaf." Brawny had set the kitchen table, and I took a seat to watch her. She was making pancakes. Already she had a leg up on winning Anya's heart, because pancakes are my daughter's favorite food. When I took a sip of the coffee, she nabbed my heart, too.

"Great stuff," I said.

"*Aye,* me mam taught me how to add a few wee eggshells to the brew. Gives you extra calcium, too. Now canna make you a pancake? There's bacon on that plate."

"What's that wonderful smell?" Detweiler wandered in, looking sleepy-eyed and hungry. After he took a chair, Brawny fed both of us with a practiced efficiency.

"I hope the sofa wasn't too uncomfortable," I said.

"Not at all. I grew up sleeping with my brothers and sisters on a thin mattress. In the service of the Crown, I often slept on a cot, if I was lucky. 'Twas actually a bit of heaven to sleep on your sofa. One of the cats joined me early this morning, the yellow tom?"

"Martin," I said. "Consider yourself complimented. Martin is my cat, and he's not interested in other people. If he sought you out, you are special indeed."

"Animals know," said Brawny, as she began a vigorous scrubbing of my sink.

I sank a little lower in my chair, because I knew how dirty my house was. I'd just been too busy to tackle the grime.

"*Aye,* with animals, their sense of character is unparalleled. That dog of yours? Gracie. What a smart hound she is. She got up several times and paced the house, checking for intruders. I bet nothing gets past her. Fearless, she is. She's been a sweetheart to Erik. He's enchanted!"

Hearing his name, Erik climbed down from the sofa and wandered in to see what we were doing. "Annie?" he asked.

"She's still sleeping, big guy," said Detweiler, lifting the boy to his lap. Someday I would be able to do the same, but for now, I knew it was best to go slowly and let Erik decide that I was worthy of his trust.

Small rant: Encouraging a child to accept a strange adult is a sure way to override the child's natural defenses. It sets the child up to be molested. We need to teach our children to honor their gut feelings. Our job is to reinforce a child's sense of security—and that comes from trusting ourselves at the deepest levels. Rant over.

From the safety of Detweiler's lap, Erik cast curious glances at me. I smiled at him. "Where's Gracie?" I asked the boy. "Have you seen her? She'll need her breakfast, won't she?"

The little boy shrugged.

"Should we go find her?" I extended my hand to him.

Cautiously, he climbed off of Detweiler's lap and tagged along with me. Together we climbed the stairs. We knocked on Anya's door, and I instructed the boy, "We always knock first, right? That's the polite way to ask if we can enter a room."

"Yeah?" Anya responded sleepily while we waited in the hall.

"Erik and I request permission to come visit you," I said. "Is Gracie there?"

A loud *thump-thump-thump* rewarded my inquiry.

"Come on in," said Anya. "Gracie was roaming around last night, so I closed her up with me."

I opened the door. Anya sat in her bed with her arms outstretched. "Erik! Come here, buddy! How are ya?"

That little guy let go of my hand and barreled into my daughter, throwing himself against her. She helped him scramble up onto the bed. Gracie got to her feet and ambled over from the rag rug. Pressing that big black nose of hers into Erik's cheek, she sniffed the boy.

My new son roared with delight. "It's cold! Her nose is cold!"

"Let's go watch cartoons!" said Anya. "What do you say?"

In a jumble of bedclothes and pajamas, they hopped out of the bed and ran past me down the stairs and into the living room. Gracie brought up the rear.

A big lump formed in my throat. I wasn't so silly as to think that they'd always get along. I knew there would naturally be quarrels and petty disagreements. All siblings tussle and jockey for their rights. But seeing Erik's hand rest so securely inside Anya's fingers, I prayed that they'd always have affection for each other. I took a mental snapshot of them that would be forever locked in my mental vault. This was a new beginning for both of them. They'd been lonely onlies, sort of. I had a hunch that the link being forged between them would never be broken.

Deep down, my gut told me that this couldn't possibly be as easy as it seemed this very moment.

12

$\mathcal{M}$y sixth sense was confirmed all too quickly. I walked back into my kitchen to see Brawny standing ramrod stiff at attention. Detweiler was sitting at the kitchen table, both hands wrapped around a mug of coffee.

"Is there somewhere that I talk to you both? Privately?" The nanny's face looked drawn and worried.

"Gracie needs to go outside," I said.

"Let me just serve the young Miss her pancakes," said Brawny. "And a cuppa hot chocolate."

I followed the nanny into the next room, just to check on the children. Anya and Erik were snuggled next to each other on the sofa.

After Brawny and I walked back into the kitchen, Detweiler said, "We could take our drinks and sit on the picnic bench under Leighton's oak tree. Would that work for you, Brawny? Let me tell Anya."

I picked up my mug, stirred the mix, and waited while he stuck his head around the corner. "Anya? We're going outside to enjoy our coffee. We're taking Gracie. Keep an eye out for Erik, will you?"

"No problemo," she said.

Detweiler turned to me. "She's devouring those pancakes. I think they're fine, but you should look in. The scene is priceless."

Erik was leaning up against my daughter as she ate. Their two heads were close together, hers with white-blond hair and his auburn curls. She was wearing a pink brushed cotton pajama set that Sheila bought her, and he had on blue PJs with trucks on them. As soon as she finished her pancakes—and that took no time at all—he'd snuggled into her lap. Anya wrapped her arms around him. Their attention was riveted to the TV screen as they watched a group of penguins waddling down to the sea.

My gosh but they looked adorable.

"*Aye,* they're going to get along just fine," said Brawny as she joined us in the doorway.

Detweiler whistled to Gracie, and she bounded over to his side. I have no illusions. She loves him best. I watched as she looked up at him adoringly. He snapped the leash onto her collar. The three of us stepped outside to where the air was crisp, with a warning of cooler temps to follow.

My sweetie helped me by holding my arm as I stepped over the bench of the picnic table. One acorn rested on a cluster of brown leaves, forming an impromptu centerpiece on the wooden surface.

"Thank you for letting me come here to St. Louis with you, Detective Detweiler," said Bronwyn. "Mrs. Lowenstein, you are as fine a lady as I was led to believe. Greeting me with such warmth. Taking me into your home. 'Twas a mean trick we pulled on the both of you, but there was a good reason behind it. A very, very good reason."

Despite her clear articulation, her Scot's heritage blurred her speech. "Very" was pronounced "verra." I found it charming.

"As you might of suspected," Brawny continued, "there's more to my presence than meets the eye. Miss Lorraine couldn't tell you all the details. Her house is bugged. Every room but one. So's her car."

"What!" I nearly spit out my decaf coffee. "You're kidding!"

"No, sadly, I am not. We sweep the front room regularly, but

we leave the others alone so they don't realize she's on to them. She's known about the listening devices for some time. That's why she insisted on meeting you at various places, Detective Detweiler, sir. She didn't want to tip her hand. She'd done her homework. Had you both investigated thoroughly."

My jaw dropped. Detweiler's grip on my hand tightened, but his expression didn't change.

"I can see that shocks you, Mrs. Lowenstein, but remember, Lorraine Lauber was handing her much loved nephew over to you both. It was the only way she could be sure that he'd be safe. Checking you out and all."

Taken from that point of view, her vigilance did make sense. "Why didn't she tell me about the bugging?" asked

Detweiler.

"She couldn't be sure that you wouldn't give it away. She didn't know you well enough to trust that you'd be a good enough actor not to reveal her secret. See, 'tis only because she knows that it's happening that she can plan around it."

Detweiler's face turned grim and his mouth flatlined. I wondered how much more he could take. From that first call, telling him that Erik existed, right up to this moment, there'd been nothing but treachery and trickery. Detweiler's ex-wife, Gina, had disappeared while she and he were still married. Just up and vanished one day. A year later, she asked him for a divorce, telling him that she was living happily in California, that she would never come back to him, and that the matter was settled in her mind.

Fast forward to the present, five years later. Detweiler gets a call that Gina and her wealthy second husband, Van Lauber, are dead. They died in a car crash. Oh, and she left behind a son, Erik. According to the caller, an attorney for the Laubers' estate, Erik is Detweiler's biological child. So my honey flies to Los Angeles to pick up the boy. But first he must meet with Lorraine Lauber, Erik's aunt, and Van's sister. Of course, Detweiler is eager to see his son. But Lorraine keeps delaying their meeting. Finally she hands him a letter from Gina, in which she admits that Erik is not his biological son. No, he's the product of an affair that Gina had with another man, an African-American. Nevertheless, Gina begs Detweiler to take the boy and raise him as his own. Since Erik was born before the divorce papers were signed, in the eyes of the law, he *is* Detweiler's child.

Lorraine loves Erik, but she has a form of MS that gets progressively much more debilitating. She wants to know if Detweiler will be able to love this boy?

Of course, he can. One look and he does.

But he has to make sure I feel the same. When Detweiler calls to ask me how I feel, I say, "Bring the boy home with you."

And so, Erik Chandler Detweiler came back to St. Louis with Detweiler. As did Brawny, the nanny who'd been with the child since birth.

As I shifted my weight on the hard picnic bench, I thought, Perhaps now we'll learn exactly why Brawny has been foisted on us. I had a hunch there was more to her continued employment than a kind gesture on Lorraine Lauber's part.

It was hard for me to get comfortable on the hard bench, and I wiggled around a bit. There was so much that I wanted to ask, but Detweiler deserved the chance to have his questions answered first. However, I couldn't sit still. I drummed my fingers against my leg impatiently as I waited to see what we'd learn next.

What else had Lorraine and Brawny hidden from Detweiler? "The long and short of it is simple. Miss Lorraine thinks that her brother and Gina were murdered," said Brawny. Her gentle gray eyes hardened to the color of cold steel. "She's sure that someone paid off the California Highway Patrol to keep the real facts quiet."

"Why does she think that?" asked Detweiler. A coiled energy had infused his posture, the precursor to him taking action.

"But after the tragedy happened, Miss Lauber paid her own investigator to go over the facts, such as they were. He came up with different results. When she went back to the CHP and pressed the matter, it appeared that key pieces of evidence were no longer available. They'd gone missing from the evidence lockers."

I couldn't help myself. "That's awful!"

"*Aye,* and it gets worse. See, you never asked Detective Detweiler, so Miss Lorraine never told you, but Mr. Lauber put money in trust for Erik. I don't know how much. 'Tis none of my business. Even Miss Gina didn't know about it. Mr. Lauber did it under the table, sort of. His first three wives took him to the cleaners, I guess that's how you say it, so he didn't much fancy letting Miss Gina know all his financial dealings. Can't blame him, can you? There's money there in trust for the wee fellow. I'd imagine it's a fair sum. But it can't be released without Miss Lorraine's say so. Hers and Mr. Thornton, who's an attorney. Only Miss Lorraine doesn't trust Mr. Thornton. Never has. So she figured it was best not to say a peep to you. That way you couldn't let on that you knew about her doubts. She also decided that getting Erik out of California was safest for the boy."

"She had us checked out?" I still marveled at that.

"*Aye.* Both of you. Character references and all. You'll be pleased to know that a whole lot of people think the world of you both! She even checked into CALA. In fact, a friend of hers is an alumnus, so really, he checked everything out for her. Since a lot of people with money send their children there, she knew Erik would be safe on the premises. Of course, she trusts the two of you implicitly."

I tried to take all of this in. Instead of speaking in a logical measured way, I babbled. "Are you suggesting that Erik is in danger? I mean, it's one thing to kill a man and his wife, but his child? And Erik wasn't even his. He's not kin to Mr. Lauber, so why would he be in danger? I'm confused."

"'Tis confusing, isn't it just?" Brawny turned so she could keep one eye on the house. She was always vigilant. In fact, I wouldn't be surprised if she owned a Gaelic version of *Semper Fi* cross-stitched and framed.

"Miss Lorraine is smarter than some give her credit for," said Brawny slowly. "Men often underestimate the fairer sex. Especially once a woman is of a certain age. Mr. Thornton thinks he's got her wrapped around his little finger. But she's never felt comfortable with the man. After her brother died, she asked for an accounting of Mr. Lauber's investments. Took a wee bit too long to get those numbers. Things didn't quite add up. Large purchases weren't registered the way they should have been. She's got a bright mind, so she put two and two together, and then she asked for an accounting of the money in Erik's trust. That took a suspicious long time to calculate. She started wondering, 'What if the money was being moved from one pot to another?'"

"What did she conclude?" asked Detweiler. "She's thinking it's more than likely possible."

"But why is Erik in danger?" I asked. I still couldn't see the link between the Laubers' funds and the boy.

"Because if Erik is gone, there's no reason for the trust to pay out to one source. Instead, it will all go to various charities, groups that would be happy for any small sum of money. If there's been shenanigans behind the scenes, Erik's death might give someone time to cover his tracks." She paused. "Of course, this is pure speculation right now. Miss Lorraine's the first to admit that she's got naught to hang her hat on. Just a lot of scurrying about that seems unnecessary when she asks for an accounting. That and a bad feeling. But I don't discount such a notion. Especially coming from Miss Lorraine. Listening to that still wee voice inside you, it's a good start, isn't it?"

"If this is true, Lorraine's in danger, too?" Detweiler's voice sliced the autumnal air with a cold, cold edge.

"It's possible. I told her as much. She's careful, you see. She's got Orson, her driver, and he's more like a bodyguard than a chauffeur. Hilda, her cook, well, she can handle a knife in places other than the kitchen. As for tracking down the money, she hired a forensic accountant, the best in the world, and he's doing it sort of backdoor-like. In a manner that won't raise red flags or tip her hand."

"But she's still alone in that big house, and she's practically immobile," said Detweiler. "I don't like that at all."

"Right. I pointed all that out to her. Because she sleeps upstairs, she's isolated. As you well know, she can't get to her first floor very quickly. Not with those legs of hers. She and I discussed it before I left. I recommended that she buy herself an Alsatian."

"An Alsatian is what we call a German Shepherd?"

"That's right, Miss Kiki. But she found something better. For her at least. A Giant Schnauzer. Won't shed. The dog will be ready in late October. She's flying to Kentucky to meet it. I wish she had it right now, today, but..."

"You both seem to think the world of Lorraine Lauber," I said.

"We both do." Detweiler nodded along with Brawny. "She's

good people. You and she will get along like a house on fire. Now, Brawny, what do you think we need to do to keep Erik safe?"

"Trust me," she said. "I'm a Celtic warrior through and through, sir. To harm you or your kinfolk, a villain will have to go through me. When he does, he'll learn where the word 'berserk' came from, and how come you don't go messing with a Scot. Not if you want to keep your guts tidy inside your belly."

13

*B*rawny and Detweiler immediately reviewed what security measures were already in place at our house. They did a survey of the lights, the motion sensors, the locks, and the alarm system.

Before Erik's first day at CALA, Brawny and Detweiler visited the school. They confabbed about the best route for her to take when dropping the kids off. They also met with CALA's newly appointed head of security and spoke for a long time with him. Maggie Earhart would be Erik's kindergarten teacher, so the three of us met with her to discuss our fears. Maggie is rock solid and pragmatic. She not only listened carefully, she volunteered a few good ideas of her own for keeping Erik safe. Among those ideas came the practice of using code words. To pick him up, a person would need to use those words.

We also agreed that Erik needed to be able to trust his own instincts, especially because he and Brawny had often discussed how important it was to trust one's intuition. If something worried him, he was to go to the nurse's station and complain about pain in his heart. If Maggie saw anything that tripped her warning trigger, she also could send us a coded message. All of this preparation was shared with Anya. Thank goodness, she took it as more of a personal challenge than a frightening development.

Detweiler bought canisters of pepper spray. One for me and one for Anya. We practiced using them on a calm day. He even helped Anya dot the lids on the canisters with bright red nail polish. "Most people panic and point the aerosol the wrong way," he explained. "Now, let's see how you do with it." He watched her give it a squirt, and then he said, "Don't extend your arm all the way when you point it."

"Why?" she asked.

"Because with your arm fully extended, you lose leverage. You make it easy for an opponent to grab you and pull you off balance. Remember, your goal is to get away. This is a deterrent. Shoot three short bursts and run."

When Anya told her friend Nicci Moore what she'd learned about self-protection, Nicci's mother, Jennifer, called me. "Would Detweiler mind showing Nicci how to protect herself? I'd really appreciate it."

Soon Detweiler was teaching impromptu classes in Leighton's yard. Anya, Nicci, and Rebekkah Goldfader, all heard lectures on self-protection. Detweiler showed them vulnerable areas on attackers. He drilled them in using their pepper spray. They discussed dangerous situations and awareness.

All in all, it was good training. Important information that every young woman—or person of any age—could use.

Bit by bit, we built an imaginary wall of security around our family. We weren't naïve enough to think we were invincible, but after the first week of our drills, the sense of panic inside me slowly eased to a bearable pressure.

The second week after Brawny's warning, I woke up in a panic. Detweiler was working late shift. Suddenly, all my sense were alert. Obeying my gut, I knew I had to check on Anya and

Erik. I climbed out of bed, padded my way to the short hall, and tripped over Brawny.

I would have gone down on my knees, except that she bounced to her feet in nothing flat and grabbed me by the arm.

"Brawny? What were you doing here? In the middle of the hall? On the floor?" I tried to keep my voice down so I wouldn't wake the kids. She'd positioned herself equidistant from the tiny room where Erik slept and the slightly bigger second bedroom that was Anya's. Despite our protests that Brawny could share a room with Anya, she had still insisted on sleeping on the sofa.

"I heard a noise outside," she said. "Gracie got up and whimpered. I decided this was the best place to be. No one could get past me to hurt you or the bairns."

"But on the floor? Weren't you uncomfortable?" I squinted in the darkness, trying to see her expression. Instead of pajamas or a nightgown, she wore black athletic pants and a black tee shirt. Even in the half-light, I could see she was ready for action if the need arose.

"No, Miss. It's not too bad. Besides, I couldn't have slept at all if I thought you weren't protected. "

"But...but..." I couldn't wrap my head around this astonishing self-discipline of hers.

"*Tutum te robore reddam*," she said. "My father was a Macavity. That's my mum's family motto."

"What does it mean?" I asked.

"I shall render you safe by my strength."

14

_D_etweiler woke up at five on Saturdays. He dressed quietly in the half light, pulling on his gym shorts, tee shirt, windbreaker, and athletic shoes. Tiptoeing down the hall, he passed Brawny as she sat cross-legged on the floor, doing her daily meditation. Trying not to disturb her, he stepped out into the crisp fall air and locked the door behind him. Acorns crunched under his feet, scenting the yard with a greenish nutty fragrance.

"Have you told her?" Leighton stepped out of the shadows of the shed, and blocked Detweiler's path to his car. A soft nicker from his donkey, Monroe, followed. The lumbering gray animal hung his head over the fence that enclosed his tiny paddock. His gentle brown eyes followed the movements of both men intently.

Detweiler stopped his progress, reluctantly. While he hadn't been avoiding Leighton, he had hoped not to see the landlord. The more he thought about Leighton asking them to move when Kiki was seven months pregnant, the madder he got.

Even as he fought the anger welling up inside him,

Detweiler noticed how frail Leighton looked. How he was wringing his hands. How stooped over he was.

"No, I haven't told Kiki. Not yet. She had a particularly rough day yesterday. You heard about the stabbing?"

"That Laurel was Kiki's Laurel?" Leighton acted befuddled. "I heard the name, but hadn't realized the connection."

Not for the first time did Detweiler wonder if the man might have a slight touch of dementia. Of course Laurel was "Kiki's Laurel." Who else would have been stabbed at a scrapbook crop? Giving in to his curiosity, Detweiler said, "How old are you, Leighton?"

"Seventy-eight in December," the man answered. "I guess I'm a little old to be acting fatherly, huh? You're right, if that's what you're thinking. But it wasn't like I entirely abandoned my daughter, Melissa. I provided for her and her mother, Ellen. I set up a trust through my agent, Ruff Booker. A portion of all royalties has always gone to Missy."

"You have a literary agent named Booker?" asked Detweiler.

"Yes," said Leighton with a short laugh. "Pretty amazing, isn't it?"

"Look, is there any way your daughter could postpone her move into the house? Just until after the holidays? Kiki's had her heart set on having Hanukkah and Christmas here and—"

Leighton turned to stare at Monroe. "Sorry."

"She won't even consider it?" Detweiler hated the whining tone his voice had taken.

"No. I asked, honestly I did, but Missy insisted. She says she's looking forward to her first holiday in her own little house and having me over as her guest."

Detweiler rammed his fist deeper into the pocket of his navy jacket. He wanted to punch out a wall. Not that it would solve anything, but he wondered, how could Leighton be doing this to Kiki?

"After all these years, your daughter suddenly decides she

wants to get close to you? What brought on her newfound desire to be a part of your life?"

True, it sounded hurtful. Detweiler didn't really mean it as such. But as a cop, he depended on his curiosity. His sense of smell. Right now, something stunk to high heavens. If Leighton was seventy-seven, then his daughter must be in her forties at least. Why would a forty-year-old woman suddenly want to live right next door to the father she'd never known? Most people had built some semblance of a life by her age. Families. Friends. A routine. A place in the world. A job.

Detweiler continued his line of questioning, "What's her profession? Is she planning to find a job here?"

Leighton turned away from the cop, shielding his face. "I don't think Missy's found her way in the world. Not yet. She worked for a while in an insurance firm. Smart as a whip, of course. Lovely girl. Got her mother's face and figure. Then she was an assistant to an executive. At a start-up. That failed. Since then, she's sort of flailed around. Not really stuck with anything."

"Where does she live now?" Detweiler persisted. "Indianapolis. Been there two years."

"Before that?"

"Chicago. But she hated the cold." "She lived there for how long?" "Oh, I'd say, hmm, maybe a year?"

A pattern emerged. This was a woman without roots. An adult who couldn't settle down. Melissa Haversham didn't know what she wanted in life. Scratch that: She changed her mind a lot about what she wanted. Right now, she wanted her father's converted garage—and that meant Kiki, Detweiler, the kids, Brawny, and their three animals would all soon be homeless.

"So she's seen this place and—"

"No," said Leighton rather curtly. "Not in person. Not yet. She flew in last night. She's still sleeping. But she saw the color photo of the cottage in my agent's office. Missy says she fell in love with the place right then and there."

Leighton pivoted to face Detweiler. "Wait until your child grows up. You'll see all the ways you've failed her as a parent. Every mistake you've made is written there on your child's face. You'll understand. You'll see that you'd give anything to change the past. To have another chance. To make things right. Don't you get it? This is my chance to do all the things I should have done, that I didn't do, because I was too selfish or too stupid or too self-centered when she was growing up. Now she's given me a second chance. Of course I'll grab at it. Why wouldn't I? It might be my last chance to win my little girl's love. Who wouldn't knock down heaven and earth for the opportunity?"

15

Later that same morning
Gold's Gym near the police station

"You mean to tell me that your landlord is evicting you? You and a woman who's seven-months pregnant? And a kid who just lost his parents in a car wreck? And a teenager? And a nanny who just relocated from California? Plus two cats and a honking big dog?" Hadcho shook his head. "Man, that's cold."

"Don't I know it." Detweiler shook his head. "What did Kiki say?"

"I haven't told her yet," Detweiler studied his protein shake. Every Saturday, he had the same thing, the peanut butter and banana smoothie with an extra scoop of protein powder.

This was his Saturday tradition. First he and Hadcho pushed each other to work out hard. Afterward, they downed protein shakes. This once-a-week session was his only "guy time," a regular meeting he considered well worth the effort. Not only was Stan Hadcho a dedicated fitness freak, but he'd also been a good friend over the years. They'd started as partners, been split up, and then reassigned as partners, to their mutual satisfaction. Hadcho was a clean cop, a good guy, and Detweiler trusted him with his life. Furthermore, Hadcho respected Kiki, thought well of her, and that made life easier for all three of them.

"Wimp," Hadcho snickered before taking another gulp of his coconut raspberry protein shake. "Here I thought Leighton was a righteous guy."

"His timing really stinks."

"Where will you go? Any ideas? Can you move in with The Old Man?"

That was Hadcho's nickname for Police Chief Robbie Holmes. When Detweiler and Kiki married, Police Chief Robbie Holmes would become his father-in-law, sort of. That was fine by Detweiler. Robbie had recently married Sheila Lowenstein, the mother of Kiki's late husband George.

Robbie had been one reason Detweiler was on the force. He admired the police chief.

Sheila, well, Sheila could be a pill, but since marrying Robbie, she'd calmed down quite a bit. Although she was still the epitome of high maintenance.

"We can't move in with Robbie and Sheila. While they were on their honeymoon cruise, they came to an understanding about her house. Rather than sell it, since it's a great place and a fabulous location, they plan to redecorate it together. Get some of that froufrou stuff out of it so Robbie will feel more at home."

"Ah, compromise. You got to love it," said Hadcho.

"It makes sense. They found a decorator they both like. One they both trust. I guess he's already started tearing up carpet and refinishing the wood floors. No way could we move in while that's going on. Besides, Sheila is driving both Robbie and the decorator crazy—"

"As is her wont," said Hadcho.

"As is her habit," Detweiler agreed. "I couldn't ask Kiki to get in the middle of that. It's probably not even safe for the kids to be in that mess. Besides all that, living with Sheila would be challenging. Kiki's lucky to have survived Robbie and Sheila's wedding intact. What with all of Sheila's demands."

"Your parents' house? Just for a while?" Hadcho signaled the young man behind the counter by pantomiming the signing of a check. Slapping Detweiler on the back, he said, "This one's on me, pal. You get my sympathy vote."

"To get from my folks' house to CALA takes more than an hour and a half in normal traffic. Anya's at an age where she wants to do after-school activities. That would be impossible for her if we were in Illinois."

"So, what's next? Looking for a rental?"

"One that will take a Great Dane? Two cats?" Detweiler snickered. "I've been on Craigslist. I've called several real estate agents. They've told me to get real. One started laughing and dropped the phone. Not exactly an encouraging response."

"Maybe the dog and the cats go to your parents' house, and you can find a place that's temporary."

"There's that..." He shook his head. "But doing without the animals would kill Anya. Really it would."

"What other choice do you have?"

"We could move in with Kiki's mother and sisters in U City," said Detweiler. As he spoke, he picked at the hem of his gym shorts. A thread had come unraveled. That's what he'd be subjecting Kiki to, unraveling on a grand scale. Still, it might work.

"Are you kidding me?" asked Hadcho. "Kiki's mother is a total whack-job."

"True, but she lives on the first floor. Can't climb the stairs. We could occupy the second floor. It's a big house. We're talking temporary, of course, but until Kiki and I can find a place, it might work."

Turning his attention to the gym proper, Hadcho stared at the mass of bodies pumping iron. Sweating. Building muscle. Getting strong. Being all manly and macho.

He struggled, keeping his face a blank, trying not to show Detweiler how bad he felt for his friend. In his brief contact with Kiki's mother, he'd come to believe that growing up an orphan might be preferable to living under the same roof as a woman like that. For Detweiler to even suggest moving into the house in U City underscored the man's desperation.

But a man had to do what a man had to do. "Wow," said Hadcho. "That bites."

16

___

Same morning
On the way to Time in a Bottle

I could almost swear that my cell phone rang differently when Sheila called. Not because I'd assigned her a ringtone. No. My mother-in-law had a way of bending the universe to her liking. Even immovable objects bowed to her demands.

Let me give you an example.

Robbie Holmes had been dead set against living in her Ladue home. He called it, "A pretentious, oversized barn."

They'd been back all of two days from their honeymoon when Sheila had us over for dinner. She looked radiant with a slight tan to her face. The extra color showed off the ivory chiffon tunic she had paired with a pair of cream silk pants. On her feet were caramel colored embroidered slippers. Every inch, a lady of leisure.

After a wonderful pot roast dinner, cooked by her fabulous

maid, Linnea, Sheila broke out a bottle of champagne. "A toast to new beginnings," she said.

In deference to my pregnancy, I had a half a sip, followed by a big chaser of H2O.

"Yes, we're going to start over," said Robbie, with a sparkle in his eyes. "We're going to redecorate this place."

I choked on my water. Detweiler watched me carefully until I quit coughing.

I thought I was hearing things. As the conversation progressed, I assured myself that I was, indeed, sane. However, Robbie had lost his mind. Moving into this house with Sheila and letting her redecorate it was the act of a scrambled brain. For sure.

As I helped my mother-in-law clear the table, I whispered. "How did you do that?"

"Do what?"

"Convince Robbie to stay here. He was totally against it!"

"Huh. He's a man. He doesn't know what he wants." She picked up a platter of steamed asparagus and headed for the kitchen.

"He sure sounded to me like he knew what he wanted!"

"I amend what I said. Robbie knows exactly what he wants. He wants me to be happy. Because when I am happy, he is, too." She carefully transferred a large portion of pot roast into a Tupperware container for us to take home.

"But how? Come on. You have to share with me. These are skills I need to know."

"I did my dance of seven veils and when he was panting for me to remove that last wisp of chiffon—"

"Too much information!" I clapped my hands over my ears.

She pulled my hands free. "It's really very simple. You give them everything they want. You make them deliriously happy. When they're lying there with a huge grin on their faces, you start to cry."

"Cry?"

"Yes, cry," she whispered in my ear. "Loud and hard and as if your heart is breaking. You tell them that everything is perfect except...except...that you helped build this house. You raised your son, who is now deceased in it. You cradled your grand-daughter and watched her take her first steps, and now you hoped to add more lovely memories. But instead, you will be saying goodbye to all those cherished memories. And it breaks your heart."

"But he had to have put up a fight."

"Not much of one. I asked him, 'Is there any concession that I could make that might encourage you to rethink your decision?' And note the use of that word, 'concession.' You see, I positioned myself as the reasonable party. Of course, I said all this with tears in my eyes. Really, I should have taken up acting."

"Sheila, don't you feel guilty?"

She raised a perfectly shaped eyebrow at me. "Not one bit. After we came home, I went through the Sunday paper and circled all the properties I wanted to tour. Every one of them would have cost more money than Robbie was willing to spend. His hands started trembling as he examined the ads for one money pit after another. On the Monday next, I had a mover come and give us an estimate. To move all my belongings would cost more than three months of Robbie's salary. When confronted by bad choices, my 'concession' started to look reasonable and thrifty to him."

I backed into a kitchen chair and shook my head. "You are devious."

"No," she said, raising a glass of champagne and toasting herself. "Well, maybe. But I am clever. Very, very clever. And if you want to be happily married, you will learn to be clever, too."

17

---

*T*hat conversation with Sheila flitted through my mind as I adjusted the phone under my ear. True to form, Sheila never began a call with, "Is this a good time?" or "I hate to bother you." Instead she launched into whatever was on her mind. Today she led off with, "You weren't at The Old Social Hall when that woman was stabbed, were you?"

"What do you think?"

"I think that 'trouble' is your middle name."

"What a lovely sentiment. Good morning to you, too, Sheila. Have you been drinking?"

"One Bloody Mary. Why? Are you keeping count? Are you all right?"

"Sort of."

"Don't tell me you were hurt! How's the baby?" A bit of panic edged into her voice. When I first learned I was pregnant, I figured that Sheila wouldn't care. After all, this wouldn't be her biological grandbaby.

I was wrong. Dead wrong. She had made it abundantly clear that she was the grandmother to all my children. Even Erik. And I loved her for it.

I just didn't always like her. Not all the time. Not when she was three sheets to the wind, and lately, she'd been drinking far too much, in my humble opinion.

"I'm fine and the baby's fine. We're all fine except for poor Laurel, the stabbing victim."

"Let me guess. One of your crafty customers got a bit frisky with her exactly knife."

"That's an X-Acto knife, and no, that's not what happened. This was a serious attack. Not your average papercut." She went quiet.

"Sheila? You still there?"

"Of course, I am. Tell me more because you don't sound fine. Not completely."

"I'm shook up. You should have seen it. On second thought, be glad you didn't. Laurel was a mess. There was blood every-where, and because this was a fundraiser for a charity, I couldn't exactly say, 'Hey, let's all go home! I've had enough for one night, how about you?' I had to tough it out. Worse luck, there's another crop tonight at the same place."

"Cancel it."

"I can't," and I explained the financial penalties I'd incur from just such a cancellation.

"Is Detweiler planning to attend?"

"Yes, and Hadcho's coming too. Unless they get a big break and nail down the assailant, they both insisted on showing up, and frankly, I'm happy to have them there."

"Serves you right," she said. "What do you mean?"

"Haven't you heard that old saying, 'No good deed goes unpunished'? Here you are, worrying about other people and their problems when you should be sticking to your knitting."

"Hmmm." Not long ago, I decided to ignore anything she said that I didn't like. "That reminds me. Do you know anybody who can teach needlepoint? I need a teacher for my store.

Someone good. Really good. Someone classy, who is familiar with elegant pieces."

She cleared her throat. "I'm perfectly capable of teaching needlepoint. Why don't you hire me?"

"Love to! I'll have Margit Eichen call you and put you on the schedule," I said. "Got to go!"

With that, I hung up.

As I pulled into the parking lot at Time in a Bottle, I was smiling. I had just won a twenty-dollar bet with Sheila's new husband Robbie Holmes. "No way she'll come teach at your store," he had said. "Although I'd pay you to have her do it. She needs to have a hobby. Some reason to get out of the house, other than going to the club and drinking. If she doesn't quit bugging the decorator, he plans to quit. And if he does, I don't know what we'll do with all this fabric and furniture that's on order."

Now my mother-in-law would become my employee. Gee, wasn't life full of surprises?

---

18

*E*ven before I had officially purchased the store, I'd been given permission to make any changes I wanted. After conferring with my co-workers Margit and Clancy, I'd knocked down the wall that separated the main sales floor from the stock room. By expanding the sales floor I was able to add a room for needle arts. Officially, the room was dedicated to Dodie. Unofficially, we called it "the yarn room," but really, it was more than that. By using every available inch, we added yarn and fiber, needles, accessories, and canvases. A small table and four chairs invited our customers to sit down and knit or stitch for a while.

The shelves went from waist high to the ceiling. Cabinets under the shelves held more merchandise and supplies. There was also a flat-screen television and a DVD player. Whenever Erik came to work with me I helped him get comfy in his small stuffed chair, a gift from Bonnie Gossage who told me that her boys loved theirs. Then I turned on the video of SpongeBob SquarePants so I could do my work.

Today, however, he was home with Brawny. I quickly went through the procedure to open the store. Those chores done, I called the hospital to see if I could get an update on Laurel's condition. After begging and pleading with the nurse in charge, I got nowhere. Drumming my fingers on the top of my worktable, I text-messaged Mert. "Any word on Laurel?"

"Great," I said to silence on the other end as I concluded my call. "Just ducky. Thanks a heap, Mert. We were supposed to be best friends forever, but I guess forever is a short hop in your books, huh?"

Margit heard me griping and walked over to where I sat. She'd come in through the back door, but I hadn't heard her entrance.

"No word?"

"Nope."

"I heard on the news that she's stable," said Margit. "That's good, right?"

"I guess."

"Are you all right? I know Clancy is. She came in the same time as I did. She's working on the kits for tonight's crop."

"I'm upset, but otherwise, okay. I figured that Laurel would be ready to talk by now. Or to write down a description of her attacker."

"But Detweiler will tell you what he learns. When he learns it."

"But he had to leave last night. It wasn't his jurisdiction.

Hadcho stayed because he was a first responder." "Hadcho?"

"Yup. I could call him. Maybe I will." I didn't tell her that the guys met every Saturday to work out together. Calling one meant alerting the other. Still, the fact that the media announced Laurel was in stable condition, well, that was reassuring. Sort of. I wondered what it really meant.

I decided that I would send Hadcho a text-message, but first I wanted to write an email to all of our crop participants. My goal was to tell them on behalf of the Diabetes Research Foundation how much we'd appreciated their contribution, and on behalf of Time in a Bottle, how much we appreciated their patronage. Of course, I would also have to mention what happened to Laurel. I hesitated when I came to that. Then I sent my text-message to Hadcho, asking if he had an update on Laurel's condition.

To my shock, the second that I hit "send," I heard a marimba riff. Behind me.

I turned to see Hadcho walking toward me. He must have strolled in through the back door.

"Great timing, huh?" he said as he pulled over a stool and sat down. His hair was still damp, and instead of his usual natty coat and tie, he had on a navy nylon jogging suit. As if answering my unspoken question, he said, "Just came from the gym. Detweiler is fine."

"Laurel?" I asked. "Not so much."

My heart plummeted. "But the radio said that she's in satisfactory condition!"

"That's true. However, we suspect that someone slipped her a heaping helping of Glucose. Her blood sugar was sky high. Glucose is a product that doesn't have any taste to speak of. Someone could have easily put it in her Diet Coke."

"Wait a minute," I said. "Stop. Are you telling me that Laurel is diabetic?"

"You didn't know?"

"No, I had no idea!" But as I protested, I also began putting together bits and pieces. This crop had been Laurel's idea! She'd proposed it and asked if I could help. There were other breadcrumbs sprinkled along the path. There was the fact that she never ate sweets. That she drank diet colas or water only. How she'd disappear into the bathroom after a long shift and always take her purse along. Suddenly, I realized she'd been monitoring her blood sugars.

"Right, well, she is. Diabetic, I mean," he said. "Every diabetic is a little different, but those can all be symptoms."

"She went into the bathroom, and then what? I'm confused. Is she worse off because of the diabetes?"

"Not exactly. Sort of. Between the stress of the attack and her blood loss, she's in worse shape than she would have been. When her blood sugar went haywire, her body reacted. First to go is your vision. Then your mental acuity. The docs are thinking that Laurel must have headed into the bathroom because she realized her blood sugar was off."

My expression betrayed that I wasn't following his logic. Call it "pregnancy brain," but I couldn't figure out what he was telling me.

"Then why can't she name her assailant?"

"Because her blood sugar was so far off, she's lost her memory. The point is that she has no idea what happened to her in the john. None. She's clueless. She doesn't even know who came in the john. I thought Murray would be able to nab the perp. A real slam-dunk, but he can't. He's no closer now to making an arrest than when it happened," Hadcho said.

"Wow." I leaned back so that I could rest my lower back against my worktable. "If you can't find the person who did this, and Laurel can't tell you who it is, that means that he or she is still out there."

"Uh-huh. Since they don't know that Laurel can't help us, they'll probably try to attack her again, to shut her up."

19

$\mathcal{I}$ jumped up, left the back room, and grabbed Clancy, dragging her from the front of the store. "You need to hear this, too. Where's Margit?"

"She had to leave. Her mother is still having problems. She raced out the door when they called."

While Hadcho repeated what he'd told me about Laurel having diabetes, Clancy listened carefully. Her face showed no emotion, but when Hadcho finished, she made a ladylike snorting noise. "I knew it. I knew she was hiding something, but I couldn't figure out what. She'd get kind of spacy and go grab her purse. Why didn't she tell us? That would have made life a lot easier on all of us."

I shook my head. "I guess because she's a private person. Like you pointed out to me a long time ago, I really don't know much about Laurel. Her background. Her friendships. Whether she dates or not. I know who she's been to me, I know what I've seen of her, and that's how I've formed my impression of her character. She's a wonderful person."

"Beautiful inside and out," said Clancy.

"Let's not hold hands and sing *kumbaya* here. Because that won't help me help her," snarled Hadcho.

"What can we do? How can we help?" I asked. "You're not even on this case, are you?"

"No, but Murray and I are friends. If I bring him something, he'll listen. You got her employment app? Any paperwork? Because of her throat, she can't talk much right now, but she can respond. I need anything in your files that might help me paint a picture of who she is. What her life is like. Where the bodies are buried." Hadcho pulled out a Steno notebook from his hip pocket. "Contacts? Next of kin? References? Former employers?" "I never looked," I explained. "Dodie hired her on Mert's recommendation. I had no reason to rummage through old paperwork." "Get it for me," said Hadcho. "Please."

He followed us to the file cabinet.

Fortunately, Margit is as obsessive about paperwork as Clancy is about organization and appearances. Shortly after she came to work here, Margit went through all of our filing cabinets, dumped the outdated paperwork, and organized the files to a fine fare-thee-well. Using the key hidden behind the filing cabinet, I unlocked the drawers.

"As secure as Fort Knox," said Hadcho with a laugh. "Like a burglar wouldn't have looked there first thing."

He was right. I made a mental note to find a better place to stash the key from now on. But for now, I was happy that I knew exactly where all our personnel paperwork was, and that I could put my hands on it.

Combing through the alphabet, I let my fingers march along until I found "Wilkins." I withdrew the manila folder and opened it. Inside were a W-2 form and another tax form, indicating that Laurel had no dependents and no withholding. Otherwise, nada. Not a single other sheet of paper.

Clancy had been watching. "What's wrong?"

"There's nothing here," I said, and I turned to show her the empty file folder.

"Let's take it from the top," said Hadcho. "What do you know about her? What can you tell me, since you obviously don't have the slightest paper trail?"

"I can tell you that I'm going to wring Margit's skinny neck," I said. "She's in charge of compliance with all regulatory agencies. We should have a standard employment app on each of us. Is there one there on you, Clancy? For all I know you're an undocumented immigrant."

"Ha!" she said. "My secret is discovered. I'm actually a recent transplant from Mars. As for paperwork, I don't remember ever filling an employment app out. Did you?"

"No, not that I recall," I admitted.

"Good work," said Hadcho. "Impressive operation you've got here, Mrs. Lowenstein."

I turned to him and growled. "I am not in the mood for your wisecracks, Hadcho. Give me a break."

"Simmer down. How about if you concentrate on what you do know? Or think you know?"

For the next ten minutes, Clancy and I volunteered information. Laurel was dating a guy named Joseph Riley, the priest at St. James Episcopal Church.

"A priest?" asked Hadcho. "Maybe the Vatican sent a hit man."

"Episcopal priests can marry," I said, "so one might assume that before they marry, they can even date."

We also knew that Laurel had taken a few classes at Washington University, but I didn't know if those were for credit or not. She was currently attending a local community college, Prairie Central. She was a friend of Mert's—and that's how we'd met her. Dodie had needed extra help, but couldn't commit specific hours. Laurel was incredibly flexible. As a point of fact, she'd sort of eased her way into our lives and into the inner circle of the scrapbook store. I couldn't remember anyone ever announcing she was one of us. It simply happened without fanfare. I also knew she was twenty-nine years old, and her birthday was in February. She didn't have any siblings, at least not that we knew of. She drove a baby blue Toyota Avalon, a newer model. She wore a size four pants and an eight top. This summer she'd taken time away from the store to finish a project that would help her in an accelerated master's degree program. Neither Clancy nor I knew what the project entailed. We knew she'd been studying anthropology and sociology with an emphasis on women's issues. Or something like that.

I knew that she and John Henry Schnabel, the ace attorney, were dear friends. They had been for years. However, I wasn't exactly sure where they'd met or how they'd grown so close. "I bet he knows everything about her."

"What makes you so sure she and Schnabel are best buds?" asked Hadcho. "I would have guessed you two knew a lot more about Laurel."

"She asked him to take on Detweiler's case pro bono, and he didn't hesitate. Didn't skip a beat. He intimated to me that they had a pact. That if either of them ever asked for help, it was like that song in Peter Pan, that they were blood brothers, or blood siblings, I guess you'd say."

"Looks like I'll be making a phone call to the good attorney," said Hadcho.

Otherwise, and this was embarrassing, we didn't know much. For instance, I had no idea where she lived. Or if she lived alone. Or if she had family nearby. Nada.

"I remember that she never had any birthday parties when she was growing up, but I don't know why she didn't. She simply mentioned that to Anya one day when we were working on a birthday party event here at the store. I admit that I found that curious. Otherwise, she's never talked about her upbringing. Not at all."

"Remember," interjected Clancy, "a long time ago when I mentioned to you that none of us knew anything about Laurel? I said it when you needed her help, and she called that lawyer friend."

"The truth is," I admitted, "we simply accepted that she was a very private person. She never tried to pry into our lives. She was always there when we needed someone, and she's beautiful. Once we learned that she wouldn't lord her good looks over us, we sort of forgot about everything else."

"Too bad," said Hadcho. "Because there's something in her life, some little wrinkle there. Because of it, some creep wants to get rid of her. Sad to say, ladies, I was kind of counting on you to point me in the right direction."

20

According to Hadcho, none of the security cameras at The Old Social Hall recorded anyone leaving the building after Laurel was stabbed. Either the cameras missed a person, which was highly unlikely, or the person left with the rest of us at the end of the crop. What we had was the iconic "locked door" mystery, a puzzle to be sure.

"Of course, could be that a member of staff did the deed," said Hadcho. "Murray's checking all of them out. But that's highly unlikely. Since the place was closed to the public for your private function, I don't have anywhere else to look, but at your guests. Could you print up a copy of your guest list for me? I told Murray I'd get it for him."

"I can do better than that," said Clancy. "I had each guest fill out a form for us with her name, address, phone number, contact info, and method of payment. Those have all been scanned into the computer along with a simple list so that we could take attendance."

"Both of them, please," said Hadcho. "But if you could print out the list of attendees, I'd like to go over the names with you."

That proved to be a totally boring exercise. Nearly half of

our attendees were new to us. The others were folks we'd come to know and love.

"How'd you advertise this?"

I opened my computer and pulled up a form that Margit had created. The checklist enumerated all the places we'd sent advertising or notices. As it printed, I reflected on the irony. Here I had oodles of info about the crop and croppers and nothing on a co-worker whom I would have trusted with my life.

"Did you find the weapon?" I asked.

"Nope, and I doubt that we will," Hadcho said. "We had a specialist look at photos of Laurel's cuts. Those wounds could have been made by your everyday kitchen cutlery. In fact, that's more than likely exactly what was used."

"Why can't you find the knife?" asked Clancy. "You obviously know what you're looking for."

"I suspect that the doer slipped the knife into a cart of dirty cutlery that was on its way into the dishwasher in that kitchen. See, right after I arrived, when I realized what had happened to Laurel, I initiated a search for any knife that might have been capable of being used as a weapon. That led to someone checking the dishwasher. That officer discovered it had been turned on just minutes beforehand. When she learned it was on, the manager was surprised."

"Angela Orsini," I said. "She's the manager."

"Right. She told me that they usually didn't run it until after the guests left for the evening. Because it's a big commercial unit, it takes a lot of water and energy. Noisy, too. So she has a rule that at any job, the dishwashers aren't to be run until they're full, and that's always at the end of a work shift. But when I asked one of our officers to check on it, someone had turned it on. But no one admitted to doing so. The button panel had been wiped clean of fingerprints."

"You're telling me that you suspect the assailant used a knife from their cutlery set, and then put that same knife back into the dishwasher and ran it? Any knives you would have checked against the wound would have been washed clean," I said.

"Precisely."

"That means you've got a victim who can't tell you what happened and no way to pin down the weapon that was used. Your victim is an enigma, and you don't have any personal information on her that would direct you as to why someone might have targeted her."

"Ding-ding-ding. Congratulations, Mrs. Sherlock Holmes, you win the prize."

21

"Round Two," Clancy said. "Our second Halloween Crafting Spook-tacular Starts at six and ends past my bedtime."

"Gluttons for punishment," was Hadcho's sarcastic rejoinder. "Anything we should look for or be aware of?"

He sighed and let his eyes roam the junction of the wall and the ceiling. "Sometimes the perp will return to the scene of the crime, hoping to relive what happened. Sometimes he or she will come back and insert herself into the investigation. It's possible that your doer will want to assess the damage. How about if you print off a list of tonight's guests?"

I did exactly that. We cross-referenced the attendees. "I only see six returning visitors," said Clancy. "Three are those members of St. James Episcopal Church."

"Why so many from one church?" asked Hadcho. "Did the good father assign attending the crop for penance?"

"Father Joe took it upon himself to suggest from the pulpit that attending this event was a good deed," I said. "These ladies signed up not once but twice."

"Keen crafters, eh?" asked Hadcho, raising his eyebrows.

Clancy and I exchanged a long look.

"No," I said finally. "They brought along a bunch of supplies, but I didn't get the impression that they knew a lot about paper-crafting."

"Why'd you say that?"

"Because one of them cut herself badly, the others ran behind and needed help with their projects, and all of them made messes of their work," I explained. "That doesn't indicate any expertise. At least not to me."

"It's possible that they love crafting and they aren't very good at it," said Clancy. "We've seen it before."

"True. I wonder if they have anything they can share about Laurel," I said. "Maybe I can get it out of them when they come tonight."

"Uh-huh. No, ma'am. I suggest you leave the interviewing to the experts," said Hadcho, making a sweeping negative motion with his hands. "Remember, there's a slasher out there. Detweiler will lose his mind if you even get the tiniest paper cut."

"Look, I can ask them questions, and it will sound natural. If you ask them, it'll sound like what it is, a police interview."

"I'm just sayin', you need to stay out of harm's way."

"Since you and Detweiler are both going to be there, I think I'm pretty well protected, don't you?"

"At least promise me that you'll keep out of the ladies' john," he said.

After he left, Clancy turned to me. "He knows nothing about pregnant women, does he? When I was pregnant, I practically lived in the john."

I got up and headed toward the back. "Where're you going?" she called after me. "Where do you think? To the john!"

_____

"$\mathcal{I}$ can't believe we don't have any paperwork on Laurel," I said. It was lunch time and Clancy had joined me at my worktable. She nibbled on a tuna fish sandwich, while I ate some leftover lamb stew that Brawny had made.

"Believe it," she said.

"I'm going to try Mert again."

"Do you want to eat a handful of Tums now or later? Because calling Mert is only going to upset your digestion." Clancy watched as I typed in a text-message. "For someone who claimed to be your friend, she's certainly left you high and dry."

Tears prickled behind my eyes.

"Kiki, don't," said Clancy. "She's not worth it."

"I figured that when she heard I was pregnant, she'd come around. She loves kids. Told me that she always wished she had more children. When I saw her at Dodie's memorial service, I thought she'd at least come over and wish me well. She did give me a slight nod of acknowledgement, but she also managed to keep her distance," I said.

"Did you always know she was this stiff-necked?"

"Sort of. She was always mad at someone or another. There was always at least one person in her life that she wasn't talking to. But I thought we were different. I thought she'd always be there for me."

I paused and reconsidered. "On the other hand, I knew that one day it would be my turn. That she'd get angry with me. When a person has a habit of getting ticked off, you have to be honest with yourself. It's just a matter of time until they get mad at you. I knew that. I pussy-footed around her. I prayed she'd never be mad at me. I thought we were better friends than that. At least that's what I wanted to believe."

I swallowed the lump in my throat and added, "I thought that if she did ever get really mad at me that she'd miss me. That our friendship meant something to her, because it sure did to me, but I guess I was wrong."

"You weren't wrong. I'm sure it meant a lot to her. Mert has always struck me as a complicated person. She's angry deep inside. I don't think it takes much of a spark to set her tinder glowing. That blaze has to burn her, and worse luck, she's fanning the flames."

While I appreciated this philosophical view of a friendship gone sour, it didn't fix anything. I still missed Mert. And yet, as time went on, I wasn't totally confident that we'd ever revive our relationship. How could I ever rely on her the way I had before? Now that I knew she could easily blame me. Easily withdraw her affection. Did I really want to put myself in a position to be hurt by her again? When she first quit talking to me, I'd lie awake at nights and rehash all that happened. But as the months went by, I'd come to a conclusion: Yes, we'd been friends. Yes, I once thought the world of her. Yes, she was a good person. But did I want to open my heart to her again? Did I want to go through her rejection? Did I want to go back to treating her with kid gloves because I knew she could get so angry?

She'd made a decision that I had done her wrong. She mistakenly believed that I'd involved Johnny in a plot that nearly cost him his life. When she learned the truth, she didn't back down. She hadn't given me the benefit of the doubt. Instead, she had attacked me. Blamed me for everything, hurling insults my way, and accusing me of things that didn't make sense. She'd painted herself as my victim, and she'd done it in a smug, self-satisfied way.

The longer this estrangement went on, the more I found myself thinking, "I can do without that sort of drama."

Really, I could.

23

———

A few hours before the second Halloween Crafting Spook-tacular

While I did prep work, Clancy called the croppers from the previous evening. We'd worked up a script that apologized for any emotional distress caused by Laurel's stabbing. Although we stressed it wasn't our fault, I knew that some of the crafters would blame us. That was human nature. As a token of our regret, we offered them a discount coupon and a free seat at one of our regular Monday night crops. Over time, we'd learned that a small peace offering could pay huge dividends.

The coupon and free crop opportunity would encourage new customers to come and visit our store. Clancy, Margit, and I were confident that one visit was all anyone needed to decide that we were the premiere St. Louis shop for almost any sort of crafting.

Why? For many reasons. At any given hour, at least one of

our management team was here at the store. We knew this place inside out, and we had the power to make customers happy.

In addition, our staff included Rebekkah, daughter of Dodie Goldfader, the original owner of the store; Brawny; Margit; Laurel; and soon we'd be adding Sheila. Brawny and Margit were keen knitters and crocheters. Laurel could do about anything, although she wasn't an innovator, once she'd been shown how to do a project, she could follow instructions and share what she'd learned. Rebekkah was a hot mess. However, whenever we needed a helping hand, she pitched in. She knew the supplies and how to work the various tools, but she was a hazard when left to her own devices. Sheila would pull in the hoity-toity crowd. Every alum of CALA owned a needlepointed belt. It was some sort of badge of honor. Sheila must have made a zillion of them for my late husband, George. I could just imagine the impact on our bottom line that an ongoing needle-point belt class could have.

The only thing we didn't have, and needed, was someone to help me with restocking, provide assistance during our evening crops, and oversee our food offerings.

I keenly missed Cara Mia Delgatto's help with that last task. Before she moved to Florida, Cara Mia organized the menus for our crops. Sometimes, she brought leftovers from Cara Mia's, the restaurant her late parents had named for her. Other times, she brought a main dish and worked with our croppers, because they almost always brought a dish to share, but often needed guidance so we didn't wind up with five dishes of green bean casserole.

On crop nights, Cara Mia also helped me by sticking around to run errands. She pitched in during the cleanup. Then we walked each other to our cars.

We really could use another helper. I knew exactly whom to call.

My long lost sister, Catherine. I texted her: Could you drop by the store? I'd like to see you.

She responded quickly and said she could come by in an hour.

"Do you think she'll be interested?" asked Clancy, when I told her what I had in mind.

"I think she might. She's in a Twelve Step Program, and she's doing well. Amanda told me that she avoids Mom as much as possible, which makes sense. I guess she's been doing yard work since she arrived. Catherine likes working with her hands."

Amanda was my younger sister by eighteen months, and Catherine by three years, because she's eighteen months younger than Amanda. Fifteen years ago, Catherine had become estranged from our family. Then, three weeks ago, she popped back into our lives.

"Did she do crafts when you were kids?" asked Clancy.

"A little. Mostly she did stuff outdoors. She loves plants. We didn't have much of a yard. The front of the lot sloped down to a broken sidewalk, and the slope was covered with rocks. There were too many trees overhanging the property and too much shade for anything to grow. But there was one sunny stretch next to the alley, and she really cultivated that strip of ground. I remember her planting sweet peas. Irises. Oh, and pinching back mums. Any cuttings she could scrounge from the neighbors' gardens, she'd bring home and try to get started at our house."

"It must have been a real shock to open the door and see her standing on your front step a few weeks ago," said Clancy. She pulled up a chair across from the desk where I was sitting.

"You can say that again. I hadn't seen or heard from her in all those years. But I knew who she was immediately."

"She kept in contact with your Aunt Penny that whole time?" "Aunt Penny rescued her. I've only gotten the story piecemeal, but when Dad kicked her out of the house, Catherine spent the night in a Greyhound Bus Station. She scrounged up enough change to call Aunt Penny, who wired her the money for a bus ticket to South Carolina, where she was living at the time."

"I can't imagine tossing my child to the curb because she was pregnant. And she was only fourteen. That's unthinkable."

"It's barbaric, isn't it? Dad didn't even listen to Catherine long enough to learn she'd been raped. As far as he was concerned, she'd been promiscuous. I guess he had the nerve to say that a woman couldn't be raped unless she wanted it. Can you believe that nonsense?"

"Your father must have been a moron."

"He was also a superb mathematician and a talented artist. But a social and cultural Neanderthal."

"Hey, don't insult cavemen," wisecracked Clancy.

"My father grew up in a rural, backwater area of southern Illinois, and he had never been exposed to erudite people. In some ways, he and my mother were a great team."

"What do you mean?" Clancy stepped around me and opened the top drawer of the desk that had once been Dodie's. From the desk drawer, she withdrew a tiny bobble-head turtle. Dodie used to tinker with the toy when she was thinking.

"My mother has pretensions, but no real substance as a person. My father had strong opinions, but no depth of thought. Neither traveled much. Neither were great readers. They never questioned their beliefs. Everything was black and white. People were good or bad. Moral or immoral. They were like two radios with very limited bandwidths."

"We're talking about a distinct lack of intellectual curiosity," said Clancy as she tapped the turtle and watched his head float up and down. "You're saying that if someone told them that the earth was flat, they would continue to believe that forever. They had no reason to challenge what they knew. Facts were facts, right?"

"Right. They believed that blacks and Jews should stick to their own kind. The man of the house was the provider, end of discussion. The woman's job was to make the man of the house happy. In return, he put food on the table and kept a roof over your head. There were two kinds of women: good and bad. Men were men, and bad behavior was part of the bargain. A smart woman didn't upset the apple cart."

"He didn't even hear Catherine out?" Clancy shook her head in disbelief.

"Nope. From what I've been told, she told our parents that she *thought* she might be pregnant. Mom knew she'd been interfered with while walking home from school. A neighbor found Catherine lying in a ditch beside the road with a bump on her head and blood on her clothes. But Mom never said a word to my dad. Never told him that Catherine had been raped."

"Did you and Amanda know that your sister had been molested?"

"No," I said, wiping away a tear with a shaking hand. "On that particular day, Amanda and I were at choir practice at church. Catherine can't carry a tune, so she didn't belong to the choir. She stayed late after school to help a teacher, Mr. Heffernan, and lost track of the time. Any normal parent would have gone looking for her child, especially when it got dark outside, but not my mother. She decided 'to teach Catherine a lesson.'"

"How did Catherine get home? Did the neighbor bring her?"

"Yes, it was an elderly woman who often saw us walking past her house. She noticed Catherine's scarf fluttering in a bush and went over to investigate. The woman drove Catherine home. Mom was furious—with my sister. Instead of taking her to a doctor or the hospital, she warned Catherine that if people knew, she would be shunned. She shamed our sister into silence. Catherine slid into a deep depression. Went to school and came home, but then she'd go immediately to bed. Amanda and I couldn't pry out of her what had happened. It wasn't that we didn't notice something was wrong; it was this conspiracy of silence. No one would tell us what was going on!"

"You were just a kid. A teenager. I'm not sure what else you could have done," said Clancy, as she laid a kind hand on my shoulder.

"Maybe," I said. "Or maybe I was just too selfish to care. Usually my mother was busy picking on me. But for those four months, she left me alone and carped at Catherine. I should have realized something was up."

24

─────────

$\mathcal{I}$ was back at my worktable when Catherine walked in. She jingled as she walked, her fingers playing with Amanda's car keys. They'd fallen into a routine where Catherine dropped Amanda off at work, which gave her use of her car, a Saab convertible, during the day. Catherine didn't have two pennies to rub together. After having her child and giving it up for adoption, she'd taken to self-destructive behavior. Since alcoholism ran in our family, that became her drug of choice. But now she'd been clean and sober for three years.

"Hey, big sister," she said as she slung an arm around my shoulder. I rose to hug her. She's taller than I am by about four inches. While my hair is dishwater blonde and Amanda's is auburn, Catherine's is coppery red, a color that most women would kill to possess. It's not as curly as mine or as wavy as Amanda's. As far as I'm concerned, Catherine is the pick of the litter when it comes to looks.

"Pull up a stool and take a load off, baby sister," I said.

"Nice place you've got here." Her soft gray-blue eyes roamed from fixture to fixture, taking it all in. "Wow, Kiki. Good for you."

"It's not paid for, but you're right. I fell into a pot of jam, sort of. I love this place."

"I can see why."

Clancy approached us from the stockroom. In one hand she held a Diet Dr Pepper and in the other a Diet Coke. I had a bottle of water. "Hi," said my friend. "We haven't met. I'm Clancy Whitehead. You're living in my mother's house."

"I'm Catherine," said my sister, rising to take the Diet Dr Pepper. "It's a nice house. Big as all get out. I'm sleeping in the room that y'all used as an office. On the first floor? I love books, so it's really comfy for me. If I wake up at night and can't get back to sleep, I just choose something from the shelves. I hope you don't mind."

"Books are meant to be read. I'm delighted to hear you're enjoying them," said Clancy, pulling up a stool.

"How'd you know I love Diet Dr Pepper?" asked Catherine.
"It's a family trait," said Clancy.

"Well," I said. "I'm going to sound very left-brained, but I invited you here, Catherine, for a purpose. Clancy and I've been talking. We desperately need more help. I was wondering if you'd consider coming to work here. I can't pay you much—"

"Offer accepted."

"Um, don't you want to hear what I want you to do? How much I can pay?"

"Nope."

"Gee," I said. "That was too easy."

"Not really," said my sister. "I need a job. I don't have any marketable skills. We always had fun together when we did crafts. I realize this is different, but I'm eager to learn. I'd rather work with family than with strangers."

She paused. "I'm trying to rebuild my life. I did a lot of dumb stuff. I have to attend Twelve Step meetings every other day to stay sober, so I need a boss who'll understand that. I also need someone who'll be honest with me if I mess up."

Clancy and I looked to each other and shrugged. "Sometimes I might not have a car," said Catherine. "At least at first. Is that a problem?"

"No," I said. "You've met Brawny, our new nanny. She can pick you up or I can."

"When can I start?"

Clancy and I spoke in chorus: "Tonight!"

25

"*Y*ou're telling me that Laurel was stabbed in the middle of your event?" Catherine was helping me sort supplies for goody bags. Clancy had purchased clear plastic treat bags from the Dollar Store. Into these went a handful of candy, some bookmarks for a series by Joanna Campbell Slan, stickers, and pens with our store name. We paperclipped name tags right to the bags.

"That is correct," said Clancy. She was kitting up paper supplies for the make-and-take projects. When you kit supplies, you break them down into the smallest portion necessary for a project. Instead of wasting an entire sheet of paper, when you only need a piece the size of a business card, so you don't hand a crafter an entire 8 ½ by 11 sheet. Kitting cuts down on confusion, and it lowers the final cost of the project.

"You don't know why Laurel was attacked?" asked Catherine.

"Nope," I said.

"I love reading mysteries," said Catherine. "Absolutely love them. I'm trying to think about what my favorite amateur sleuths would do."

"What would they do?" asked Clancy.

"Snoop around. You said Laurel was a student at a local college, right? I'd start by talking to her classmates."

"But how would I find her classmates?" I asked.

"Was she attending class this semester?" Catherine asked. Clancy and I looked at each other. "The trash can!"

I raced away from the worktable and into the back room. Two days ago, Laurel had asked to use the printer stationed by Margit's desk. "Mine is out of ink and I need to turn in my assignment," she'd said.

"No problem," I'd said.

But I'd forgotten to swap out the blue paper I'd put in the paper tray. As a result, Laurel's assignment wound up being printed on blue sheets. We'd quickly rectified the problem. The first run of her homework was tossed into the recycling. Since our recycling was always collected on Mondays, the blue papers should still be there. Sure enough, the papers were nestled at the bottom of the bin.

"Tada!" I said, as I walked back onto the sales floor. "Looks like her class is with a professor named Brian Overmeyer. This is an assignment about social classes in Regency England. Her class meets on Wednesday mornings."

"Okay," said Catherine. "May I use your computer?" "Be my guest," I said.

"With this information, I can go to the campus directory and see what other days the class is meeting and what times. Also, I can find the professor's office hours."

With lightning strokes of her fingers, my baby sister did just that. Grabbing one of the sheets of discarded blue paper, she wrote all the information on the back. When she finished, she handed the sheet to me.

"What else would one of your amateur sleuths do?" asked Clancy.

"She'd pretend to be a floral delivery person and visit Laurel in the hospital. She'd track down Mert and make her spill her guts. After all, Mert's the link, here, right? Oh, and she'd go on Facebook and see what she could learn about Laurel's circle of friends."

I knocked myself in the head with my fist. "Why didn't I think of that? Anya is always telling me to check out Facebook."

"Does the store have a Facebook page?" asked Catherine. "No? Hey, sis, time to make the leap into the twenty-first century. I'll put one up for you. Meanwhile, spell Laurel's last name for me."

I did. Once again, my sister tapped out a message on the keyboard. She opened Laurel's page. Sort of. Since we weren't friends, we couldn't see much of it. Except for the photos. When Catherine clicked on Laurel's photo album, Clancy and I almost fell off our chairs in shock.

26

———

"Holy guacamole," I said. "So she's an exotic dancer? A stripper? What gives?"

"Read more carefully, big sister," said Catherine. "She's a belly dancer. That's entirely different from an exotic dancer. She dances under the name Sharina Azid. And for your information, belly dancing is a noble profession. In Egypt and other Middle Eastern countries, the entire family goes to restaurants where the dancers entertain. It's only here in the Puritanical US of A that we associated it with stripping, like you just did."

"Sorry!" I held up both hands in a gesture of apology. "Do you think that Hadcho knows about this, Clancy?"

"I would imagine that he does. Checking out people's Facebook pages is one of the first things that any law enforcement officer does these days. I read an article about it somewhere. I think that what you put up on Facebook is fair game for use against you, but don't quote me on that."

"But her dancing isn't a reason to stab her, is it?" asked Catherine. "Unless you were the jealous type and your husband paid too much attention to her wiggling around in costume."

"Who knows?" I wondered. "What else is Laurel hiding?"

I tried to text-message Mert again, and got no response. "Here's a question for you," said Catherine. "Why did someone decide to stab her right now? In the mysteries I read, the sleuth pays attention to the timing of the attack. What significant event was occurring in Laurel's life? It's clear she's been a belly dancer for a while. At least, I get that impression from the photos. Some of them look recent, but others weren't taken with super-duper cameras. Why did someone decide that she had to be taken out ASAP?"

Clancy explained to Catherine how little we knew about Laurel. "It's embarrassing, really. She's always there for us. Always a good friend, but we never got past the surface with her. She kept us at arm's length."

"I can't help but wonder why," I said. "We didn't even know she had a boyfriend until last week!"

"As someone who's been there, I would guess she was fighting her own demons," said Catherine. "I don't think you should take it personally. I think you should trust that she told you what she could, what she was comfortable sharing. And I don't think you should speculate as to why she kept a portion of her background to herself. Just trust that she was doing what was right for her."

I turned to my little sister and put both hands on her shoulders. "I trust you. I trust that you did what was best for you, and you were young and scared and without guidance. As for what happened next, you had to heal. I'm sorry that you went through the healing process alone, and that I wasn't there for you, but perhaps that's what you had to do. If in the future, I can do more for you, I hope you'll put your trust in me. I love you."

27

___

"Another night, another stabbing," muttered Clancy under her breath as we dragged the big cart on rollers into The Old Social Hall. Catherine pushed from behind. "Don't you dare say that," I fussed at her.

"Doesn't it give you the creeps to be here?" she asked. "Yeah, sort of."

"I brought a sage smudge stick with me," said Clancy. "I used a ton of these after my divorce."

"You believe in that stuff?" Catherine asked.

"You betcha. I believe in anything that might help. At the very least, it clears the air. Adds a nice fresh Western smell. Kiki, you hold the door open. Catherine and I will get the cart through."

With a mighty heave-ho, they shoved our stuff into the hallway.

Angela came around the corner and opened her arms to give us hugs. I introduced Catherine, who also received a quick embrace. Angela said, "I heard from Mert that Laurel is better."

I bit back a retort. Would it have killed Mert to share the news with me? I hated this sort of passive-aggressive baloney.

But Clancy was onto my tricks. She pinched my upper arm, just hard enough to snap me out of my nasty slump.

With all the drama yesterday, I'd forgotten that Mert and Angela knew each other. In fact, it had been Mert who suggested to Cara Mia that she give Angela a job in her catering business.

"Laurel is better?" asked Clancy. "Tell us more."

"Mert told me that Laurel had gone to the bathroom to test her blood. Sadly, that's the last thing she remembers. She woke up in the hospital this morning and couldn't tell them what happened. She was shocked when she realized that she'd been stabbed."

"Will she be okay?" I asked. As Angela and I talked, Catherine and Clancy dragged the heavy case on casters into the private dining room. Angela had done a wonderful job of getting the tables set up as I'd requested. I propped a small doorstop under one of the wheels of the case and unlatched it. Clancy and Catherine started unloading the kits and supplies. I wasn't supposed to lift anything heavy, so I waited until we got down near the bottom of the box. From the last box, I withdrew the overhead projector cells that I'd printed with pictures of our projects in progress. I also grabbed the manila envelope with the list of attendees, and our master schedule. But as I moved, I listened for Angela's response, although I took care to shield my face from her because I didn't want her to see how ticked off I was.

Really?

Was Mert so angry with me that she didn't have the decency to ease my mind? I'd apologized and apologized for something that wasn't my fault. What more should I do?

The answer was: *Fuggedaboutit.*

I thought she was my friend. But friends like that I could do without.

Angela paused and lowered her voice. "Of course, there's

always the possibility that her attacker might try it again. If he or she doesn't realize that Laurel didn't recognize the person who stabbed her, that creep might try to finish the job. Mert's decided to stay at the hospital around the clock until Laurel is released."

"She can do that?" I asked. "I figured they would give the bum's rush to anyone who wasn't family."

"But she is," said Angela. "Is what?" I asked.

"Mert is family."

"She is?" I felt my voice go up a notch. "Mert is related to Laurel? How?"

"They're mother and daughter."

28

———

I felt my jaw flap open. Clancy must have seen my expression because she stopped what she was doing and hurried to my side.

"Did you know that Mert and Laurel are mother and daughter?" I asked my friend.

Clancy frowned. "No, but remember how I kept saying they looked alike. That they had certain mannerisms that were the same? You just didn't see it because you'd known Mert for so long."

"But...but...if Laurel is Mert's, and Laurel is twenty-nine, that means that Mert got pregnant when she was thirteen," I said.

Clancy stared at me. She didn't say a word, but I knew what she was thinking. My own sister had gotten pregnant at age fourteen. Fortunately, Catherine was on the other side of the big dining room, so she couldn't hear our conversation.

Without words, Clancy and I came to the same, sad, silent conclusion: Mert must have been molested or seduced to have had a child so young. No wonder she didn't talk about it. Then it struck me. Three years ago when Sheila and I were at our worst, relationship-wise, my mother-in-law had called protective services on me. One outcome could have been for Anya to go to a foster home. Mert had turned paler than a sheet of typing paper and begged me not to allow that to happen. I was aware that Mert had been bounced from one foster care home to another, but she'd never shared the details. Now it occurred to me that one of the "details" was the birth of her daughter, Laurel.

I would have asked Angela for more information, but right then Detweiler came walking in. "Sorry I didn't get here sooner to help you unload. I hope you didn't carry anything, Kiki." He stopped talking as he caught sight of Catherine.

"Hey, girl," he said, as he gave my youngest sister a hug. "It's good to see you."

The two of them had clicked from day one. Even though Detweiler hadn't had the chance to talk to Catherine very much, what with the arrival of Erik and Brawny, he seemed to have an instant affinity for my youngest sister. Probably because he had two younger sisters of his own.

I couldn't wait to tell him what I'd learned about Laurel being Mert's daughter, but I didn't get the chance. Thanks to the media reports that Laurel had been stabbed, our croppers not only showed up early, they showed up eager to chat. A part of me wanted to label them all a bunch of ghouls, but their questions were so considerate and sincere that I quickly dropped the attitude. Of course, many of them knew Laurel. Others didn't, but had heard of her second-hand. I did my best to delay my answers to their inquiries, telling them that I'd address the group when we got started.

Meanwhile, women continued to file in. Mary Martha, Patricia, and Dolores arrived in the middle of the pack. "Ladies!" I said. "I'm so glad to see you again."

"It's for a worthy cause," said Patricia rather stiffly.

"We didn't get all our projects done last night," said Dolores. "We hoped you'd have time to help us personally tonight."

"Sure. I'd be glad to!" I said, with rather too much gusto. "Let's find seats for you. How's your hand, Mary Martha?"

"A little stiff. I can't use scissors, but Patricia and Dolores said they'd help me if I need it."

I got them seated and turned to see Faye Edorra grinning at me. "Ready for Round Two? I just love touring the Lemp Mansion. So many haunting vibes. Absolutely delicious!"

Tonight she was dressed in another Lavender Lady outfit, complete with faux blood smeared in dull streaks on her torn dress. The person who did her makeup was a real pro, because her skin color was sallow and the circles under her eyes convincing.

"Glad you're here," I said. Of course, she was being paid to come, so it wasn't likely that she wouldn't show up. However, I figured being thankful never hurt.

"Wouldn't miss it for the world," she said. "Last night went down as just one more calamity in the long history of local tragedies. I could almost feel the uneasy spirits accompanying us from the Lemp Mansion back here to The Old Social Hall. You know, there really are ghostly hitchhikers. People think Disney made that stuff up."

"Uh, well," I stuttered. "I'm glad the stabbing didn't scare you off."

"Oh, no! Never! I can regale my audiences with a firsthand account of it!"

"Right," I muttered. At least one person found the silver lining of our dark cloud. Now to address the concerns of my other guests.

"Before we begin with the night's activities, let me say something about the tragedy that happened here last night. Our dear friend, Laurel Wilkins, was stabbed in the restroom right around the corner. Tonight we have Detective Chad Detweiler with us. He'll be stationed in the hall between this room and the ladies room. We also have Detective Stan Hadcho arriving any minute. If you see anything or hear anything that doesn't seem right, don't hesitate to call one of the officers to help you. While we certainly don't anticipate a problem, we'd have been negligent not to worry about your safety."

A hand shot up. Lottie Feister was asking my permission to talk. "How is Laurel?"

"Thank you for asking. I've been told she's stable and doing better. However, she's still in need of your prayers."

Another hand requested acknowledgment. "Do you have an address where we could mail her a card?"

"If you'd send them to the store, I'll make sure that Laurel gets them."

Detweiler stepped forward, and as he did, I moved back and away from the center of the room. "We have every reason to believe this was an isolated and personal attack. There's absolutely no cause for your concern. That said, if you know something, anything at all, no matter how small, that might help our investigation, it would be much appreciated. Any information would be kept in confidence. I'll pass around my business cards. There's a phone number on them in case you want to speak to me privately."

I didn't realize it at the time, but I'd stepped out of the line of sight for the women closest to me. I was still tired from the long day before, so I leaned against the doorsill.

"She got what she deserved," said a voice.

My head spun around. Where'd that come from? Who'd been talking? Had I heard what I thought I heard? Was it possible that I'd misunderstood?

I thought about what Faye had said about ghostly vibes. Was

it possible that the angry ectoplasms that roamed the Lemp
Mansion had decided to stake out a wider territory?

Ugh.

29

It wasn't until our first snack break that I was able to tell Detweiler what I'd learned about Mert and Laurel. "Can you believe it?" I said. I also told him about the comment I'd overheard as I stood in the doorway. "And here's the best part. I went on Facebook. Laurel has a page. Did you know she's a belly dancer?"

His smile was gentle. "Yes, babe. I knew about her dancing. Hadcho pulled that up first thing. I guess he'd known about her second career for a long time."

"Really?"

"Yes, but it's not what you think. He loves Middle Eastern food. He's sussed out all the best Greek and Lebanese restaurants in the area. He was eating at one when Laurel came walking out of a back room, a private party, dressed in her belly dancing costume. They practically bumped into each other."

"That rat! He never told me."

"He didn't have any reason to tell you. Or me." "Did she ask him to keep it quiet?"

"No, but look. He's a private person, and she is, too. Why would he go around blabbing about what he'd seen?"

"Does he think that's why she was stabbed?"

"No, he doesn't. She's kept her real name secret. To hire her, you have to call and leave your number with a talent booking agency. They vet the requests. She's no fool. Although most of her customers understand what she's doing and respect her, there's the odd weirdo who sees belly dancing as an invitation to lewd behavior. To keep that sort of creep out of her life, Laurel has put a barrier between herself and her public. She also charges a hefty fee for her time. That helps sort out the riffraff."

"Haven't you learned anything that's helpful to the investigation?" I asked. I probably sounded huffy. I was tired. Scheduling two events had made sense at the time. I really did care about our ability to make some money for charity. And now that I knew Laurel was diabetic, I felt an even deeper commitment to our cause.

But I'd drastically underestimated how much these late events were taking out of me. The stabbing had added extra stress, but it was late nights that were doing me in. Before I was pregnant, I could stay up for two crops in a row with no problem. But now, not so much.

The truth of the matter was that I hadn't considered the fact that I was nearly fourteen years older than when I'd had my last pregnancy.

I'd had Anya when I was twenty. Now at thirty-three, I tired more easily. Of course when I was expecting Anya, I'd dropped out of college only to sit around in a tiny apartment staring at four walls and watching soap operas. Today, I had two children and a business to run. Somehow I'd failed to take all of that into account.

Detweiler came over and brushed my cheek with his hand. "Sweetie, why don't you go sit down? You look ready to fall over. Quit worrying about Laurel. Let Murray and his detectives do their jobs. You've got enough on your plate. Tell me, why's Catherine here?"

"Because Clancy and I decided that we really need more help. Especially now that Laurel's not available. Once we discussed it, I decided that I knew the perfect candidate. Catherine accepted immediately."

"I'm glad. I like both your sisters. But Catherine needs you and Amanda doesn't, so I'm especially happy that she'll be spending more time at the store."

"Yeah," I said. "I guess you're right."

Detweiler knew what had happened to my sister. He'd become furious when he heard that my mother had let my father toss Catherine out of the house. He'd gotten even angrier when he heard how she'd gotten pregnant. "Your mother isn't a real mother," he'd fumed to me. "You know how they call bad fathers 'sperm donors'? She's nothing more than an 'egg donor.' You and your sisters raised yourselves. Do you realize what would have happened to Catherine if Aunt Penny hadn't stepped in? She would have been snatched up by a human trafficker. With that gorgeous hair and being pregnant to boot? They could have sold her to some pervert for big bucks."

I'd pooh-poohed that idea. "Come on, Detweiler. We live in the United States of America. Not Thailand!"

"I know perfectly well where we live. The US is one of the world's biggest markets for human trafficking. Let me pull up the statistics."

When he handed them to me, I couldn't believe what I read. In our country alone, more than one hundred thousand women and children were thought to be the victims of traffickers. "But here? How does this happen?"

"Believe me, all it takes is a little negligence. Once the predators find out that no one cares, they swoop down. They act like they are being friendly, by offering food and shelter, and then they drug their target. For others less fortunate than Catherine, there is no Aunt Penny who comes to their rescue. Just a life of misery."

"I didn't realize," I said. "That's...awful."

Detweiler pulled me close and planted a kiss on my hair. "The past doesn't matter. We live in the moment. Catherine is safe now. She has the two of us, Aunt Penny, and your sister Amanda. I'm glad you gave her a job. I figured that you would need help at the store, but I didn't want to push you because I know you're worried about making the payments on the business. But I think you did the right thing, babe. Really I do."

I nodded. "I think so, too. Everything will work out. Catherine didn't hesitate. She seemed thrilled that I asked her to join us. See how good she is with people?"

"I see," said Detweiler. "Why shouldn't she be good with people? She's walking in the footsteps of her older sister."

30

I purposely devoted a lot of time and attention to anyone who'd joined us the night before. I figured those croppers deserved extra brownie points for daring to return to the scene of a crime. In particular, I'd hovered over Mary Martha, Patricia, and Dolores, the hapless three-some. They all needed a lot of help with their projects, and I supplied as much assistance as I could without doing the work for them.

"When's your baby due?" asked Patricia in a very casual tone. She looked to be in her mid-forties, but she could have been younger. The way she dressed and wore her hair aged her. I guess you'd say that the "bloom of youth" had faded.

"January fifteenth, but he might come sooner," I said. "Just think, maybe you'll see me on TV, holding the first baby of the New Year."

The women exchanged sidewise looks of distaste.

"And the father? Is he in the picture?" Mary Martha raised her head from her work to boldly lock eyes with me.

"Absolutely. See that tall cop over there by the door? The one with the wavy dark blond hair and the green eyes? Detective Detweiler? He's my baby's father."

"But is he excited about the birth?" asked Dolores. "He couldn't be happier," I said.

"Um, does he intend to stick around? After the child is born?"

I worked hard at keeping my cool.

They were fishing for details of our relationship. They wanted to know if we were getting married. However, they'd raised my hackles, and when that happens, I dig in my heels. I wasn't going to give them what they wanted. No way, no sir. Whether I was married, unmarried, engaged, or acting as a surrogate mother wasn't their business.

"How do you three know each other?" I asked as I pulled up a chair to make myself more comfortable. If I was a scarlet woman, why not let a little of that sinful coloring rub off on my guests?

The three backed away from me and my chair. Evidently scarlet was contagious. Who knew?

"We are members of the altar guild at St. James Episcopal Church," said Patricia, primly. "We used to belong to another denomination, but that church didn't live up to God's teachings. So we went looking for a church home. Once we found St. James, we all took instruction at the same time. At last, we've come home to the one, holy, catholic church, but catholic doesn't mean—"

"Roman Catholic. It means universal," I said. "As per the Nicene Creed and the Apostles' Creed, right?"

The three converts looked surprised.

"We had heard that you are a Jew," said Mary Martha in a chilly tone.

"My late husband was," I said. I continued to play havoc with their mistaken impressions of me by adding, "I was raised in the Episcopal Church. High church."

That shut them up. The three women chewed air for a while.

However, I now felt mean and petty. I'd shut them down, and I'd shown an unkind side of myself, for which I was truly ashamed. "I've met Father Joe. He's a delightful man. Tell me what exactly he said about this crop. He certainly must have inspired all of you since you decided to join us again tonight."

We were back on *terra firma*.

"If you've met him, you know that Father Joe is wonderful!" gushed Patricia. "So spiritual, loving, kind, and, um, awesome!"

"Not to mention easy on the eyes," added Dolores.

"Good thing that Episcopal priests can marry, huh? It would be a waste if a man like that couldn't take a bride," I said, more to myself than to the croppers.

Dolores got a dreamy look on her face. She was the youngest of the three. I'd put her age in the early thirties, probably the same age as Father Joe. She spoke almost as if she were in a trance. "What an asset he is to our church community. He has totally turned the place around. People are filling the pews to listen to him. He's revitalized the choir."

"The vestry loves him," Patricia continued. "His outreach to members, old and new, has changed the entire makeup of our church community. Before he came, the church was nearly insolvent, but since he arrived, the collection plates are full every Sunday."

"What do you think of him, Mary Martha?" I asked. She had been suspiciously quiet while her friends prattled on and on.

"Mary Martha is Father Joe's personal assistant." Patricia giggled. "He calls her 'God's secretary.' Isn't that the cutest title?"

"I do what I can to serve the Lord." Mary Martha's neck turned red.

"More like, you'd do anything you could to serve Father Joe," said Patricia, as she elbowed her friend. "Admit it, he's like a rock star!"

"When you see him walk among the people, you can

imagine how it was with Jesus," said Mary Martha. "His touch sends chills up the spine. When he talks to you, it's as if no one else in the world exists. His sermons are absolutely life-changing!"

"Wow," I said, and I meant it. I'd grown up with slightly dusty, doddering old priests who snoozed off during hymns. Good men, all, but not what you'd describe as "rock stars."

"Sounds like you are convinced that Father Joe is a wonderful spiritual leader," I said. "I hope sometime to hear one of his sermons."

"You really should come and join us one Sunday. That man has breathed new life into our church community. He's eased our financial burdens, he's touched our lives, and he's brought the spirit of Christ back into our lives," said Patricia.

"As you can see, he means a lot to us," and Dolores flipped open her album to show me pages she'd made. Along with photos of the stained-glass windows and the exterior of the church, there was one picture of Father Joe.

The priest certainly was a good looking man. After the party at the Detweiler family farm, Clancy had remarked on what a gorgeous couple he and Laurel made.

He did have that whole rock star vibe. Joe Riley wore his dark auburn hair long and curled loosely around his collar. Most compelling was his blue-green eyes. More than the shade, there was an intensity that held your interest.

"I have a better picture right here," said Patricia, flipping open her album.

Neither woman handled a camera with a lot of skill, but Patricia moved closer to her subject, which gave her tighter shots. One photo of Father Joe showed a man who obviously enjoyed life. His eyes crinkled with happiness and his head was thrown back, emphasizing those gorgeous dark curls of his.

I smiled, thinking of how he had laughed at something that Laurel had said when we were on a hayride at the farm.

"Mine are better than hers," said Mary Martha, pushing her album my way. "I also have this set of photos that I haven't put on pages yet."

I looked through her album. Candid shots are usually better than posed pictures, and I love candids for just that reason, but these were all candids, which struck me as odd. I made the appropriate sounds of approval and then gave her the album back and opened the paper envelope full of photos. Being careful to cover my fingers with a paper napkin to keep natural oils from ruining the photos, I held the stack in one hand. But I didn't get to go through them because I paused to watch Clancy.

She was up front, instructing people to find a stopping place. Since this was nearly the same point in our schedule when Bonnie had discovered Laurel, my mouth went dry with anticipation of another scream. Clancy, too, must have felt the energy shifting, because she paced at the front of the room, stopping only to fiddle with the overhead projector. From the far side of the dining area, Catherine raised an eyebrow at me, silently questioning the odd buzz. There weren't that many people from the previous night's crop, but the small sampling would never forget what had happened. I couldn't blame them. I tried to swallow, but it was as if someone had slipped a noose over my neck.

"The photos?" Mary Martha prompted me. "Aren't you going to look at them?"

She didn't seem at all bothered by memories of last night's tragedy. I certainly was, but perhaps because of my pregnancy, I was keyed up.

"Oops." Nervously I shuffled through the stack of photos, noting once again, how intrusive the camera angles felt. These were pictures taken from off to the side, surreptitiously.

In these shots, Father Joe interacted with children, seniors, and members of the choir. The pile included pictures of him in the pulpit and at coffee hour. I whisked through them, and then I stopped because the photo in my hand caught my attention.

It had been torn in half. I studied the portion of the photo that had been salvaged. To the right was Father Joe. His head was turned and the expression on his face was one of great affection. Love even. But the object of this admiration had been torn off. All that remained was a hand resting lightly on his forearm. Squinting and turning the picture toward the light, I looked more closely. A little bell went off in my head.

"Isn't that Laurel Wilkins' hand? I think I recognize the ring she's wearing."

Mary Martha frowned at me. "You mean in the photo?"

"Yes, right here," and I pointed to the portion of the picture before I passed it back to her.

"That's her." Mary Martha frowned. "Hanging on Father Joe."

Dolores sniffed. "Par for the course, I'm afraid."

31

Sunday morning

$\mathcal{O}$nce the stress of the Halloween Crafting Spook-tacular crops was lifted from my shoulders, I felt giddy with relief. Of course, I didn't hit the sack until three in the morning, but once I snuggled under the covers I was out like a blown light bulb. I didn't open my eyes until Detweiler climbed out of bed. I drifted between wakefulness and sleep. The promise of much needed rest kept me burrowed under the covers. At one point, I lifted my head and reached for the vinyl blinds. A quick peek outside told me that the day was rainy and blustery, perfect snoozing weather. No one would be in a hurry to walk Gracie in the park.

A short time later, the savory fragrances of butter, bacon, and sugar tickled my senses awake. Brawny was making pancakes and bacon. Knowing that both my little ones were taken care of allowed me the luxury of rolling over and going back to sleep a little longer. As the world faded around me, as I smiled to myself. No wonder rich people hire nannies!

Thank you, Gina, for this legacy! If you hadn't agreed to hire a nanny, I would never have been in this enviable position.

"Coffee? Be careful, it's hot."

I woke up to Detweiler sitting on the side of the bed with a big mug in his hands. Easing myself toward the headboard, I sat up and took the steaming beverage from him. He was wearing an old tee shirt and a pair of running shorts. His hair was damp, as was his shirt. He must have gone running in the rain.

"Gosh! It's ten o'clock! I can't believe I slept so late."

"You needed it. I hope you don't have any more marathon scrapbooking sessions like that planned for the future."

I didn't answer. Of course I had long crops planned for the future. To keep the store profitable, I intended to squeeze in every event I could between now and when the baby came.

"Did you have a nice run?" I asked, plucking at the damp fabric of his shirt.

"Yes, I got out and did my five miles before the rain started in earnest," he said. There was a weird look on his face. I could tell that something was seriously wrong. "We need to talk, honey, and I don't know how to tell you this, so I'm going to blurt it out."

Stars swam around the edges of my vision. Oh, no, I thought. He's leaving. He wants nothing to do with me. He's bailing on us. On me and our baby!

"It's about Leighton," Detweiler continued.

"Leighton?" My voice sounded like a frog's croaking. "Is he okay? Is something wrong with him? Is he hurt? I've told him he needs to tack down those stupid rugs in his house."

"No."

I shivered, despite the hot drink in my hands. "Then what is it?"

"He's asked that we move out." "What?"

"He's given us until this coming weekend."

"*What?*" I couldn't be hearing this right. "Is he having work done on the house?"

"No."

"When can we move back in?" "I don't know. Possibly never."

"B-b-but I don't understand." My eyes filled with tears. "Did I do something to make him mad? Did we do something wrong? Is he in financial distress? Why?"

"Did you know he had a daughter? Melissa?"

I hesitated. "Yes, I remember him saying something about her. They're estranged. She won't return his calls. He was married, young. This happened before his books took off."

"Right," said Detweiler, taking the coffee cup out of my hands and moving onto the bed so that he was right next to me. He wrapped his arm around my shoulder and pulled my head to his chest. "She's certainly returning his calls these days. Melissa visited Leighton's agent in New York City. While she was at his office, she saw an article describing how Leighton had remodeled this place, to turn it into a writing studio. She's decided that she wants to move in."

"But she doesn't even talk to her father. He hasn't seen her in years." I said with amazement.

"Things change, sweetheart. You know that. I guess she's come to the conclusion that she wants to have a relationship with dear old dad, because she's here right now."

"Okay, I'm all for family, but couldn't she wait until after the holidays? Moving now will be so hard on Anya! And Erik. And me. And the baby. Not to mention what this'll do to my work schedule. Moving is horrid. It took me months to move out of our big house in Ladue. This one isn't that big, but it'll still be a nightmare. This is my busy season at the store! How on earth am I going to tell Anya? Erik is just getting settled and he loves

Monroe! And...and..." I burst into tears. I cried and cried and cried.

On one level I was thinking ahead to all the work and feeling totally overwhelmed. But deep down, I was reliving a past wound. This was too much like my father throwing Catherine out of the house. Sure, Amanda and I never knew exactly what happened, but we'd heard shouting and the slamming of the front door and—*poof!*—our sister had vanished into thin air. Now it felt like another father was tossing me to the curb. I'd truly become attached to Leighton, and I thought that he'd come to care about me, too. The fact that he'd cold-bloodedly decided to evict me hurt. Was there something wrong with my ability to judge people?

"He told you all this but he didn't tell me!" I wailed.

"Right. He says that he thought you'd be able to take it better this way."

"That mealy mouthed, white-haired coward. How dare he stick you with his dirty work?"

"Kiki, if I could have punched his lights out, I would have. I can't remember the last time I was so angry with anyone. You know that I'm not a violent person by nature; it was all I could do to keep from going for Leighton's throat. I can't believe that he's doing this to you. To us. He gave me some cockamamie excuse about how as a parent, you'll do whatever you can to rectify the mistakes you've made in the past. Instead of making it better, he only made the situation worse. At least for us! Why hurt someone today because you made a poor choice yesterday? You've treated him like a loving daughter, but where was this woman, huh? She has nothing to do with him until it's convenient for her. But she's blood. Big deal. Maybe blood isn't all it's cracked up to be, because she sure hasn't acted like his blood kin. Not until now when she wants something from him."

"Yesterday at the crop, you were staring at me with this weird expression on your face. Was it pity? You do still love me, don't you?" and I gripped his tee shirt as though I could force him to stay with me forever.

"I love you more and more each day. That look on my face? I was worrying about this very moment. About telling you the bad news. About how we'd deal with it. And I felt so bad for you because you're marrying a man who doesn't have a big bank account. If I had lots of capital, we'd have more options, but we don't. Most of the time I don't worry about money. But yesterday, watching you work so hard, seeing you bust your backside for your customers, and knowing what I had to tell you, made me physically ill. Babe, I am so, so sorry that I can't fix this for you. For us."

32

"Before we spring this on Anya," I said, "we need to come up with an idea about where we'll live. Sheila's house is out of the question. She called me the other day, and I'm worried about her."

"Why? Isn't the decorating going as planned?"

"I guess. It's her drinking that's got me concerned." I shrugged. "Anyway, we can't go there. Not with everything all torn up. We'd only get in the way of the contractors. That's not an option."

"I agree," he said.

"I've got that lump sum from Dimont Development," I said. "It's not a lot but it could be a nice down payment."

"Right, but we can't rush into anything. Especially not into a big purchase like this. I've been looking online and I even talked to that friend of yours, Pamela Bertolli? She says there's nothing available right now that would work for us. Especially in our price range. We need to be patient and maybe grab a foreclosure. We also need to sit down with a map and consider exactly which areas we're interested in."

He was right. I tended to rush into decisions, and he was

more methodical. That made us a good pair, as long as we respected each other's needs.

"Then we need to find a rental, right?"

"I'm not sure that's possible. First of all, I don't want to give up first and last month's rent and a deposit. Not when we've worked so hard to save money for the baby. Second of all, it's not likely that any landlord would take us. You had a hard enough time when you just had a dog, remember? A big dog. Now we have two cats. The only solution there would be to send the animals to my parents' house. Although I know my mom would help us in a heartbeat, sending the animals away would kill Anya. Probably upset Erik, too. Have you seen how he's taken to Martin? And Seymour?"

I nodded. "This reminds me of that old conundrum. Maybe you've seen it? It's a triangle. The sides are labeled fast, cheap, easy. You can pick any two sides, but not all three. We need animal friendly, within a reasonable distance of CALA and my store."

"Available immediately." "Financially doable."

"With at least two bedrooms, two baths, or more." "With a fenced-in yard."

"In a neighborhood that's safe."

"We're talking Clancy's mother's house, aren't we?" I asked. "Speaking of big decisions, I also think we need to revisit the timeframe for getting married. Anya's come around to the idea. That means we ought to get hitched earlier rather than later."

He lifted my chin and kissed me. "You know how I feel about that. Say the word and I'm there."

I buried my face in my hands. "I just can't add more to my 'to do' list. Not now."

"Take a deep breath. Let's deal with housing. That's an immediate need."

I reached for the mug and finished the last of my coffee. "I can't imagine that any place other than the U City house would work. Not for us. Not under the circumstances. The space we need is there, being unused. My mother is in one bedroom on the ground floor. Amanda is in another room on the ground floor. Catherine told Clancy that she's been sleeping in the office, because she likes knowing that if she wakes up at night, she can grab a book and read. The second floor is unoccupied right now."

Detweiler nodded. "That's the way I figured it. I didn't know where Catherine was staying, but even if she was upstairs, I knew most of the second floor was empty. Why's Amanda sleeping on the ground floor?"

"Because she fell in love with that particular bedroom. It faces a romantic old willow tree, and there was a bird's nest there that she liked watching. Also because it's close to the backdoor, so if she had a late date, Mom didn't need to know."

"Can you stand living with your mother?" asked Detweiler. "Because as stressful as all of this is, I don't want to make it worse for you."

"I don't know." I twirled a lock of hair, an old habit from childhood. "That's the honest answer. She's been better since I told her to back off. I think she's actually a tiny bit afraid of me."

"Well," he said, as he stretched his long legs so that his bare toes touched mine. "If I need to scare her into good behavior, I will, because frankly I think we're out of options."

"Me, too," I said, leaning my head against his shoulder. "Thank goodness you have a big gun."

"Want to see it?"

33

I messaged Amanda and asked if we could meet her for lunch. Alone. Without Mom or Catherine.

Although my sister Amanda and I had been at odds for years, we'd mended our fences when she came to live in St. Louis. We'd also taken vows to love, honor, and respect each other. When I sent her a text-message asking for a meeting, she cleared her calendar and didn't ask a lot of questions and vice-versa.

"Brawny, would you mind holding down the fort while my wife and I go out together for lunch?" Detweiler asked the nanny.

"Hold down the fort?" She looked confused. "Watch the kids and animals," I explained.

"Of course. Anya was going to interview me for her creative writing class, so we had plans for this afternoon anyway. I can easily make the children sandwiches and macaroni and cheese."

"Great," I said.

"I'll get the laundry done while you're out." "That's even greater!"

More and more with every passing day, I was thinking that I needed to send Lorraine Lauber the biggest thank-you card ever crafted. Brawny was an absolute treasure.

"Where you going, Mom? Detweiler?" Anya asked.

"We have a few housekeeping items to iron out. Adult stuff," I said, trying to be vague without lying. Telling her we were being evicted would be hard, but not having a place to go would be the absolute pits. Detweiler and I had decided to work out the details and present this as a done deal, rather than to add further turmoil to her and Erik's lives.

Of course, I hugged her goodbye and walked over to the sofa where Erik was playing Angry Birds on Anya's phone. "Goodbye, honey," I said, and I offered him a hug. Absentmindedly, he accepted it and gave me an air smooch. I guess seeing Anya hug and kiss me had encouraged him to do the same. This transition had been hard for him. Erik still cried for Gina, his mother. But his acceptance of my affection showed he was feeling ever more comfortable with me.

As we headed for my car, I glanced over my shoulder. The curtains twitched at Leighton's backdoor. Detweiler saw the movement, too.

"I certainly hope he has the good sense to stay away from me," I said.

"I hope so, too. Because I am definitely not happy with him, and if he does anything else to upset you, I might have to tell him what I really think."

Detweiler opened the door on the BMW for me and took me by my arm as I lowered myself onto the passenger side seat. "Kiki, I can't remember the last time that I was this disappointed by someone."

I didn't say anything until Detweiler climbed into the driver's seat and moved it back to accommodate his long legs. "Disappointed? I'm more than disappointed. I'm downright crushed. At the very least, why couldn't he have told her that she had to wait until after the holidays?"

"Because he feels guilty," said Detweiler as he looked over his shoulder while backing out of my drive. "As well he should."

34

"*L*eighton Haversham seemed like such a nice man," said Amanda, as she opened her paper napkin and set it in her lap. Around us, happy patrons grabbed their brown

trays and searched for tables. St. Louis Bread Co. is a favorite any time of the day, but at lunchtime, it's packed.

She continued, "Just goes to show you, appearances can be deceiving, I guess. And to spring this on you at the last minute? What does your lease say? Have you checked it?"

"I never had a lease with him," I said. I took a large long gulp of my iced green tea because I didn't want to burst into tears. While we were at home, I'd managed to keep a smile on my face. I didn't want Erik or Anya to realize how upset I was. But as Detweiler drove us away from that little cottage and as I stared at the mums I'd tended so carefully, I thought I'd burst into sobs. Since moving into the cottage, I'd put a lot of sweat-equity into the place. I couldn't believe what Leighton was doing to me. To us. To my children.

I wasn't in a forgiving mood.

So he'd messed up with his daughter. Big deal. That didn't

give him the right to make my children miserable, or to ruin our holidays.

"When Kiki moved in, Leighton promised to come up with a lease, but he never did," explained Detweiler. "As time went on, it didn't seem to matter. Anything that came up, Leighton dealt with fairly. He told her over and over how much he enjoyed having her live nearby. He told me that she was like a daughter to him."

"Right," Amanda said with a smirk. "That's exactly why I work for an attorney. People can talk until they're blue in the face, but when push comes to shove, if you don't have a legal document, all bets are off." She buttered a piece of sourdough bread. "What are you planning to do? Where will you go? Sheila's house?"

"Not possible. She and Robbie decided to redecorate. They have hot and cold running painters, carpet layers, and a decorator. It's not an option, I'm afraid," I said. My turkey with cheddar smelled delicious, but my tummy wasn't cooperating. Part of the distress was morning sickness and part was agitation.

When I wasn't fretting over moving, I was stewing over Laurel. When I wasn't worrying about Laurel, I was wondering how I'd get everything done in time for Christmas. When I wasn't freaking out over the holidays, I worked myself into a tizzy, wondering how I'd manage to keep up with all the demands the store was making on me. Right now, I needed to set our Plan B for housing in motion. At least that would give me breathing room. If Amanda was agreeable, I could cross our lodging off the list. If she wasn't, Detweiler and I would have to reconnoiter.

"Actually," said Detweiler, taking my hand in his, as a signal that he'd do the talking for both of us. "We've been over all our options, and none of them are good. Leighton's really put our backs against the wall. We'd like to buy, but this is too big of a decision to rush into. If we hurry the purchase process, we might not get something that will work for the long haul. On the other hand, renting does not look feasible."

"You're right," said Amanda. "I can't imagine you renting. Who's going to rent to a family with two kids and two cats and a miniature horse? Not to be disparaging of Gracie. She's wonderful, but most landlords will take one look at her and think, 'Big dog, big problem.'"

"So true," I said. "She needs a fenced in backyard. Great Danes are sight hounds. They see it; they chase it. She's pretty good about coming back when I call her, but if a squirrel teases her, she's off like a shot."

"I wish you'd told me that sooner." Amanda gave a rueful laugh. "She's usually so calm, but the last time I took her for a walk, a squirrel ran across our path, and zoom! Away she goes. I must have done a four-minute mile, running behind her."

Detweiler and I both laughed. We knew exactly how it felt to be on the wrong end of Gracie's leash when she took a squirrel detour.

"Amanda, I have a favor to ask. I'll understand if the answer is no, but would it be possible for us to move in with you? Just until we can find another place to live?"

"Of course you can, but are you sure you want to?"

Her quick acceptance of the idea brought tears to my eyes. I felt overwhelmed with gratitude that she'd respond so favorably. I dabbed my eyes and said, "I can't think of any other solution. Not with such a short turnaround time. We could stay on the second floor. It's actually more room than we have now. Brawny is a wonderful cook, so you might enjoy coming home to hot meals and waking up to homemade breakfasts."

"Sounds divine. And you're right. The second floor is unoccupied. I suppose you could put most of your furniture in storage. Some of it would fit into the garage, I guess. But can you stand being around Mom? She's so mean, Kiki. You wouldn't believe the things she's said to Catherine. Cathy said that even the Twelve Step folks found it hard to believe how nasty our mother is. That's saying something."

I nodded. "You're right, but I figure that if I keep the kids on the second floor, we don't need to interact with Mom. At least we can keep the interactions to a bare minimum. Our only other option is giving up our pets for a while. We think that would actually be harder on the kids than living in the same house with Mom. They're both emotionally dependent on their furry siblings."

"Brawny can act as a buffer," said Detweiler. "I have no doubt that she can hold her own against your mother. In fact, I'll go one step further. I'd never agree to this if I didn't think that you, Catherine, and Brawny could help protect the kids from her antics. With the three of you helping us, I don't think she'll get away with much bull."

"Of course, we will make a contribution toward your monthly rent payment," I said.

"Pooh. If you pay your share of utilities, you can consider this an early wedding gift. Do you think we need to talk this over with Clancy? She's your friend. You know her better than I do," said Amanda.

"I'll call her," I said.

"Meanwhile I'll talk it over with Catherine," Amanda said.

We moved to other subjects, including the possibility of taking a trip over to Eckert's Orchard to pick the last apples of the season. But I struggled to focus on such a pleasant activity. The thought of packing terrified me. I remembered how difficult it had been when I first moved into the big house George built for us in Ladue. Anya had only been a toddler at the time. Moving with a little one made a tough situation nearly unbearable. Of course, back then, I wasn't working full-time either.

Amanda noticed the panicky look on my face.

"You worried about packing up? I can understand that. But remember, it's daunting to you because it's your stuff. I'm not emotionally involved."

She had a point.

"Here's the plan," she said. "I'll call a temporary caregiver to watch Mom. Catherine and I can come over Friday night and get started. We can finish up on Saturday. Can you get people to cover the store? Okay, good. I suggest that you get Anya out of the house. Have her stay at her friend's place. Brawny can take care of Erik and the animals. Your place is small. If we have enough people, we can pack you up in one day, two at most."

"Do you really think we can get this done in a day and a half?" I asked.

"Nothing to it but to do it," she said, as she hugged me.

35

While Detweiler drove us back to the house, I called Clancy. When I told her what Leighton had decided about moving us out that weekend, she went ballistic. "How dare he? I have a good mind to come over and pin his ears to his head!"

"Whoa," I said. "Before you do that, I need your help."

I explained our limited options and asked, "Is it all right with you if we move into the second floor at your mother's house? You need to be honest with me, Clancy. If you have a problem about us bringing in a dog and two cats, I need to know."

"I have no problems with that whatsoever. Although I couldn't stand to live with you, you'll keep the place clean enough. Besides, now I have a good reason to come over and get you organized."

We both chuckled at that. During every visit to my house, she manages to cull through my belongings, organize them, label things, and generally tidy up the place. She can't help it. She's borderline OCD. We've come to an understanding. Anytime she feels a burning desire to clean or pick up while she's visiting, she can have at it. I'll get out of her way.

"Thanks a million," I said as I gave her an air-kiss loud enough that she could hear it over the phone lines.

"Thanks from me, too," said Detweiler, raising his voice so Clancy could hear him.

"Why don't I call Rebekkah and see if she and Margit could run the store this weekend?" Clancy asked. "That way I can help you and your sisters pack? If you let me in there, you'll know exactly where everything is. Besides, you shouldn't be lifting anything, Kiki. Let the three of us do the hauling, wrapping, and packing."

I opened my mouth to protest, but Detweiler reached over and covered it with his hand.

"Clancy?" he said. "I've always thought you were pretty terrific. Now I'm revising my assessment upwards. I agree with you one hundred percent. Kiki should not be lifting boxes."

I thanked my friend again and ended the phone call. There was only one hurdle left to climb. We had to tell Anya. When I'd first learned I was pregnant, Anya had been spending the night at her friend Nicci Moore's house. Nicci's mother, Jennifer, had broken the news about my pregnancy to Anya for me. I'll never know exactly what Jennifer had said or how she'd put it, but she'd managed to convince my daughter that being a big sister was the coolest job on earth. I wondered how could I structure our announcement so that Anya felt strong and capable of handling this change?

"What am I going to tell Anya?" I asked Detweiler.

"I don't know. I suppose we could start by explaining this wasn't our idea."

"Throw Leighton under the bus?"

"He deserves it, but no," said Detweiler. "On second thought, that's not a good strategy. I don't want Anya to have trust issues."

"I have trust issues."

"Right, see?"

We laughed. I twined my fingers through his. Having him to share my burdens certainly made life better.

"How about if you tell her that Leighton came to you with a problem, and that he's really, really sorry," I said.

"I won't do that. I won't make excuses for him. He didn't say that he was sorry, Kiki. Not even once. In fact, he's sort of decided that his wayward daughter comes first and that he doesn't owe you anything. I'm not going to lie for the man or sugarcoat what he's done. I'll tell her honestly that I'm disappointed in him. Sometimes even people we like and trust let us down."

"That's a good point. I'll tell her that our long-range plan is to buy a house. I'll emphasize that we'll choose one as a family."

"Right," he said as he stroked his chin. "I think it's important that we be honest. Yes, we'll regret leaving this place. Yes, we're sad at how Leighton made his decision. But on the other hand, we're looking forward to finding someplace that's perfect for us. Particularly because our family is growing," he said.

"But for the near term, we'll have to lump it, because we have pets. We don't have many options."

"Blame it on the critters, huh?" said Detweiler, giving me a sideways glance.

"No, but it's true. When she sees that this is really a choice between giving up the animals or living..."

"In the same house as your mother..."

"She'll see that we're making the right decision," I said, and then I stopped. "Or not."

"Babe, we're doing the best we can. She might throw an absolute wobbly, as Brawny says, but at the end of the day we're her parents. She'll have to move with us and make the best of a bad situation."

"Uh-huh," I said. However, I had a sinking feeling that "wobbly" wouldn't begin to cover how upset my daughter was going to be.

36

"How did it go?" asked Clancy on Monday morning after sticking her head inside my office. As usual, she was dressed in classic style, gray slacks, a pink twin set, and pearls. But the black booties on her feet jazzed up the outfit, making it more trendy than retro.

"Not well," I admitted. "At first, Anya thought this was a practical joke. Then she wanted to run over and fuss at Leighton. Of course, she cried. That got her wound up. She started to spiral out of control because to her, this place is home. At the very least, it's her favorite house, and here she was being asked to make all these adjustments."

"Sharing it with a new brother and a baby and a nanny," said Clancy.

"Plus a new father figure. The whole kit and caboodle."
"That must have been distressing."

I grinned despite myself. Only someone like Clancy could use the word "distressing" in a sentence and sound totally sincere.

"It was," I agreed. "For a while, I thought we were on our way to a full blown meltdown, and then something miraculous happened. Erik walked over, put his hand on Anya's shoulder and said, 'Peas don't cry.' She recognized that he was puckering up, and suddenly there was more at stake that just her own welfare. I give her credit: She hasn't been a big sister for long, but she's taking to the role just fine. This was a horrible shock to her, and she handled it pretty well, all things considered."

"What about Brawny? What did she say?"

"Detweiler had forewarned her, but even so, she surprised me. She put an arm around Anya and said, 'We'll all be together, Annie. That's what counts. You know what a blessing it is to have your family by your side. You can see that your mother is plenty upset about this. She's made up her mind to be polite and kind to Mr. Haversham, even though he's hurt her something fierce."

"How about you?" Anya asked. "Are you okay with all this, Brawny?"

"Right as the spring rain on heather," she said, "although if he crosses my path in a dark alley, I might use my dirk to carve out that black heart of his.'"

"Uh!" Clancy covered her mouth. "She did not!"

"Oh, yes, she did. To make her point, she pulled out a tiny knife from the garter holding up her knee socks. I thought I'd keel over on the spot, but Anya was fascinated. Erik took one look and said, 'Dirk,' so I suspect he's seen it before. Next thing I know, the kids are out in the yard, and Brawny's showing them knife tricks."

Clancy sank down in the chair across from me. "I don't know whether to laugh or cry."

"Well, it does explain one thing. I wondered why she never wears slacks, only a plaid skirt. Now I see that if she had on pants she couldn't grab that knife in the blink of an eye."

"Is she still thinking that someone might hurt Erik?"

I'd warned everyone in the store that Erik could be a target.

To my mind, forewarned was forearmed. Since he often came here to play, they needed to be on their guard.

"Yes, in fact, while Detweiler and I were out talking with Amanda, Brawny got a call from Lorraine Lauber."

"News?"

"Sort of. Lorraine ordered a guard dog. A smart idea, actually. The breeder's in Frankfort, Kentucky. Since that's close to us, she's planning a short visit. Should be here on Friday."

"You really do have your hands full, don't you?" said Clancy.

"Yep. Should be interesting, huh?"

37

"**K**nock, knock," said a voice outside my office door. Clancy and I pivoted in our seats to see Hadcho.

"I didn't come to do a security check, but now that I'm here, you need to either keep your back door locked at all times or have some sort of dinger that rings when it's open. I'll talk to Detweiler about it. In the meantime, lock up, okay?"

Clancy rose with the intention of moving over one seat, but before she could, Hadcho asked, "Got any coffee in here?"

"So now I'm your personal secretary?" Clancy doesn't take any guff off of anyone. I like that about her. I would have gone and poured him a cup without a second thought. Not Clancy. She's very good at drawing lines and keeping boundaries.

"No, ma'am, you aren't. If you'll point me in the right direction, I'll make coffee for all of us."

She did, getting up and walking past him. To my surprise, she was back in a few, but she took the seat farthest from the door. Her mouth twisted as she tried to resist the urge to smirk about her victory.

Sure enough, Hadcho returned with three coffees on a tray.

"I made instant decaf for you, Kiki. I know you miss the real stuff, but that's the breaks."

I thanked him and took my mug.

"Clancy, you take yours black with two sugars." He set the mug in front of her. I sipped mine and realized he'd doctored it just right.

"Now that we're all set with our refreshments," he said. "I call this meeting to order. I am no fool, so I've decided to work with you rather than against you."

"What exactly does that mean?" I asked.

"Murray told me that he's running up against a brick wall with Laurel Wilkins' stabbing. Detweiler will be here any minute, and he'll fill you in on what we've learned."

As if on cue, my honey joined us. He grabbed a chair on wheels from Margit's desk and rolled it to the outer edge of the office.

"I made fresh coffee," said Hadcho.

"No, thanks," said Detweiler. "Brawny has spoiled me rotten. She fixes a 'to go' cup for me every morning."

"Here's the deal," said Hadcho. "Both of you ladies have to agree to keep your lips zipped. We can't tell you all the details, but you have to tell us everything you learn."

"Wait a minute," I said. "That hardly seems a fair trade." "Take it or leave it."

Clancy and I both shrugged. I said, "Okay, spill it."

"Here's what Murray has told me. So far none of the forensic evidence has been helpful," said Hadcho. "As you know, we combed that bathroom for anything we could find. In fact, we even removed the sink trap. There was all sorts of blood in that john, but without a warrant, we can't match it to any one person. Laurel Wilkins' clothes had two types of blood on them. Hers and someone else's. But Murray can't figure out who that second person might be. Or even if it's human. He's running DNA tests, but as usual, that'll take a while."

"We gave Murray your list of attendees, but he could use more background on them," continued Detweiler. "As you're aware, that's a long list. We're wondering who knew Laurel and who didn't. As best you can tell us."

"Okay," I said. "I can print another copy of the guest list and tell you what we know, although it's possible that there were people in attendance who knew Laurel outside of the store. If that's the case, we can't tell you much."

"Of course," said Hadcho. "But it's a start."

As the list of attendees printed, I told my friends, "I saw a photo yesterday. Mary Martha Delaney had it. The picture showed Laurel and Father Joe. But it had been torn to exclude Laurel. The women made it clear that they didn't much care for her."

"Not care for her?" asked Detweiler with the sort of expression that suggested he found this confusing.

"Um, right."

"Are you holding back on us?" asked Hadcho.

"No, I mean, sort of. I don't want to accuse anyone of anything I can't confirm, but these women definitely did not like Laurel."

The two detectives said nothing.

"What about her belly dancing? Could that be a link?" I asked.

"We're checking into it," said Hadcho. "And her studies?" asked Clancy. "Ditto."

Clancy cut a sidewise look down at my desk. I knew she was considering whether to tell them about the purloined homework. I was wondering about that, too.

"We found this in the recycling," and I opened the desk drawer to hand over the papers.

"We knew she was taking classes from this guy," said Hadcho as he studied the stack. "We're trying to talk to her friends, classmates."

"Have you questioned her mother?" I asked.

"She's in assisted living," said Hadcho, passing Laurel's homework assignment to Detweiler.

"I meant Mert," I said.

Hadcho and Detweiler glanced at each other. The message was obvious. They'd known Mert was Laurel's mother for some time, and they hadn't intended to share that with Clancy and me. But now it was out in the open.

"That's a dead end," said Hadcho. "The whole mother thing. Both biological and adoptive."

"Did you look into her friendship with John Henry Schnabel?" I asked.

"They were in foster care together," Detweiler said. "Laurel wasn't adopted until she was seven."

"You have to tell us what her status is," said Clancy. "That's only fair."

"She'll be released tomorrow," said Detweiler. "She still can't remember anything that happened to her or who stabbed her."

"We asked the police force over in her neck of the woods to keep an eye on her place. She's got a small place in an apartment complex," said Hadcho.

"Good." I nodded my head. "She should be safe."

"Not exactly," said Detweiler. "The local force didn't sound very interested in watching over her. In fact, they came up short of declining our request."

"What on earth?" Clancy spat out.

"You have to remember that Laurel's uncle is Johnny Chambers. Johnny has made a lot of enemies in the law enforcement community," said Detweiler.

"But that's Johnny! That's not Laurel!" I said. "Can't they tell the difference?"

Hadcho sighed. "Unfortunately, in this case, they don't seem to *want* to tell the difference."

"You're telling us that they won't keep an eye out for Laurel's assailant?" asked Clancy.

Detweiler looked down at his feet. Hadcho took his sweet time answering, "That's pretty much the way it is."

38

---

*A*fter I kissed Detweiler goodbye and gave Hadcho a peck on the cheek for good measure, I closed and locked the back door. Hadcho was right. We needed to keep it locked, but that would only work if all my employees had keys. Catherine was due to arrive at one. She would be working her first "in store" crop. Margit wouldn't be in today because she was meeting with one of the doctors at the assisted living facility where her mother was a resident. Margit's aging mother had dementia, and from what little Clancy knew, the woman's health had taken a turn for the worse.

I still needed to prep for our crop, but I planned to involve Catherine in that, which would be good because she'd learn the ins and outs of what was necessary.

"I need to run an errand," I told Clancy. She was taking a quick inventory of our inks and Tim Holtz paraphernalia. Since tonight I was teaching our croppers how to make paper beads, these supplies would go fast.

"Let me guess," she said, smiling up at me from her spot on the floor. "You're running by the hospital where Laurel is."

"Actually I wasn't, although that's a good idea."

"I think so, too," she said with a nod. "Especially given that the local law enforcement community isn't interested in protecting her. Why don't you take money out of petty cash? Drop by Dierbergs or Schnucks and pick up a bouquet. I'll make a fake name badge for you."

I stifled a laugh. "You are too funny. By day, Miss Prim and Proper, but by Night—"

"I'm Emma Peel from *The Avengers*. I always loved her sense of style!"

Twenty minutes later, I had flowers in hand, a fake badge that would have fooled anybody, and I stood in front of a positively ancient volunteer at So Co (which is what the locals call South County General Hospital).

"Delivery for Laurel Wilkins," I said. "She's in Room 252."

Eyes magnified to cartoonish proportions gave me the once over. "Room 354."

"Oh," I said and pretended confusion. "I guess someone copied it down wrong on my form."

Without waiting for directions, I scooted right past Methuselah's grandmother.

The door to Room 354 was ajar. A television set hummed, and James Earl Jones announced, "CNN. The most trusted name in news." Since I'm in love with Anderson Cooper, I took this as a good sign.

I rapped quickly on the doorframe and stepped inside.

Laurel looked awful. She had a huge bandage wrapped around her neck. Her regulation hospital gown barely covered another bandage that peeped out of the neckline. At the sound of my entrance, she turned toward the door.

"Kiki! What a wonderful surprise! Flowers, for me? That's so nice!"

Since I'd had the foresight to buy an inexpensive vase, all I needed to do was unwrap the cellophane.

"These are from everyone at the store. How are you feeling?"

"Pretty punk. I guess you know I have diabetes."

"Right," I said. "I wish I'd known that in advance. If something had happened to you, I might have done the wrong thing." She colored slightly. "I don't like having anyone know. When I was young, I was teased about it. I guess I should put that aside and act more grown-up about it. But I feel like people already look at me and make all sorts of assumptions. They think that because I've been blessed with good looks that my life is perfect. So I hold back on the diabetes info, because it's my way of reminding myself that they don't know as much about me as they think they do."

I took both her hands in mine. "Laurel, when I first met you, I found it hard to get past how beautiful you are. But now I look at you and just see Laurel, my friend. You are beautiful to me for all sorts of reasons. I hope at some point, you'll feel comfortable to share more of yourself with me. Because you couldn't tell me anything that would make me like you less. That's impossible. However, I would like to know you better."

A tear slid down her cheek. "I grew up in foster homes. After being bounced around, I had a hard time feeling I was really worthwhile, you know? It's better now, but I learned bad habits. When you don't have any champions, people bully you. I kept as much to myself as possible. I shared next to nothing. I figured that if I didn't give my housemates any ammunition, they couldn't hurt me. Mostly that worked. But now, I need to recalibrate? Or what is it that the GPS lady says? Recalculate?"

"I'm sorry you went through that. I didn't know. In fact, I didn't know that Mert was your biological mother until yesterday."

"That's because I don't think of her as my mother," she said. "She didn't raise me. Of course, it wasn't her fault that I was taken from her. After she looked me up, I told her that we could be friends, but that Edith Wilkins was my mother. Edith adopted me, and even though her husband left us shortly thereafter, she kept me. Edith will always be my mom."

"I hope that Erik will feel the same about me one day. That I'm his mom."

"He will."

I cleared my throat. "Do you need anything? Want me to run down to the gift shop or the vending machines?"

"No. Thanks. How did the rest of the crop go?"

I laughed. "Let's put it this way, they'll be talking about that particular crop for years and years to come!"

"Someone tried to take me out." Her voice was raspy. Another tear trickled down her cheek and hung suspended from her chin.

"I know. Any ideas who it might have been?"

"I wish I could remember. I started feeling sick. I knew I needed to check my blood sugar. I opened my purse. Next thing I remembered, I woke up in the emergency room."

"Okay," I said. "Was there anyone at the crop who didn't like you? Any enemies?"

"Hadcho stopped by and asked the same thing. Do you have a list of the participants?"

I did. I pulled it out of my back pocket. Smoothing it flat, I handed it over. "Where are you going after you leave here, Laurel? I'm worried about you staying alone."

"Mert insisted that I come stay at her house. I told her I wanted to be in my own apartment with my things around me. Hadcho told me I shouldn't be on my own. The doctor was concerned, too. So I guess Mert will come and stay with me."

She picked up the list and scanned it. "Everyone on this list has been really nice to me. I can't imagine anyone taking a knife and..."

"Could someone on the staff of the talent agency have had a

problem with you? I looked on your Facebook page. I didn't know you had a second career."

"Oh, that," she laughed. "I took lessons after I broke up with a boyfriend. I was so depressed I couldn't get out of bed. When I started, I was awful, but this other girl in the class needed help with her business, so I went with her on a couple of gigs. Then she left town, and I took over her clients. It's fun. You should try it."

"Maybe I—"

"What are you doing here?" A sharp voice interrupted me.

Mert Chambers stood in the doorway, glaring at me. "You aren't family. You ain't supposed to be here. Nurse!"

That's how I got thrown out of South County General.

39

"*I* can't believe her!" I said over my cell phone to Clancy. I was so angry that I shook with rage. "She treated me like I was some sort of stalker. Some creep. Not like she and I had been friends for years or like Laurel and I were close."

"She's a mom doing her Mama Bear imitation," said Clancy. "I wouldn't let it worry you."

"First she blames me for what happened with her brother. Now she blames me for what has happened with Laurel!" "You don't know that." Clancy was trying to sooth me.

"Yes, I do! You should have heard her. Mert yelled, 'Haven't you done enough damage to my family?' I think that message is perfectly clear. She's found another reason to blame me."

"She'll get over it."

"That's what you said after Johnny got hurt. And she hasn't." "Are you driving?"

"Kind of."

Clancy sighed loudly enough that it came through the phone and over the ambient noises outside. "Then you need to end this conversation and concentrate on what you're doing. You

156

can't change Mert's mind, Kiki. Getting in a car accident won't help Laurel."

She was right. I sort of hung up on her. I didn't mean to, but I nearly sideswiped a parked car as I shut off my phone. I wasn't sure whether I wanted to cry or bang my fist against the steering wheel. How could this woman have been my best friend! Who turns on you like that?

I pulled into a parking lot and reopened my phone. I'd recently installed the Google Maps app. Now I hit the search function and typed in St. James Episcopal Church. The nice lady who gives me earthly guidance told me that I was ten minutes away. I did a U-turn. At the very least, I could pray once I got there. I'd pray for my family and our move. I'd pray for the health of my baby. I'd pray that guardian angels would watch over Anya and Erik. Especially Erik. I'd pray that my mother wouldn't be too miserable for us to live with. I'd pray that our move went smoothly.

Of course, I'd pray for Laurel's health and safety. Would I pray that Mert changed her mind about me? I mulled that request over.

I'm not a big believer in dumping friends. Okay, sometimes you have to go your separate ways. You have to agree to disagree. Or you simply fall out of contact. You discover your interests have changed.

Once in a while, you recognize that you were deceived. That you only knew one aspect of a person, and that there were other sides to her, sides that are unacceptable to you. For example, I remembered a neighbor who moved next door a couple of years after George and I built our house in Ladue. Her name had been Mary. She had seemed perfectly nice. I had admired Mary's ability to throw a party. Then we attended a neighborhood event together, and she lied to someone just because it suited her to do so. Later I asked her about what she'd done. Mary laughed about the situation.

I didn't.

I had gone home and crossed her phone number off the paper list in my kitchen.

George had told me I was being childish, but I had disagreed. "That woman has no conscience. It's one thing to make a mistake and feel badly about it. It's another to simply not care about someone's feelings. Mary had that other woman twisted in knots. It was cruel."

What I should do about Mert. Should I cross off her number? I understood that she'd been upset when Johnny was shot. She blamed me. I figured once the truth came to light, she'd slowly get over her temper, and our relationship would normalize. But this afternoon showed me another side of Mert. She didn't care about what was good for Laurel. She didn't stop to see if Laurel wanted my company or not.

Clancy was wrong. This wasn't Mama Bear behavior. This was something else.

I couldn't figure out what.

Frankly, I was sick and tired of trying to come up with excuses for the woman I once called "my best friend."

40

St. James Episcopal Church reminded me of the church I'd attended growing up. A stately edifice of limestone with a red door, hinged with black wrought iron. Twin locust trees bracketed the entrance. A sign announced, "All are welcome!" I sincerely hoped that was true.

Bright yellow mums edged the foundation of the building and sent up clouds of spice-scented perfume. A glass case protected a sign that listed the hours of Holy Eucharist and other services. At the bottom in smallest lettering was a legend proclaiming that Father Joseph Riley was the "priest in residence."

Most priests and rabbis spend an inordinate amount of their time doing office work, writing sermons, and supervising myriad details of church work. They can typically be found in an office, rather than in a sacred space. Walking into the church proper would ease my soul, but I doubted that I'd bump into the good father on bended knee. As I stood by my car, my eyes followed the bulky stonework to my right, and sure enough, there was a second door. Much plainer but with a groove worn by the pressure of many hands. My guess was that this door led the way to the business offices, the assembly hall, and the Sunday School rooms.

What to do?

I decided to go inside and pray. I was here as much for my needs as for Laurel's.

The front door opened easily to the narthex. Once inside, I waited while my eyes adjusted to the dim light. A small greeting area held pamphlets of all sorts and another one of the ubiquitous glass cases, displaying the hymn numbers in the order they would be sung. After I could see a little better, I clasped the huge wrought iron door handle and yanked the door open.

The wonder of the nave sent chills down my spine. A soaring stained-glass window depicted Christ surrounded by children. A simple wooden cross was suspended from the ceiling. Although many Episcopal churches prefer a crucifix, I appreciated the stark simplicity of this rugged wooden icon. Dust motes danced in rays of sunlight that streamed through stained-glass windows on each side of the nave. Red carpet dulled my footsteps. The lingering fragrance of incense brought back memories.

About halfway up the aisle, I slipped into a pew. The kneeling cushions had been needlepointed in a true labor of love. The place was peaceful and quiet, so I rested my head in my hands, and cleared my mind.

When I opened my eyes, I saw Father Joe at the altar rail. His head was bowed and his hands pressed in prayerful supplication.

If I stood or moved, I might disturb him. He probably had a lot to pray about. So I sat there quietly, but he seemed to realize he was not alone. Or maybe he'd seen me hunched over and he decided to let me pray first before greeting me.

Whatever the sequence was, he raised his head. Slowly, he

rose to his feet. With a small bow of his head, he saluted the altar. I sat there quietly and waited.

"Kiki Lowenstein," he said, when he turned to face me. "I've been hoping you'd stop by."

41

"’m afraid that I can’t offer you any Diet Dr Pepper, but I guess that’s for the best, isn’t it? How about a bottle of water?" Father Joe escorted me down the backstairs and into his office. Once he got settled behind his desk, I perched on a surprisingly comfortable modern chair of navy leather with brass tacks. As he reached down under a credenza and opened a small refrigerator and withdrew two bottles of water, one for each of us. While he served us, I admired the streamlined shelving units, the uncluttered décor, and the silver lamp with a long arm extending over his desk space.

"Ikea," he said, with a sheepish grin. "The old desk had a footprint as big as a zip code. No one could fit in here but Father Conrad. I suspect that was done on purpose. Not big into counseling. Or listening. Or tending to the flock. Quite the showman, though. Enjoyed high church and all the trimmings. That man went through incense like Barnum & Bailey goes through sawdust."

I laughed. I couldn’t help myself.

"I just talked with Laurel. She figured you’d stop by. I can’t believe someone took a knife to her." He paused as a shiver shook his body. "Sometimes I forget I'm a priest. When I heard what happened to her, when I saw her in that hospital bed, I thought I'd go ballistic."

The water came in handy, as I took a drink to cover my own emotions. When I felt in control, I said, "I am so, so sorry. You can't imagine how—"

He waved away my apology. "You didn't hurt her. You saved her life."

My vision blurred as tears prickled behind my eyes. I swallowed more water and pinched the bridge of my nose. I would not allow myself to feel sorry for me. Not right now.

"Hey, let's be grateful she'll live and move on. We sure had a great time at the Detweilers' farm," he said. "It was a perfect evening. Good friends, good food, great scenery. Here's to many more such times together in the future." He raised his water bottle and we tapped them together in a silent version of a toast. "And here's to good friends who love Laurel. Thank you again for saving her life, and for being such a wonderful influence on her. She really looks up to you. I can totally see why.

You're everything she aspires to be."

"Come on," I said. "That's spreading it on a bit thick. No wonder you've charmed all your women parishioners," I said.

"Aw, that," he blushed. "I hope to make them feel important and welcome. For too long, the church has pushed women to the outskirts, excuse my pun. But the women do most of the daily running of the church. Without them, I couldn't keep the doors open on this big barn. No, really! I once did a calculation on the man hours—man hours, can you believe that?—that it took to keep the average sized-church running. You would not believe it! No way could we afford the overhead. Women are the lifeblood of the church, and most of them either work for free or next to nothing."

"Well spoken, sir. Hurrah, hurrah!"

"Like you doing that crop for the Diabetes Research Foundation. If men gave as much of themselves and their time, this would be a better world."

"Speaking of the crop, that reminds me. I owe you a thank-you note. You helped our cause tremendously by telling people about the crop. That was very kind of you. Three members of your church showed up both nights. There might also have been other church members, but I know specifically of three, Mary Martha, Patricia, and Dolores."

With a quick gesture of his hand, he signaled for me to shut the door behind me, and I did.

"Did they behave themselves?" he said. His face had turned solemn.

"Excuse me?"

"Come on, you know what I mean." "Sorry. I'm not sure that I do."

He sighed and steepled his fingers. "All three of those women are lonely, unhappy souls. I've tried to work with them. I worry that they've taken any kindness on my part the wrong way. Entirely."

"I see."

"Do you?"

"Yup, I do. We live in a society where a woman is marginalized unless she has a man in her life. I suspect that all three of those parishioners are single, right? You are young, good looking, and in their eyes, available. There's a reason that *The Thornbirds* was such a hit on TV. And *The Borgias*."

Father Joe shook his head and rubbed his eyes. "I hate this. I hate it. It was never my intention to mislead any of them. But I couldn't shun them! I had the sick feeling that they misunderstood. One of the male vestry members mentioned as much to me, but I laughed it off. I figured that if I kept them really busy, they'd come to hate me. Or even decide to back away. Instead, they think they have the inside track on everything that happens in my office."

"You're going to need to straighten them out," I said. "This is a community. Problems will spread like wildfire through the prairie."

"I know."

"Let's change the subject, okay? Have you seen Laurel today?"

"I stopped by the hospital this morning."

"They let you in? Because of your clerical collar?"

He laughed. "I'm sure that helped, but it was probably this collar that convinced them."

Reaching into his pocket, he pulled out a small velvet box that opened to display a diamond ring.

42

Back at Time in a Bottle

"So what did he say next?" asked Clancy. She looked as stunned as I had felt when Father Joe told me he planned to marry Laurel. "They haven't been dating that long, have they?"

"He got this huge grin on his face and told me that they'd met this summer when she was doing her special project. Although he hasn't asked her to marry him yet, they've been talking about it. He didn't want to propose in the hospital," and I paused. "Did you ever see that episode of *House* where he says that a ten marries a ten? That's exactly what we have here: a twenty. They're both absolutely gorgeous!"

"Okay, next question. Whom does he suspect as having stabbed his sweetheart? Surely the man has an idea or two."

"I'd say the gleesome threesome is right at the top of his list. I suggested that he talk to Detweiler. Father Joe also promised not to tell Detweiler that I'd been snooping around. I reminded him that I'd been praying, not snooping. So, it's all good."

"What did he say to that?"

"He threw back his head and laughed. You know him, Clancy. He was one of your favorite students. He's just the cutest thing. The women are right. He could have been a rock star. Total hottie. I can't blame him for thinking it might be one of them. They were worshipful when they spoke of him, but I get the feeling that they hold him to an almost impossible standard. And I can back up my intuition with observations. They were very concerned about the fact that I'm not married. They wanted to know what my future plans are. There were a lot of dark looks of disapproval."

"Then you better be careful tonight." "What do you mean?"

"As you know, all three of the women from St. James are coming to this crop. Maybe you should pat them down for shivs."

"Take away their X-Acto knives?" I shook my head. "Not hardly. Sounds risky to me."

"Speaking of risky business, Faye Edorra called. You forgot to give her a check for her appearances."

"Crud, I knew I was forgetting something! Did you apologize for me?"

"Sure did. She was a little miffed, but she'll get over it. I think she's planning to stop by tomorrow to pick it up. I pinned it to the corkboard. You still need to sign it."

"What would I do without you?" I said, and I gave her a hug. Clancy always accepts and gives affection stiffly, but I don't care. I'm still going to hug her. Whatever her reasons for feeling awkward about personal contact, I suspect she's trying to get over them. Clancy speaks her mind, so I have to believe that if affection really made her uncomfortable, she'd let me know.

"You're just buttering me up because Mert has been treating you like bird poop on a windshield." Her smile was warm.

"It hurts. It really hurts, but I can't fix it. She's made a decision and that's all there is to it."

"She's acting like a witch," said Clancy. "You deserve better."

"I thought I did," I said. "I guess she sees things differently."

43

———

ime flew past. I didn't realize I'd missed lunch until I heard someone pounding on the back door with both fists. "Hey! Let me in!"

I opened it and apologized to my sister Catherine. "Hadcho warned me about leaving it unlocked. Come on into the office. I have a key for you."

"A skeleton? Isn't that a bit ghoulish? Even for you?" My sister held up the black key with the white skull printed on it.

"I thought it was funny. See, it's a skeleton key!" "Kiki, you are nuts."

"Yup. Did you bring me any lunch?"

"Of course. I know you're always hungry, so I made us both a salad. They're in the Tupperware containers. I assume you can supply the beverages?"

We took the food and two bottles of water to my work table. In between bites of salad, I explained to Catherine about our crops. How we always included meals, but how the scrapbookers also brought a dish to share.

"The most important difference between our crops and the events held by our competitors are our make-and-take projects.

Not only do our guests walk away with a completed project, they also learn a new skill. Because these are add-ons to our crops, I try to keep them as thrifty as possible. Otherwise they would cut into our profit margin."

Next I showed her tonight's offering, paper beads. Catherine held up the necklace I'd created and cooed, "Cool!"

"I think it will be fun. Not only can you string the beads to make jewelry, but you can also add them to a page for embellishments. Best of all, the project costs next to nothing. We'll use pages from old magazines, toothpicks, glue, and Diamond Glaze."

Of course, she didn't know what Diamond Glaze was, so I showed her the dimensional adhesive that dries to a glass-like finish.

I pulled out the laminated form that Margit had created, the one that went through the steps for setting up the physical space for our crops. My sister was amazed at how we could roll our display units to one side to give us more room for tables.

"Did you tell her that someone might be gunning for you?" asked Clancy. She turned to Catherine and explained what I'd learned that day about the three women from St. James Episcopal Church.

"Come on, Clancy. You're taking this too far. They were obviously offended that I was pregnant and not married, but I doubt that they plan to do me any harm."

"Not really. Look, somebody stabbed Laurel. We don't know who it was, but it had to have been someone on the catering staff or someone in our group. Your sister happens to be a lightning rod for trouble," Clancy said to Catherine, as she pointed at me. "We both need to be watchful."

"I have no idea what to do if someone pulls a knife," said Catherine.

"I do," said Brawny as she walked through the front door.

"Detective Detweiler thought I should attend your event tonight."

"Who's watching Erik and Anya?" I asked the Scotswoman. "Your mother-in-law-to-be, Detective Detweiler's mother,

Miss Thelma. She tried to text-message you, but she's got a new iPhone and doesn't know how to use it very well. Her errands brought her into the city, and she came by the house. Detective Detweiler asked his mother if she could pick up the bairns after school and stay with them until your crop was over. Overjoyed she was. He planned to go back into work, and he asked me to come here to the store."

I wondered why, and my face must have telegraphed my curiosity.

Brawny leaned in and asked, "Could I speak to you in private?"

Since Catherine and Clancy had the prep well in hand, I could easily escort my son's nanny to the office. There I closed the door and plopped down in the big, black leather chair. "What's up?"

"Detective Detweiler spoke to the priest at the Episcopal Church seconds after you did. Seems that the more the young man thought about his overly amorous parishioners, the more he worried for your safety."

"Me? Mine? Why?" This struck me as preposterous.

"Sunday morning after services, the women asked Father Joe the definition of adultery. Standing right there at what they call coffee hour? They pinned him down. He tried to avoid the conversation, but they rather pressed the point on the issue. In the strictest interpretation, they believe you committed adultery."

I could feel the heat gathering under my collar. Who were these women and what right did they have to sit in judgment of me.

"Right, and Detweiler was separated and trying to get a divorce when that happened. Even so, haven't they ever heard that only those without sins should cast stones? What's up with these whackos?"

"It gets worse. The priest wouldn't go into specifics. The sanctity of the confessional and all. But at least one of the three women has had serious mental health issues. Hears voices and what-naught. In this case, what-naught includes violent behavior."

Brawny's demeanor did not change throughout this recitation. As she finished, she looked just as unruffled as she'd begun. But her words had caused me to panic. My hyper-vigilance kicked in.

Was I in danger? I didn't even have to ask the question.

Brawny read my face.

"It's possible that whoever stabbed Laurel Wilkins could now be targeting you. Although she hasn't remembered what happened when she was attacked, she did tell Detective Hadcho that she's had several other mishaps. A problem with her car. Messages on her phone. At her home. Through Facebook. All of them called her a Jezebel, a tempter of upright men."

"She didn't mention a word of this to me!" I felt betrayed, but instantly, I realized I was being silly. Laurel was struggling. She'd come within an inch of losing her life, and my appearance forced her to go back over that harrowing event.

"She figured it was probably some woman whose husband seemed a little too interested in her belly dancing routine. So she ignored it," said Brawny.

I swallowed. The edges of my vision blurred.

"But that was then and this is now. You can't ignore it, Miss Kiki. The villain who did this struck once. She might strike again, and your bairns depend on you."

44

When I announced that Brawny would be joining us for the crop, Clancy and Catherine welcomed her. Then I dropped the nuclear bomb and explained why her presence was important.

"The threat to Kiki is real?" asked Clancy. "What do we need to watch for?"

"I hope not. Just keep your eyes open. There's also a concern for wee Erik's safety," and Brawny went on to explain what worried us.

"If this is really dangerous, shouldn't a cop be watching the boy 24/7?" Turning toward our nanny, Clancy added, "I don't mean to be unkind, but you aren't a cop, Brawny. How could you possibly hope to protect Kiki?"

"I was trained in Britain as one of the few women members of the SRR, the Special Reconnaissance Regiment. That's your equivalent to being a Navy SEAL. If a situation arises, I'm up to it."

Clancy's eyebrows flew up to nearly touch her scalp. Catherine's jaw dropped. I stifled a giggle. In her tartan skirt and ponytail, it would be easy to dismiss Brawny as a strange character.

One might even want to laugh. After hearing of her training, you sobered up immediately.

Brawny took a seat at the head of the crop tables, next to where I usually stood at the front of the room.

As the scrapbookers showed up, hauling their supplies, I recognized a flaw in our plans. "You need to be working on a project or you won't fit in. What sort of album might you like to create?"

Brawny been admiring the scrapbook pages that decorated our store, and she'd seen the memory book I'd completed for Detweiler to take to California when he first met Erik. Her decision came swiftly. "I'd like to start an album about St. Louis. I've never been here before, and that might help me get better acquainted with my new home."

"Great idea, since I happen to have lots of photos of area sights," I said. After printing a dozen of them, I helped her choose an album.

"Red," she said. "I'd like it to be bright and shiny and full of promise."

Catherine shadowed me as I trooped around the store, gathering the necessary items. "You need to make an album, too, baby sis," I said. "That will teach you what scrapbooking is all about. What subject would appeal to you?"

Confession: Since I didn't know much about how Catherine had spent the past fifteen years of her life, this seemed to be a great way to find out what happened. I knew that Aunt Penny had given her bus fare that covered a trip to Summerville, South Carolina, where Aunt Penny owned a small double-wide trailer. Catherine completed her high school education, although I'm not sure whether she attended a regular school or did the work required to pass her GED. I hadn't had the nerve to ask what happened to her baby, but Amanda had, and she had told me that our sister had given up her child, a girl, for adoption.

Amanda also warned me that this was not a subject to broach with Catherine.

How Catherine had become an alcoholic, I didn't know. Of course, the genetic propensity was there. But had she started drinking when she was pregnant? After she give up her child? In response to her guilt and grief? That remained a great big question mark. Now as my sister thought over my question about making an album, I hoped I'd learn a few more answers. I didn't want to spook Catherine and make her withdraw from me, but I certainly wanted to know more about her past.

"I love animals, so could I do a book about our pets growing up? Do you have any pictures of Sabbath? Or Secant?"

Sabbath had been the stray black tom who adopted us. Secant was a beagle and basset hound mix who'd shown up in our yard and stuck around. Fortunately, I had photos of both. I also had a few pictures of Merrily We Roll Along, Aunt Penny's famous pet, a chow/hound mix who ran with an odd circular pumping motion of her legs. Hence the bizarre name.

As the photos printed from the computer, Catherine looked over the albums, trying to choose one to house her pages. Brawny stood at her side, quietly conversing about the merits of each style and color. There seemed to be an affinity between the two women. Almost as if they were kindred spirits waiting to discover each other. That brought a smile to my face. Brawny was as strong as my sister seemed fragile. It wasn't that Catherine was unhealthy, but she did exude vulnerability. If they could form a bond, both being newcomers to St. Louis, it might prove useful to each of them. They both could use a bit of companionship. Detweiler and I had told Brawny that we expected her to take time off for herself. Whether that meant driving around aimlessly, going to a movie, or meeting a friend for lunch, we didn't care. She'd cocked her head, considering and said, "I don't know anyone, so I doubt that I'll be tramping off, but I appreciate your thoughtfulness."

Perhaps she and Catherine would pal around together. They were both newcomers to this very insular place. It would be lovely if they could find common ground.

45

"*L*adies, our special project tonight will be making paper beads. Of course, as the name implies, we'll be using paper. Our source material will be magazine pages. But you can use almost any paper as long as it will bend easily," I said, as I picked up a necklace to show to the group.

"This one was made from old state maps. As you might guess, this was a state with a lot of lakes. Wisconsin, to be specific. Since the original papers displayed a lot of blue, these beads are primarily blue, with touches of green." I handed the necklace off to Brawny so she could examine it and pass it around.

"An Ikea catalog provided the inspiration for this necklace. The pages used featured red-orange, tan, and black furnishings. Notice how the finished beads have an ethnic vibe to them. I chose to string these beads with tiny red-orange glass beads to pick up on their coloring." Again, I offered the necklace to Brawny so she could begin handing it around.

"Finally, I want you to guess what this necklace is made of. Anyone?"

My croppers squinted at the gray beads with the delicate

JOANNA CAMPBELL SLAN

patterns. No one even ventured a guess, so I held up a security envelope. "These were originally old security envelopes. I upcycled my mail by using the inside of my correspondence for the outside of my beads."

"I can't believe it," said Nena Hanna as she stared at the necklace in her hands. "This is absolutely beautiful."

"Yes," said Frances Walker as she took the ethnic looking necklace from Nena's fingertips. "But what does this have to do with scrapbooking?"

"Good question," I said. I held up a scrapbook page. The embellishments were beads that I'd made from scraps of paper.

The buzz was instantaneous. All the croppers talked at once. Clancy and Catherine passed out old magazines we'd been saving.

"I'd like for you to pick a scrapbook page where beads might be a cool addition to your layout. Either pick an old page you'd like to gussy up, or one that you'd planned to work on anyway. Or you could choose a color combination that you've wanted to tackle for an upcoming page. And if that doesn't work—"

Laughter.

"Just pick colors that you like. With those shades in mind, go through these magazines and tear out two pages. That's all it takes! Remember that your magazine pages should predominately display the colors you want. How can you tell if there's enough of your desired colors? Squint. That's right. Hold the pages at arms' length and squint. If you can't see enough of the color you want, try again."

Rip-rip-rip. The sound of happy tearing filled the store. This was the first chance I'd had to walk around and chat with my customers. As I did, I helped several of them make decisions about the magazine pages they'd be using. Several signaled to me that they wanted my help. I knew that Brawny wasn't thrilled to see me walking around, but this was my job, and I intended to do it to the best of my ability. However, her concerns were uppermost in my mind, as I kept a careful distance between myself and my guests. Instead of leaning over their shoulders, I stood a respectful foot or two away from them. It certainly did feel awkward.

Dolores waved to me. "I want blue. Virgin Mary blue." "Um, I'm not sure I know which color that would be," I said.

"Of course you wouldn't know," snickered Mary Martha. "But scarlet, that's a color you're familiar with."

My face probably turned just as red as that particular color, but I decided to take the high road. "There are many variations of any primary color. We all see and interpret color differently."

Patricia smirked as she ripped two pages from a catalog. "I hope to make prayer beads, in gold and white, the Holy Spirit descending like a dove. Filling a pure heart with his grace and beauty. But perhaps you didn't realize that, Kiki. That spiritual beauty outshines temporal earthly good looks. All of us rot in the ground when we die. But the good souls among us will be crowned by the King of Kings. Those of us with righteous souls will be glorified for the true beauty within."

Patricia absolutely glowed with self-conceit. In response, her friends also assumed smug smiles.

"Mark my words," said Dolores. "The humble shall be uplifted. Those who put their appearance before the sanctity of their souls shall be revealed for the ugly creatures they are."

"You'd be amazed, Kiki," said Mary Martha in a conspiratorial tone, "how often the devil uses good looks to lure people into evil. The Bible tells us that Satan was the most beautiful of all God's angels. By the same token, many whom the masses consider lovely are really demons in disguise."

"Did Father Joe condemn corporal beauty?" I said, wondering out loud. "Was that one of his sermons?"

The gleesome threesome exchanged shifty glances.

"He said that beauty is vain." Mary Martha stuck out her lower lip. Boy, when it came to ugly, she had the corner on the market.

"In Genesis," I said, "it says that we are made in God's image. Wouldn't it follow that we would be beautiful?" "How did you come up with that?" asked Patricia.

"From reading, listening, and studying," I said. Just because I spend most of my time playing with paper and glue, doesn't mean that I'm a complete dunce.

"I believe that God leaves us love notes everywhere we look," I continued. "He sprinkles beauty on this earth in the most unlikely places, as a reminder that his hand has touched everything we see. I think that beauty elevates us. It calls us to look up with appreciation, rather than keep our gaze on the muck and mud under our feet. So beauty is not necessarily a sign of great evil. On the contrary, it can be a sign of God's love. For example, Father Joe is a beautiful man, and I think he's exactly the way God intended him to be, don't you?"

That shut all three of them up.

Taking advantage of their stunned silence, I moved on to other customers who'd both been listening to our conversation intently. It tickled me when Amy Gill bent her head close to mine and whispered, "You go, girl."

This was entirely unexpected and very much appreciated. I hadn't intended to start a ruckus. Really I hadn't. But I wasn't going to let "haters" gain a foothold in my store. This was my store. I had the payment book to prove it. Nope, as long as these women were under my roof, I wouldn't tolerate letting them spew foul, unChristian hypocrisy. This would be a place where people came together to cheer each other on. My aim was to encourage people to create not destroy.

Then and there I hatched a plan. I'd been meaning to have Rabbi Sarah come by and bless the store. Now I decided to hold an ecumenical gathering and include Father Joe, too. This place would welcome all good people of all religions to come together in harmony.

I would invite the Gruesome Threesome—Mary Martha, Dolores, and Patricia—so that they could have front rows seats. In fact, I'd even make a little speech and say that the idea came to me while talking to them.

Yeah, that was the ticket.

You live by the nasty word, you die by the nasty word.

Boo-yah!

46

The rest of the crop went smoothly. Liz Cohen brought her fabulous Robert Redford, also known as Better Than Sex, two pans of it. Any crop where you can stuff yourself with chocolate and sugar is a good crop, in my humble opinion. Julie Spinelli brought a dish called Mexican Lasagna. It was so amazing that I begged her for the recipe.

Cara Mia Delgatto had sent me a FedEx box earlier in the day after text-messaging me that the box was not to be opened until my crop. She'd also text-messaged Clancy and asked her to pick up a couple of loaves of Ezekial bread and a pound of butter. Her directions included, "Let the butter sit out and the bread defrost."

Of course I'd been curious. Clancy had slapped my fingers away twice already.

I'd been instructed to open the box when we took our break for food. With all the drama surrounding Laurel, that instruction had been pushed to the back of my agenda. However, now I opened the FedEx package with a craft knife. Looking down into the box, I didn't know what I was looking at. Not exactly. Six glass canning jars sat like a row of gold helmeted soldiers. I picked up one and held it to the light. The pinkish-ruby color amazed me and brought the croppers to a complete standstill. They'd been loading their plates with food, but one glimpse of that gem-like color stopped them in their tracks.

"What is that?" asked Liz Cohen.

"Looks like homemade jelly," said Amy Gill.

I picked up the index card taped to the top of the jars. With a yank, I freed it and read, "What we have here is seagrape jelly. It was made just this week by Cara Mia Delgatto." I twisted open the lid and took a sniff.

"These are Cara's instructions," said Clancy, holding up a piece of paper that had been snuggled between two jars. "Toast a piece of Ezekiel bread. Butter it. Add copious amounts of the jelly."

"I'm game," I said.

In seconds, Clancy had a piece of toast ready for me. I had opened my mouth for the first bite when Nena said to Amy, "Did you know that seagrapes were edible?"

Amy smiled. "Yes, I knew that because Bill and I have a place in Florida. Even so, I don't think I've ever tasted the grapes in a jelly.

I bit down and savored the robust grape flavor. "My golly, they sure are edible. This stuff is fabulous! Wow!"

That started a rush for toast and jelly. I blinked as I worried it would disappear before I could put any aside for Detweiler.

"Don't worry about them eating it all," Clancy whispered in my ear. "Cara Mia told me to tell you that she's making more batches, and she'll send another batch to you next week."

"Thank goodness because I'd have to twist some arms and grab the rest of the jelly away from our customers. Can you believe how good this is?"

"If Cara Mia makes it, you can count on it being scrumptious."

The crop ended at midnight. A half an hour later, we hustled the last of our customers through the checkout process and out the front door.

"How did you do? May I see your albums?" I asked Catherine and Brawny.

Catherine took to scrapbooking right away. She suffered the usual beginners' worries about matching paper and photos, but once she started creating her pages, she gained confidence and quit asking for my opinion.

Brawny, on the other hand, moved slowly. She was a devoted measurer who put things together very deliberately. Her color combinations were very, very conservative.

Whereas Catherine loved heaping on the embellishments, Brawny's pages were stark. Catherine tended toward cute, but Brawny would emphasize one striking element of her page and be done with it.

They put their albums side-by-side. "Did we do it right?" asked my little sister. "I'm not sure of the rules."

"That's because there are no rules," I said. "No scrapbooking police. No one who'll come to your door in the middle of the night and fine you. You do what you like. I can see that both of you are developing your own style, and as you can tell, your styles are as different as you are. That's good! These albums should reflect your personalities."

"But you do so many different things on your pages," said Catherine. "While I was gathering paper, I looked at a lot of the pages you've done, the ones on display. You use all sorts of stuff and I only used premade embellishments."

"You are just starting out," I said. "When I was starting out, there weren't as many premade embellishments to choose from. Besides, it's part of my job to come up with cool ideas that my customers can re-create. That's not what you're trying to do. That said, look at the page you did with your beads. You found pages with black-and-white print. You made the black-and-white beads, and you edged your page with them. That's pretty upscale work for a newbie."

"I'll say," said Clancy as she joined us. "I didn't try anything other than premade embellishments on my pages for a year. Kiki basically forced me into it. Otherwise, I'd buy it and slap it down. I just didn't have the confidence to think outside the box."

Brawny looked admiringly at Catherine's pages, and Catherine oohed and aaahed over Brawny's. "I like how clean and simple your pages are," I told the nanny. "You emphasize what's important to you. I love that page with the picture of the Arch. Now all you need to do is take time off and go photograph places around town. Go explore. Discover. This really is a fascinating place."

"I'll go with," Catherine said. Then shyly, "If you don't mind. Since I'm new here, too, I'd love to have someone to poke around with."

"I'd like that very much," said Brawny, and the two exchanged phone numbers.

While we were cropping, Detweiler had text-messaged me that he and Hadcho were working late, helping Murray by going over lab evidence and witness statements. I messaged him back that I understood. I reminded him that his mother was at our house. He responded that he'd run home long enough to give her a hug. "She's enjoying spending time with Erik," he said via text.

Brawny and I locked the store up and walked Clancy and Catherine to their cars. As soon as the car door on the Saab was unlocked, Catherine threw her arms around me for a big hug. The spontaneity surprised me. "Big sis, this was the best! I loved it!" she said before hopping behind the wheel.

"*Aye,* 'tis a grand time. You must be very proud of yourself,

Miss, knowing that you make so many people so very, very happy."

"I love what I do," I said.

"I can tell," Brawny said, walking me to my BMW. "I'll stay right behind you on the road, Miss Kiki. Don't get out of the car at your house until I signal to you."

I nodded, but in truth my mind was elsewhere.

Was it really possible that one of the three women from the St. James Church had hoped to hurt me? Had they stabbed Laurel because they thought her beauty was a gift from Satan? Was it simple jealousy? Clearly all three were smitten with Father Joe, but he was in love with Laurel. Did they know that? Had he said something about his intentions?

Putting myself in their places, I tallied what they might perceive as black marks against Laurel. She had been illegitimate. She didn't have a proper family life for years. She had diabetes. She made money belly dancing. She was beautiful. Oh, and Father Joe loved her.

Taken all together, I could imagine one of them striking out at her.

The first question was, Which woman did it?

The second was, How could I prove which person was responsible?

47

When it comes to worrying, I'm a real pro. After I worried about finding Laurel's killer and seeking justice for the crime, my nimble mind moved on to fretting about our move. Should I go through our belongings and cull out what we didn't need? Otherwise, I'd be paying to store items that we weren't going to use. I'd also be paying for boxes and packing paper.

But what did I need and what could I pack away?

I'd never been on the second floor of Clancy's mother's house, because I'd never had a reason to poke around up there.

First thing tomorrow, I would go and see what was on the second floor. I could use my phone and take pictures. Then I could better decide what to pack and what to store.

But then my plans came to a screeching halt as I thought, What should I do about the kitchen?

Amanda and Mom didn't cook. Once a week Amanda took Mom grocery shopping. My mother would buy pre-cooked meals from Schnucks or Dierbergs. She also stocked up on TV dinners. On occasion, she and Amanda would buy a Domino's Pizza, but that one pie would last for several meals.

Were there any cooking utensils in the kitchen? Which ones? What might we need?

What was Catherine doing for food. Was she making a weekly grocery trek? As a kid, she loved macaroni and cheese. Soups out of the can. Had her tastes changed? She sure chowed down this evening.

Granted, I still had plenty to worry over, but for the rest of the drive home, I indulged myself. I re-lived that hug from Catherine, and a big grin spread my mouth wide. Knowing that I'd found a way to help her made me feel great. Seeing how well she'd fit in made me proud! Watching her budding friendship with Brawny gave me hope. Things were really looking up when it came to my baby sister.

I made a mental note to call Aunt Penny and thank her. At first, I'd been angry that Aunt Penny hadn't told us where Catherine was or how she was doing. In fact, neither Amanda nor I knew that Aunt Penny and Catherine had stayed in touch. But now I realized that Aunt Penny had done what was right for Catherine, even though Amanda and I resented her for it. Catherine had been struggling. She told Amanda that she had "hit rock bottom." I couldn't imagine what that was like. I vaguely recalled Aunt Penny cancelling a trip to visit Mom in Arizona. Mother had been quite put out. Aunt Penny had said, "Something's come up."

Shortly thereafter, my aunt sold some stock.

In hindsight, I put two and two together. I've never been good with math, but I thought I could reasonably write down "four" as the answer. I bet that whatever happened to Catherine, Aunt Penny had bailed her out. Furthermore, that "rock bottom" stumble had been costly.

Did I want to know what happened? I wasn't sure that I did.

Catherine would tell me if she wanted me to know.

Meanwhile, I decided that I would enjoy this interlude with her.

The older I got, the more I realize that you have to soak up all the happiness you could, whenever it presents itself, because who knows what the future would bring?

With that settled in my mind, I drove the last few blocks to my house. Sad to say, I'd completely forgotten that Brawny told me to stay in my car. Instead of doing as she had asked, I caught sight of Thelma Detweiler's car and ran to my back door. I pulled it open and stepped inside.

An unpleasant scene awaited me.

"So this is the fabulous Kiki Lowenstein," said a woman, standing in the middle of my kitchen. Her weathered skin suggested that she'd spent too much time in the sun. She stank of cigarette smoke and alcohol. My impression was of an aging party girl.

"Who are you and why are you in my house?" I asked the intruder.

"Kiki." Thelma rose from her seat at my kitchen table, her hands moved toward me in a wordless expression of regret. I gave her a hug and asked, "Are the kids okay?"

"Yes. Both in bed. Fortunately they fell asleep before Melissa walked in."

"Melissa," I repeated. "Melissa Haversham?"

"This will be my house," she said, invading my personal space. She practically stepped on my toes in an effort to get right up in my face. "I came to look it over. Of course, some of the furniture won't work for me, but—"

"All of what you see is mine. The place came unfurnished."

"Hmmm. Let's see what Dad says about that."

"There's no 'Dad says' to it. I have friends and family who can vouch for these items being mine," I said, suddenly aware that Brawny was at my side. Melissa shrank back a step. Brawny hadn't said a word, but her presence had intimidated the interloper.

"I'll be out of here on Sunday. Until then, I'd appreciate it if you stay out of this house."

"My house," she repeated.

"It will be. I'm asking you to stay away out of common courtesy."

"That's rich!" She threw back her head and hooted. "I have the right to come over and take measurements. You can't expect me to buy furniture without knowing what will fit."

I dearly wanted to say, "Who cares? Sit on the floor! Bring a sleeping bag!" But that would have only inflamed the situation. Instead, I took a deep breath and said, "If you need to take measurements, please call me and let me know you are coming. As you can probably understand, my daughter and my son are stressed out enough about the move. Your presence will only further upset them."

From under the kitchen table came a *ggrrrrrrrrrrr*. I turned and stared at Gracie. She never, ever growls, but sure as that day was long, she'd bared her teeth and grumbled at Melissa.

"That dog—" started Melissa.

"Is very big and very strong. You won't want to upset her. So again, I ask that you call me first before you come over to take measurements."

"If it's convenient for me, I will."

"I suggest you make it convenient. I'd hate for you to have a run in with my dog."

"Or your nanny," said Brawny in a gruff voice. "I don't take well to people I don't know. Not when the children's welfare is mine to see to."

190

Melissa raised a haughty eyebrow, one that had been totally over-plucked. The few skimpy hairs looked like someone had drawn on her forehead with a Sharpie pen. Staring at Brawny, she said, "Are you threatening me?"

"No, Miss. I'm simply explaining that I get a bit overwrought when it comes to protecting my charges. Think of it as apologizing in advance."

"You know what? I think we need to talk this through with Leighton," I said. "Maybe I need to make it clear to him that I expect you to respect my privacy."

"Dad's asleep. He's been tired lately. I helped him to bed myself, and I checked on him before I came over here." She lifted her chin defiantly.

"I'll go over and talk with him tomorrow," I said.

"Call first," Melissa sneered at me. "After all, this is our property. You're merely squatting on it. Like one of those homeless people who takes up residence in someone's house while they're out of the country. A freeloader."

48

helma's face was white with fury. As for me, I couldn't even find words for how angry I was. The room shifted under my feet, but Brawny caught me on my way to the floor. I sank down onto a kitchen chair that Thelma shoved under me. Brawny forced me to put my head between my knees. From that awkward position, I heard the back door slam behind Melissa.

"Next time," Brawny said, "let me go first. I coulda dealt harshly with her, and you'd have not been bothered by such carryings on. Not in your condition. When's your next doctor's appointment?"

"Next week."

"Might have a touch of high blood pressure. We'll need to keep an eye on that. Can't have you coming down with preeclampsia."

Thelma took the chair next to mine and reached out for my both my hands. "I'm so sorry. Chad trusted me to take care of the kids, and I botched the job. I feel horrible. But Melissa had a key, so I undid the dead bolt thinking it was one of your sisters."

"What a horrible person!" I finally got my wits about me.

"How on earth could she be Leighton's daughter? He's so nice. Well, he was so nice until he decided to evict us."

"Hon, are you sure you don't want to come live with us? Maybe you could enroll Anya in a nice school over in Illinois. She could always switch back later."

Thelma was trying her best to help, but I couldn't imagine taking both Anya and Erik out of CALA, relocating them, and then moving back to the area. In fact, I couldn't imagine taking them out of school. Currently, it offered stability. They both had friends, although admittedly Erik didn't have as many as Anya. But Anya's best friend Nicci Moore was an important part of her life. Jennifer Moore, Nicci's mother, was another parent I'd come to depend on. That counts for so much in this world. Hillary Clinton was right: It takes a village to raise a child. Jennifer was part of my village.

All that aside, I couldn't imagine commuting back and forth from Illinois. Especially not with the holiday season upon us. The drive alone would kill me. The time crunch would eat me alive. And the roads? Sheesh. There are only two seasons in Illinois. Winter and road construction.

"Thelma, you are such a sweetheart. If it comes to that, I'll take you up on your offer. Meanwhile, we're planning to move into the second floor of the house my sisters and mother are renting from Clancy. It's in U City, so that's not too far from CALA or the store."

She pulled me close and hugged me. "You have to do what you think is best. I'm sorry I let you down this evening. It'll never happen again. The next time a key jingles in the lock and Gracie growls, I'll call the cops and let the dog do her worst with them."

"Miss Thelma, what else did Miss Haversham say while she was here?" Brawny bustled around in the kitchen, making me one of her endless cups of tea, I presumed.

"Talked on and on about herself. About how she hadn't

gotten a fair shake in life. How Leighton owed her. How things were going to be different. How she was taking over." Thelma waved a dismissive hand. "A bunch of hooey. Fortunately both kids were tuckered out. They'd been in bed for an hour when she showed up. The minute she stepped over the threshold, I knew there was something off about her. She's either mentally ill or high on something. She was acting like Brenda did."

Brenda, of course, was Detweiler's dead ex-wife, his second wife after Erik's mother, Gina. Brenda had been a nasty piece of baggage who'd been a drug addict.

"I smelled alcohol on her breath," I said.

"Yes, there was that, too, but her movements were uncoordinated. Her speech was slurred, and she rambled. I think there's more to her problems than a drink or two." Thelma accepted a cup of peppermint tea. While I dumped a half a bowl of sugar in mine, Thelma sipped hers straight.

"I don't understand this 'poor me' attitude," I said. "The past is the past unless you insist on dragging it around with you. Then it becomes your present and your future. So Leighton wasn't the best of fathers. A lot of men fail in their responsibilities. She can't possibly expect him to make up for everything now. Giving her a house is a pretty big concession, but that's just me. I can't imagine my parents giving me a home, much less a house. Much less, a house on such a desirable piece of land."

"What nonsense about your furniture!" said Thelma. "Chad will take care of that. I plan to tell him that he needs a couple of uniformed officers here on the premises on moving day. We'll just see about her getting her mitts on your things!" She had moved from shocked to indignant. A good sign.

"Yes, well, a lot of this might have to go into storage. First on my list tomorrow is a visit to the house in U City. I know that Clancy left most of her mother's furniture in the house. I need to see what's available so we know what to pack away and store."

"*Aye*, can you wait until after I drop the bairns off at school? You shouldn't be driving around alone," said Brawny.

"That's right, Kiki," said Thelma. "Chad told me about your friend being stabbed. How about this—it's late for me to be driving home, and Chad said he might crash at the police station. What if I spend the night and take the kids to school tomorrow. I'll text Louis and tell him what's up."

That seemed like a good solution. I told Brawny where to find the blow up mattress that I keep on hand for sleepovers. Once it was inflated, and I'd loaned her some pajamas, Thelma, bless her heart, slept on the floor next to the sofa that Brawny claimed for a bed.

"Dear God, I know it's not right to pray for things, rather than for people, but we really need a bigger house," I said before I fell asleep.

49

Tuesday...
Kiki's little cottage in Webster Groves

*I*n the wee hours of the morning, Detweiler slipped into bed beside me. "Shh," he said, as he slipped his arm around my shoulders. "We'll talk later. You need your rest." He was right; I was far too tired to rouse completely.

When sunlight brightened our bedroom, I turned to him. He was awake, staring at me. "I heard you had a visitor last night. Melissa Haversham. I almost tripped over Mom on the floor."

"Yes." I struggled to grasp what he was saying. "Mom on the floor?"

"She spent the night on the living room floor in a sleeping bag."

I groaned. We had so many bodies under one tiny roof that we were beginning to look like a youth hostel, minus the youth.

Detweiler continued, "I need to have a talk with Leighton. This is unacceptable."

"I agree. Thank goodness Anya and Erik were already asleep. I'm going to call Jennifer tomorrow and ask if Anya can spend a couple of nights at her house this weekend."

"It might be hard for Erik to be without her, although maybe he can go spend some time on the farm with Mom and Dad. They would love to have one-on-one time with him. Brawny can go with him to keep an eye out. Although I hate the thought of separating the two of them, another visit from Melissa Haversham might push both kids over the edge."

"You can't imagine how creepy she was! That woman was acting as if she owned the place. In fact, she seems to think that everything she sees is part of the house. Good thing she didn't set eyes on you."

"I wish she had. I would have set her straight."

"I tried to do just that, but I have a feeling that she plans to challenge me about my furniture. It isn't much, but it is mine." Unexpectedly, I started to cry. "This is a nightmare! I trusted Leighton. I would have gone over and talked to him myself last night, but she informed me that he was asleep—and it was late."

"Honey, don't cry. Please. This is breaking my heart," said Detweiler, as he pulled me closer.

I hiccupped, held my breath, and finally calmed down. I couldn't do this to Detweiler. I wouldn't. We'd get by somehow. "Your mother said she'd drop the kids off at school this morning. Brawny and I will go over to the U City house and see what furniture we can take and what we need to put in storage. Then I'll call Jennifer."

"While Mom's taking them to school, I'll have a talk with Leighton. Just in case there's a problem with his daughter, I'll have two uniformed officers here on Sunday when we do the actual move. It's one thing for her to muscle her way into this house while you and I are away from home, but it's another thing for her to face down two officers."

"I'd love to see her arrested, but can you do that? I don't have a lease! It would be my word versus Leighton's, and I'm on his property without a legal document. How could I have been so stupid?"

"You weren't stupid. You were trusting. You might be right about the legalities, and certainly we don't have the time or the money to hire an attorney, but I have to believe that the presence of uniformed officers will prove an intimidating factor." He rolled away from me and covered his eyes with his arm. "I just cannot believe this. It's one thing to want to help his daughter, but it's another to mistreat you! Especially when you're pregnant!"

"I know, I know. Okay, this is making me more upset. Let's change the subject. Any progress on Laurel's case?"

"No. Not from a forensics standpoint. We're sifting through all the pieces of information, trying to see how it fits. We're also trying to get information about the mental state of those three women, but as you can imagine, that's pretty tough sledding."

"What will you do? How can you move forward? Whoever did this is still out there."

"I know it. Believe me. I haven't forgotten what happened to her, but we don't have enough information to help Murray bring any of the three women in for questioning. Father Joe can't tell us anymore. Crummy as it is, I respect his position."

I propped myself up on one arm. "Okay, he has to abide by the sanctity of the confessional, but all three of the women originally attended the Church of Christ Our Shepherd, a non-denominational church. I know that because they were working on religious scrapbooks, and all three included photos of that particular church. Maybe the pastor there won't be so scrupulous. Or even a board member might be able to tell you more. A board member from either church."

"I'd thought of a board member. Worth a try to talk to the other church members, I guess."

I told him about Mert seeing that I was tossed out of the hospital. "I can't believe her! To think she was my best friend!"

"I don't know what to tell you, sweetheart, except that she's the loser. She really is. You were a great friend to her."

The fact that he put it in the past tense was enough to slam the door on that relationship. I was tired, hormonal, lonely, afraid, pregnant, and nearly homeless. Fortunately, I was also in the arms of a man who loved me and who held me while I cried.

50

*C*lancy was scheduled to open the store. I text-messaged her and said I'd be coming in a bit late. Next on my list was a phone call to Jennifer Moore. I badly needed a shoulder to cry on. However, I didn't want to air my dirty laundry in front of Brawny. She didn't need to hear that my mother was nearly impossible. Or that I hated the fact we were moving. But I did need her help with Anya.

If I whined to Jennifer about our living arrangements, might the Scotswoman misinterpret my complaints?

In the end, I decided the call couldn't wait. "I have a problem," I told Jennifer. "We need to move. Leighton's daughter is coming home, and she's told him she wants to live in our house, so we're basically out on the streets as of Sunday. Could Anya come spend the weekend with you? Starting with Friday night?"

"Of course she can. Let me guess. It's Melissa. She's back?"
"You know her?"

"Of course I do. I went to school with her."

"Um, Jennifer, do you mind if I put you on speakerphone? I have Brawny here in the car with me. Last night Melissa dropped by the house. Thelma was watching the kids. Fortunately they were both asleep, but by the time I got home, Melissa was eyeballing my furniture and talking about what she wanted of it."

"Sure, put me on speakerphone. I don't care." Brawny said hello, as a courtesy.

"Melissa is bad news," said Jennifer. "You probably already know that by now. Her mother milked Leighton for every cent she could get her hands on. Leighton only owns that house because it belonged to his parents."

"I didn't realize that!"

"Yes. He grew up in that house."

"But he says he didn't do enough for Melissa when she was growing up."

"He's right, of course. Here's the thing: No one could have done enough for her. She has this unrealistic sense of entitlement. Thinks that he should pay and keep on paying. Her mother taught her that. The stories I could tell you! Melissa was always complaining about teachers. About her classmates. She's a sociopath. I think that's the right term. Has no conscience when it comes to other people."

"Does Leighton realize that?"

"I doubt it. He's too busy feeling guilty."

"Does she have a history of drug or alcohol abuse?" asked Brawny. "Last night when we arrived, she seemed to be under the influence of something or another."

"Melissa drank, did dope, and smoked cigarettes in high school. She also slept with any guy who'd have her. Vandalized school property."

"Wow. What a mess. I can't believe she's acting like my possessions are hers! And that Leighton is giving me the boot! I have to be out of the house by Sunday. Can you believe that?"

Jennifer chuckled. "Let me guess. You don't have a lease." I felt my face redden. "No, I don't."

"Listen, girlfriend. You and I are going to a tattoo parlor. We're going to get you a big old tattoo across your butt. You know what it's going to say? 'Trust but verify.' I know you're more likely to be a flaming liberal than a conservative, but Ronald Reagan was right, my friend. And the best sort of verification is a legal document signed by all parties."

"I guess I'll be paying for that tattoo," I said. "I think you already have."

BRAWNY CRANED her neck from the passenger's seat and took in the stately brick two-story building in U City, which is what the locals call University City. "Good lines," she said. "Easily defensible despite the fact your neighbors are rather close. No shrubs along the edges of the place. That means no one can hide in them."

When considering a new home, most people worry about the color of the carpeting, that strange stain in the bathroom sink, whether the appliances come along with, and how large the closets are. Not me. Not my tribe. No, sir.

We looked over a new domicile and asked that all-important question that should be uppermost in everyone's mind: How defensible is your home?

Oh, well. As much as I hated to admit it, Brawny was right. The place did look like a fortress. "Do you still think Erik is in danger?"

"The best time to overpower your opponent is when he or she becomes complacent. I refuse to let down my guard. The forensic accountant is still looking into Mr. Lauber's finances. Until then, Miss Lorraine cannot spring her trap—and young Master Erik is at risk."

"Um, Brawny, you remember when you met my mother at

the airport?" I would remember it until my dying day. My mother had taken one look at Erik and screamed, "That child is black!" And that was only a highlight.

To her credit, our nanny maintained a pleasant look on her face even while thinking about my mother. "Of course, I remember."

"I hate to tell you this, but Mom was on her best behavior that day. I know that's shameful. But it's the truth."

"*Auck*. You're giving me fair notice, aren't you?" "That's one way to put it."

"I shall do as you wish, but I could use a bit of direction, Miss Kiki. How much should I tolerate?"

I'd been thinking about that. "I'm not sure. Come on, let's face the dragon."

Amanda anticipated my knock on the door and welcomed us inside. "I called work and told them I'd be coming in late. I figured this was as good a time as any to lay out the ground rules for Mom. Let's go into the kitchen."

My mother had taken a seat at the head of the kitchen table. In front of her was a cup of cocoa. Forewarned is definitely fore-armed, as was proven by the glower on her face.

"Hi, Mom," I said, trying to keep it casual. "You remember Brawny."

"Good day to you, Mrs. Collins."

My mother sniffed. "I prefer Montgomery. That was my professional name."

I rolled my eyes.

Amanda poured a cup of decaf for me and a cup of coffee, black, for Brawny. She warmed her own cup of coffee in the microwave. "Mom, Kiki and Detweiler are going to be moving in this weekend. They'll be taking over the second floor."

"It's only temporary," I hastened to add. "We're looking for a house to buy as we speak."

"I know you don't like change, Mom," said Amanda, diplomatically, "and this won't be easy for any of us, but I want you to make Kiki and Detweiler and their kids feel welcome."

My mother didn't say a word. She used a spoon to drown a tiny marshmallow.

"Mom?" I said. "I'd really like to try and get along." Still nothing.

Catherine came down the stairs; her footsteps announced her arrival as she joined us. After giving me a hug, she poured herself a cup of coffee, added cream and sugar, and pulled up a chair next to Brawny.

"Look, Mom," said Amanda, keeping her voice calm and pleasant. "I was hoping we could get off to a good start."

"A good start? With Kiki? What did you expect? I wasn't consulted. My feelings weren't considered. You three cooked this up without any regard for how I feel. None! Is that any way to treat your mother?"

Instantly I was four years old. The sense of panic that swamped me was that raw. I fought to tamp down my emotions as I said, "Mom, please. The truth is that I don't want to move in. I'd rather not. But I'm in a sort of a bind. So I'm asking you—begging you—please, just tolerate me and my family. It's only for a short time. Only until we can find a place suitable to rent or buy."

"This is *my* house," Mom proclaimed. "Do you really expect me to live under the same roof as a little black boy? Have you really sunk so low?"

"Your house?" Amanda's voice edged up a notch.

"Erik is my son," I said, and stopped for a second. Actually Detweiler and I needed to check on the legalities of that. "Erik's not 'a little black boy,' and he's as white as he is black. Just like our president! Not that it matters. I think if he can stomach living in the same house with you, you can manage to be considerate towards him. Mom, you go to church every Sunday! Haven't you learned anything about being kind to other people?"

"I've learned an eye for an eye," she said stiffly. "I also know that the commandments say to honor your mother and father. You wouldn't know that, would you? You went and married a Jew!"

My sharp intake of breath could be heard in the next county, I'm sure. My mother's prejudices had always been covered over with a veneer of good breeding. She would be kind to people's faces and mutter darkly about them when out of their presence. However, this assault on poor dead George stunned me. I began to see why Amanda thought Mom was slipping a cog, because my mother had always proclaimed loudly that the Jews were God's Chosen People. This sudden change of attitude was unlike her. Was it possible she was suffering from Alzheimer's? Or some other form of dementia?

Then I remembered something my friend Ned the Nurse told me when I had talked to him about my mom. He'd explained, "Old age exaggerates people's personalities. So the guy who was a bit sarcastic is really sarcastic and cruel. The woman who was vain can't go five minutes without fishing for compliments. The man who had a bad temper now throws tantrums. That's how it goes."

Was it possible that this was simply a by-product of the aging process?

If so, I hoped to die young.

"You're being silly, Mom. The Ten Commandments were handed to the Jews," said Amanda in a disgusted voice. "Of course Kiki knows that. She can probably even recite them in Hebrew."

I couldn't, but that was a great bluff.

Catherine's eyes had swiveled from one speaker to the next.

But now she sat as rigid as a porcelain statue and stared at our mother, practically looking right through her. In the silence, I could almost hear Catherine panting, like a wild animal after a chase. To my surprise, I watched Brawny put a hand on my sister's shoulder, the sort of companionable gesture that tells you that you aren't alone in the world. In response, my sister relaxed a bit.

"Whatever," said my mother in a pale imitation of my thirteen-year-old daughter. "I'm not interested in having two children under foot. I especially don't want the mess and fuss of animals, stinking up the place. I am not willing to let Kiki and her boyfriend move into this house to carry on their tawdry affair."

I literally saw red. I'd heard people say it, but I had never felt anything so vividly true. How dare she!

Since the day I left for college, I'd asked nothing of this woman. Nothing! She hadn't given me a penny, hadn't helped with babysitting, hadn't visited me, hadn't asked about my child or my life, and hadn't even offered me a shoulder to cry on. Now I was in a tough situation. I was asking her to help my family, even though it wouldn't be any skin off her nose, and she was flat out refusing!

"Those two children are your grandkids!" I said.

"Huh," she huffed. "One of them certainly is not. The other? Marginally so."

Catherine turned her chair backwards so she could lean against the rungs. Once done, she leaned the chair so that she got right up in my mother's face. "You let my father throw me out. You let him act inappropriately with my sisters. Amanda is kind enough to let you live under the same roof with her, despite what a mean, despicable woman you are. You don't want to live with my sister, fine! Let's take a vote. There's three of us and one of you. I vote that we toss you out onto the street."

Brawny shifted her weight. I didn't even need to turn and look. I could feel her next to me, absorbing energy like a battery does when you turn over the engine. The hairs on my arm, the one resting nearest her, prickled with energy. I shivered with fear. Slowly, I turned to stare at our nanny. She was not a happy bunny. Not at all.

"Catherine has a point," Amanda said.

Catherine's lower lip trembled as she paused for air. Her fingers knotted into fists that rested on the table top, not two feet from our mother's face. "You are some unnatural excuse for a parent. Y-y-y-you—"

"Out!" Brawny jumped up. "All of you. Leave now." "Pardon?" Amanda looked up at the Scotswoman, who towered over where my sister was sitting.

"Ladies, I'm asking you to leave me to talk to your mother. Alone."

"Why?" asked Catherine, her voice husky with anger.

"Trust me, please. I've had a wee bit of experience with such things."

I was so sick of my mother, and so worried about my sisters, that I quickly agreed. "Okay, Brawny. If you think you can talk sense into her, go right ahead, because I give up."

"Don't do that, Miss Kiki. No giving up. Not when your cause is just," said Brawny, as she stepped next to my mother. My mom stared up at Brawny, pouting at the nanny, until dismissing the woman with a "huh."

"You want all of us to leave?" asked Amanda. "You aren't going to hurt her are you?"

"Please, please, please, hurt her," Catherine mumbled under her breath. "Give her a taste of how that feels."

"No," said Brawny. "I'm not going to hurt your mother. I'm simply going to talk sense into her. She needs an attitude adjustment, you see. I'll help her with that. Sort of like a Vulcan Mind Meld."

That broke the tension. We laughed. Sort of.

"I should have guessed you're a Star Trek fan," said Catherine with admiration. "Come on, guys. We need to talk among ourselves anyway."

"You all go first," I said, pointing to the door. Once they were out of hearing range, I said to Brawny. "Promise me you won't hurt her."

"Isn't that the way of it? This woman has abused you, mistreated you and your sisters, attacked your family, and impugned your reputation, but still you worry about her? Does it look like she's worrying about you?" Brawny sounded puzzled.

I could answer that without glancing at my mother. "I know she's not."

"You should be," said Mom. "If you and your sisters weren't so selfish, you'd care about my feelings."

"But I do care," I said. "I always will. That's why we held this meeting. I care and I want you to be happy and I want you to get along with my family."

"That's a lie," said my mother with a sneer. "You want me out of your way so you can do exactly what you want with no concern about me or my needs."

"Mom, can't you meet us halfway? Couldn't we find a middle ground? I really, really need a place to stay. So do my kids. It's only temporary. I'd be happy to do what I can for you. Take you shopping. Watch movies with you. Brawny here would cook for you. But I need your assurance that you'll be civil to Detweiler and to the kids."

"I am always civil. I am the most civil person you'll ever meet. Everyone knows that."

"You don't sound civil when you refer to Erik as 'that little black boy.'"

"What else would you call him? A mulatto? A mixed breed? A mutt?"

I gasped. How could she? When did she become such a bigot? At the same time, it struck me with surprise that over the years, I'd overcome such prejudices. I'd met wealthy folks who were nice and some who were mean. I'd met Jews who were nice and Jews I didn't like. Ditto Baptists, Moslems, Jehovah's Witnesses, members of the Amish community, Mennonites, Christian Scientists, Hindus, Mormons, and others. Certainly I'd met blacks and Latinos who were charming as well as those who were jerks. People could embody the best and the worst of humanity, regardless of their creed or culture. That was the way of it.

As for calling my son a mulatto. A mixed breed. A mutt. I couldn't believe the language my mother was using. "Can you really be talking about Erik? Cute little guy? Five years old? Just lost his parents? Big brown eyes? Loves to sing 'The Wheels on the Bus'? Wants to be a cowboy when he grows up? Did you actually meet that wonderful child and not fall in love with him?"

"Don't be silly," said my mom. "I'm not about to fall in love with a little black boy. That's the most ridiculous thing you've said all morning."

Her words were a hard hit to the pit of my stomach.

"Please leave now," said Brawny, pushing me out of the kitchen.

My palm itched with the desire to slap my mother across the face. Hard. I wanted her to feel the sting of my anger. To know how it stung and burned. How humiliating it was.

I turned on my heels and started for the door. Just before I got to the dead end of the hall, I pivoted so I could look back. Brawny was squatted down so that she and my mother were eye to eye. Brawny was talking. A gold circle flashed, moving back and forth like a metronome. My mom was listening. Her head inclined. Her eyes narrowed, following the gold coin.

Hmmmm. I wondered what Brawny was saying.

My sisters had stepped out the side door, off of the dining room, which led to a brick patio. Catherine's eyes were red-rimmed. I put my arms around both of them. "Thank you both for standing up for me and my family," I said. "All for one—"

"And one for all!"

Despite how miserable we felt, we laughed with this remembrance of a childhood chant.

"OKAY, that got my mother's attention." I phoned Detweiler once Brawny dropped me off at the store. Clancy tactfully went to the sales floor so I could close my office door and talk to him with some privacy. I still couldn't believe what had happened. It probably sounded like I'd lost my mind when I told Detweiler about the meeting. He was livid when he heard how abusive my mother had been. That turned to sadness when I shared what Catherine had said.

"I wish I'd been there," he said. "I shouldn't have let you go alone. I would have forced your mother to listen to reason. I don't know how, but I would have done it. At least I would have given her a real talking to."

"No need," I said. "Brawny took care of it." A silence. Then, "How?"

"I believe she hypnotized my mother." More silence. Finally, "Come again?"

"You'll have to ask her, but after the fact, Brawny explained to us that she had hypnotized my mother. The father of modern hypnosis was a Scottish neurosurgeon named James Braid. Brawny says she used a trance-like state to help Mom become selectively attentive. With Brawny's help, she would only focus on happy thoughts. On positive feelings."

"Did it work?" he asked.

"I can tell you that when the three of us walked back into the kitchen, Mom seemed peaceful and cheerful. She asked me when we'd be moving in. I told her and she nodded. She actually said, 'If I can do anything to help, let me know.' Can you believe it? Then Brawny and I went upstairs and took pictures and measurements. She has an app on her phone that functions like a measuring tape. Turns out, we don't need any of my furniture. It might actually be best to store all of it and concentrate on packing and unpacking our clothes and toilet articles."

"My parents said we can put everything in their garage."

"That's great! It will save us a bundle. We don't need the furniture now, but we will want it eventually."

"I can't believe it. You actually sound upbeat," he said. "Considering what you just went through, I'm amazed."

"Yep, me too. The thought of spending more time around my sisters makes me happy. As long as Brawny can keep Mom hypnotized or whatever, this might actually be an interesting adventure. One of the rooms upstairs used to be Clancy's. It's done up in pale grey and yellow. Anya would love it. There's a large bedroom at the front of the house that would be perfect for us. Big bathroom attached. I'll put Erik in a bedroom that they used for guests. It has a daybed with a navy rib cord spread on it. Catherine volunteered to make a couple of pillows out of red bandannas."

"And Brawny? Our own Mary Poppins?"

"There's a room with a sleigh bed and an old-fashioned quilt on it. I wish you could have seen her face light up. She loved it. I could tell she was determined not to ask for it, so when I said, 'Gee, this would be perfect for you,' she sighed with joy. There's a Jack and Jill bath separating her room and Erik's. Really, this will work out perfectly. The kitchen has everything that Brawny needs for cooking. My sisters volunteered to work with her to come up with a schedule of menus. They'll pitch in with the food costs, but we'll all eat together."

There was another silence. One so long that I thought I'd lost him. "You there?" I asked.

"I just wanted to say that I know this has been hard for you. Adding Erik to our lives. Surprising you with Brawny. And now, having to move. And I want you to know that you've been a real rock throughout this. You've really been wonderful. I can't wait to marry you and spend the rest of our lives together."

51

*M*argit would be in at noon. She would look over the paperwork from all three crops, the two for charity and the one Monday night, and work up an analysis of our profits and losses. I did my portion of the assessment, calculating the costs of our materials, estimating my time, and then making a note about any extraneous factors. Regarding charitable crops, I wanted to use a big red marker and write STABBING on the form. But I didn't.

I did draw a red box and write, "Laurel." Then I added a frowny face.

Usually I perk up pretty quickly when I started thinking about my next project. Today, I couldn't muster the energy. Even though I needed to work on a make-and-take for Friday, I was creatively out of steam.

"I'll take over the sales floor," I told Clancy.

"Good," she said. "I've still got a few calls to make. People who were at that first crop."

I groaned.

At my worktable, I pulled out a Zentangle® tile and started to practice a new tangle. We'd added Zentangle sessions to our offerings, and I now presided over one each Thursday night. I really couldn't call them classes because I had yet to take the training, but I hoped to soon. So instead, we took turns teaching each other a new tangle. That made the session lots of fun, but it was still a profit center for the store.

Bent over my tangles on the square of paper, I didn't immediately snap to attention when the door minder rang. When I looked up, Johnny Chambers was standing in front of me.

"Johnny!" I squealed and ran to him, throwing my arms around his neck.

He laughed. "How's the baby bump?" "Getting bigger every day," I said. "How are you?"

"Can't complain," he said. However, his face is still thinner than it once was. He was still hurting from the gunshot wounds he'd taken at the slough, right before I shot and killed my husband's old business partner. "Of course, if it hadn't been for you, I wouldn't be standing here. I won't never forget that."

I let go of him and climbed back on my stool. "Your sister—" "Has her head up her butt. She cain't back down from her

high horse. I love her. She's kin, but she's always had a terrible time saying she was wrong. It's a shame." Usually he didn't talk with such a backwoods twang, but speaking about Mert sent Johnny into some sort of default. I don't know why.

"I went to see Laurel yesterday," I began.

"And my sis made sure they ejected you from the hospital." "Word travels fast."

"Right. I told her not to be so proud of herself. She didn't do Laurel any favors at all. There's no reason she should be angry with you."

"Let's change the subject. How's Laurel today? She's getting out, isn't she?"

"Yeah," he nodded slowly. "That's how come I came to talk to you. We've asked the cops to keep an eye out, but they don't seem interested. They're sort of holding a grudge against me."

What we call St. Louis is actually a metropolitan area made up of many different municipalities. Each has its own governance and law enforcement community. Unfortunately, these entities don't always operate in sync. In fact, a lot of important information slips through the cracks.

I could sort of understand the police department being fed up with Johnny. In his younger days, he'd been a hooligan. But he'd served his time up in Potosi. Now he and his family deserved the same protection that any law-abiding citizen had a right to expect.

"I'm so sorry," I said, sincerely. "That's got to be scary." "It sure is."

I waited. What was his point? Was he here to ask me if I could get Robbie to phone the local law?

"I heard tell that the police don't have much to go on. That the forensics hasn't given them a line of inquiry." Johnny rested his hands in his lap as he sat half on and half off his stool.

I didn't know how to answer, so I said nothing.

"I was thinking that maybe you could poke around. No one will expect a pregnant lady to be asking questions or playing cop."

I bit my lower lip and tried not to smile. Actually I'd been thinking the same thing myself. "What do you know about Laurel? Her life? Anything that might offer a clue as to the name of her assailant?" I said. I'd pulled out a sheet of white copy paper. Now I prepared to take notes.

"You've met Father Joe," said Johnny. "Since they're a couple, she's been going to St. James on Sundays. She's taking classes over at Prairie Central. I got the name of her teacher here." He passed me a slip of paper with Brian Overmeyer's name, phone, and office hours.

I added this to my list, but I didn't let on that I already knew about the teacher or her class.

"This here is the name of the talent agency that books her for modeling and such." He handed over a business card that read: Star Bright Talent. Because he didn't say she was a belly dancer, I didn't ask any more about her second career.

He squirmed a little on the stool. "You, uh, know that Mert's her real mom?"

"I'd heard something like that."

"Our parents split up after we were born. Ma took me, just to spite our dad. She sent Mert to foster care because she didn't have enough money to feed both of us. Mert bounced around from home to home. I ain't never got the sense of all of it, and she don't talk about it none, but it must have been pretty awful. She got raped. More than once. Got pregnant. More than once. She had Laurel, and they took the baby from her straight away. Laurel did okay with her first foster family, until she started having problems because of her diabetes. Then they didn't want to deal with a sick kid. So she bounced around from place to place until Edith and Jasper Wilkins took her in. Edith has diabetes, too, so she knew how to care for Laurel. It were too much for Jasper. He up and left them both."

Emotions pummeled me. I couldn't imagine what Mert and Laurel had been through. Two generations of women who'd been tossed into the system and passed around like ash trays for people to put their burning cigarettes in. Clancy had once told me that she thought the old orphanage system was actually a better choice for kids than foster care. "At least at the orphanages, there were checks and balances. But once a child goes to a foster home, they are at the mercy of their foster family."

"What about the social workers who visit the kids?" I asked. There'd been a social worker assigned to take Anya from me when Sheila decided I wasn't a fit mother. It had been the lowest point in our entire relationship. Mostly I tried not to remember the incident, but this unpleasant conversation brought it to mind.

"That's like spitting in a lake," he said.

"Johnny, you don't know how distressed all this makes me."

"It's a big lump to swallow, ain't it?" he said. "I know it

sickens me. It's a wonder that Mert ever forgave me for what happened to her. I was just a little shaver, but she coulda hated me because Mom kept me and gave her up."

I nodded. "I've been wondering if she'll ever forgive me, and now, hearing her history, I can sort of see why she might not. She's been let down by too many people."

"That's true, but you don't deserve how she's treating you. It's just not fair, and she knows it." Johnny's smile was wistful. "And my sis misses you. You were a good friend. She jest don't know how to kiss and make up."

"Maybe if I figure out who stabbed Laurel, she'll forgive me."

"Maybe."

"Or maybe not," I admitted with a sigh. He shrugged in agreement.

AFTER JOHNNY LEFT, I shared my new information with Clancy. We drew up a chart and listed all the people we knew who were a part of Laurel's life. We brainstormed motives. In the end, we decided that we didn't have enough to go on. We simply didn't know that much about Laurel's life. Without better information, we couldn't formulate any useful theories as to who stabbed Laurel or why she'd been attacked.

"Maybe there's a rival belly dancer," said Clancy. "Or a classmate who's angry. Or an old girlfriend of Father Joe's. Or a parishioner."

"I have to admit that all those women from the church are pretty scary. They're like priest groupies, and they're just plain hateful."

"And at least one of them has mental illness," said Clancy. "But wouldn't that be sort of obvious? They haven't made any secret of how they feel about Laurel."

I had to agree with her. "Of course, maybe they don't care if they're obvious. They seem to think they're doing God's work. They had a real martyrdom complex going."

"They've signed up for the Thursday night Zentangle crop," said Clancy.

"Really?" I hadn't looked at our list of attendees.

"Yes." She handed me the paperwork. "Whatever else you think about that horrible night, we sure came away with a bunch of new customers."

"Wow," I said. "That's just creepy."

"Sort of," said Clancy. "Not any creepier than gapers' block on a highway, is it? People love seeing an accident as long as they aren't involved in the carnage. It's just human nature."

"Let's get back to our brainstorming," I said. "Could be that Laurel helped clean with Mert, and someone got angry. She and I have worked as part of Mert's crew before. Could it be that someone on the wait staff hates her for some unknown reason? Or possibly she was in the wrong place at the wrong time and any one of us could have been attacked? The officers who inter-viewed the wait staff didn't have any leads, but that doesn't mean that the waiters are all terrific, peace loving people. One or two of them might be working under false names."

"Or it could be that one of our croppers had it in for Laurel," said Clancy. "Maybe that cropper could have been biding her time, waiting for the chance to get Laurel in a situation where she could stab her."

"Or someone from her past could be holding a grudge

against John Henry Schnabel. Since they're such close friends, maybe that person has been hoping for the chance to hurt someone who matters to John Henry."

"Or it could be that Laurel's assailant once asked her for a date and got shut down. It's not like she doesn't attract attention."

"This is overwhelming," I said. "What's even worse is the realization that no one will be watching over her when she goes back to her apartment. Here's the address. Johnny told me it's in South County."

I handed Clancy a piece of paper in Johnny's scrawl with a street address that neither of us recognized.

"Yes, well, South County is a big piece of real estate," said Clancy. She massaged her temples, because she's prone to headaches. She was elegantly dressed. Her black pencil skirt grazed the bottom of her kneecaps, exposing a small swath of black hose that ended at a pair of nice boots. "Maybe you ought to turn all this over to Detweiler and Hadcho."

I had on a man's blue oxford cloth, button-down shirt and another pair of black maternity pants. Yes, I do most of my shopping at Goodwill, and it probably shows.

"I could give this to the guys, but as you know, this isn't their jurisdiction. They're just helping Murray as much as they can. Since Hadcho was a first responder, that's the excuse they're using to stay involved. If Laurel had died, God forbid, they might have assigned the case to the Major Case Squad. That would have allowed them to go wherever they needed in search of evidence. But since she's alive and recovering, the investigation is staying in the same jurisdiction where it occurred. Hadcho and Detweiler can ask how the investigation is coming, and follow up when Murray requests, as a courtesy to him, but they can't do the legwork. They can't work the case itself."

Clancy stared down at the list on the desk. Her handwriting

is incredibly neat. "There has to be an answer in here some-where. Or with Joseph Riley."

"Or with Mert."

I stared at the list and then closed my eyes. "I have an errand to run. I need to hire a belly dancer for Detweiler's bachelor party"

"Really? So you've decided to marry the guy and make an honest man out of him?" asked Clancy. A mischievous smirk played on her lips. Given that she was wearing a cashmere twin set and pearls, that grin looked totally out of place.

"Yes, ma'am. As soon as I can get a spare moment, I think I will tie the knot."

"You better hop to it and go get your errand done," said Clancy, "because Margit will be here in an hour. You know how she gets when you aren't ready to go over your paperwork with her."

52

"Tell Margit that I might be running late," I said to Clancy, as I grabbed my purse and headed for the back door. "Or distract her, okay?"

"Right. She's like a fine Swiss watch. I repeat. You risk the wrath of Margit. She won't like it if you aren't here."

"Remind her that I'm now the big kahuna, won't you?" Clancy laughed, and I headed for my car.

Before Johnny had left, I'd asked him what Mert was doing today. "Cleaning over at the Moores' house. You recommended her, and they've been using her ever since."

That gave me an idea.

A few minutes later, I pulled up in front of Jennifer Moore's huge house in Ladue. Sure enough, Mert's pickup truck was parked on the street. Jennifer has been working from her home office lately, so I wasn't surprised when she answered the door and hugged me.

"Are we still on to host Anya over the weekend? Or has something come up?" asked Jennifer.

"Hang on a minute," I said. I slid my hands down her arms to grab her fingers. When she's really nervous, she has a bad habit of chewing off the skin on her fingertips. To my delight, there wasn't a dab of blood. "Good for you!"

"Yeah, I've been meditating in the morning. Doing my Zentangle tiles at night." She linked arms with me and led me into her living room. Overhead I heard the noise of a vacuum cleaner.

"Actually, I didn't come to visit you, Jennifer. I know that sounds awful, but I came to see if I could corner Mert."

"Is she still not talking to you?"

"Worse. She made sure the authorities threw me out of Laurel's room at the hospital."

"She never!"

"Huh," I said. "She sure did."

"So you're hungry for another go around?" Jennifer sank down into one of her gracious stuffed chairs. I stayed on my feet. I knew that if I got comfortable, I'd want to bail out on this whole mess.

"Not really, but a girl has to do what a girl has to do."

Jennifer snickered. "She's upstairs. Although you probably guessed as much."

I trudged up the carpeted stairway, thinking to myself as my hand moved along the polished oak bannister, what if Mert rejects me again?

She didn't hear me approach. Her back was to me as she used a feather duster on the knickknacks on Stevie Moore's dresser. Stevie is gay, and recently out of the closet, so included was a colorful rainbow of clay that his sister Nicci and Anya had found for him.

"Mert? Please, could you just listen to me a second?" I asked. She froze. Her hand was raised, but she didn't bring it down.

She froze in that pose like one of Disney's fairies getting ready to grant a wish, but with a duster rather than a wand. "Make it snappy."

"I want to find the person who attacked Laurel. As you know, they aren't calling out the Major Case Squad. I'm not entirely certain that the cops in that municipality are up to the job of tracking down her assailant. You know and I know that they've got a beef with Johnny. Now that they know Laurel is his niece, I worry that her case won't get the attention it deserves. Will you help me?"

Then I waited. It must have been the longest thirty seconds of my life. I counted, "One Mississippi, two Mississippi, three Mississippi" until I got to twenty and lost track, so I started over. Mert slowly brought her arm down to her side. She kept her back to me. Finally, she spoke through clenched teeth.

"Why should I trust you?"

"Because you know that I did not purposefully endanger Johnny. You can blame me all you want, but in your heart of hearts, you know better. I've always thought the world of you, Mert. I've always thought you were an honest, decent person. This has gone on long enough. I know you're stubborn. I get it. You don't have to like me. You don't have to be my friend anymore. But if you ignore me, don't blame me if Laurel gets hurt again. I'm putting myself on the line here. Are you big enough to meet me halfway—or are you going to keep sulking?" She whirled on her heel. A smudge of dust marred her work uniform of black slacks and white polo shirt. To my surprise, she'd aged about ten years since I'd last gotten a good look at her. The brief encounter in the hospital didn't count.

Her eyes were red-rimmed and the tip of her nose was pink. She'd been crying.

"Okay," she said. "What's your plan, smarty-pants?"

~

From my back pocket I pulled the chart that Clancy and I had been working on. Mert and I sat on the edge of Stevie's bed. I knew this was a breach of cleaning lady etiquette, but I also knew that Jennifer wouldn't mind. Stevie was off at college, University of Tennessee. Even if he had been home, he wouldn't have minded.

"The women at St. James Episcopal Church acted really nasty when they were at my crop. They kept saying things about the devil being beautiful. I know they have unfulfilled crushes on Father Joe. What has Laurel said about them?"

My shoulder barely touched Mert's. She didn't pull away, and I counted that as a win.

"Them heifers are like cows in heat looking for a bull in a barnyard," snorted Mert. "Sure, they're jealous of Laurel. She's been nothing but nice to them."

"I'm wondering," I said carefully, "if they know that he's planning to marry her."

"You're kiddin' me!" She turned to stare at me. "He is?"

"That's what he's told me."

Her hand flew up to cover her mouth. "Great jumping Jehosaphat."

"He seems like a nice man."

She worried a seam on her pants. "He surely is. But to marry into our family? I cain't help but wonder what the Pope will say."

"Uh, Mert, it doesn't matter."

"It might not matter to you, but it shorely will to him! They'll drum him outta that black skirt quicker than you can say, 'Bring me a fatted calf.'"

I put a hand on her forearm. "I was raised Episcopalian, remember? They don't follow the Pope. King Henry VIII put an end to all that. Didn't you ever watch *The Tudors*? Sure, there's a bishop over Father Joe, but he won't care about...well...I'm not exactly sure what you're worried about. But Episcopalians are incredibly tolerant. Liberal."

"Oh," and she hunched over with relief. "That's good, I guess."

"I know that one of those three women has had mental health issues in the past. I don't know which one. Is it possible that one of them is enough of a crackpot to want to kill Laurel?"

"I don't know!" she choked out a sob. "I been trying and trying to figure all this out."

"Next on my list is anyone who's a rival belly dancer. I don't even know if there is such a thing, but I assume there is. Or even a wife who's seen Laurel dance and who got her nose out of joint." I hesitated and then plunged ahead, "I was even thinking of going to the talent agency and saying I wanted to hire a belly dancer for my future husband's bachelor party. I thought I could weasel some information out of them."

"Now that's a good idea," she said, perking up considerably. "Laurel never talks much about that, but I know that there was some fierce competition a while back, and she got picked while another gal got sent home."

"Okay, then I'll pursue that."

"What's this about her teacher?" Mert underlined Brian Overmeyer's name with a shaking fingernail. Although she cleans for a living, Mert always keeps her nails talon long and polished in bright colors. Today she wore silver and blue chevrons.

"I don't know. Clancy and I were just trying to put together any sort of a list of people who might be jealous or have a gripe. Admittedly, Laurel keeps her personal life quiet, but brainstormed every area we could think of. Laurel had printed out an assignment on the wrong sort of paper, so we dug it out of the trash. This is what we found."

Mert took the paper from me and studied it. "She had a

problem a couple of semesters past. Something about an inappropriate email."

"Was it from this teacher? Because this is a class she's taking now."

"I disremember. Might have been from another student. She's patched together her education. Taken classes from as many community colleges as she could because the tuition is lower."

"Do you remember all the schools' names?"

"Prairie Central, Wash U," she said, using the local nickname for Washington University, "and Charbonneau Community."

That was another avenue to pursue. I folded the paper. "Can you think of anyone else who has a beef? I know most people would immediately be jealous of her because she's so beautiful, but once you get to know her, you can't help but like her. Is it possible that someone in the store gave her a hard time? I'd like to think that I'd know if that happened, but still..."

Mert shook her head. "Not that I've heard of. She's used to people being put off by how she looks. She's coped with that her whole life."

"Is there anything about her adoptive mother? Or the nursing home? Anything at all?" I was fishing and I knew it.

"Nope. But I'll ask her about it tonight. She's insisting on going home to her apartment. I told her I'd hang out with her. At least for a while. Roger is fine at home with Johnny."

"I'll visit the talent agency and see what I can learn. Will you ask her the name of the girl who lost out?"

"It's Abbysinthe I remember it because it's a sort of play on the liquor. Her cards say she'll make you forget your troubles."

I shoved the chart in my purse and stood up. "Yeah, I just bet she can."

53

The Star Bright Talent Agency sat like a frumpy *hausfrau* smack dab in the middle of a block in the West End. Around it other brick and limestone facades with broad display windows, showcasing eclectic art, fair trade goods, hippy style clothing, trendy eateries, and a bookstore that was closed more often than open. Despite the optimistic name, Star Bright looked more like the last star you'd see any night with its dirty vinyl blinds pulled down over windows that needed cleaning.

The door opened with a hard yank. I stepped inside and changed my mind about the place. As grubby as the outside had seemed, the waiting area was well-appointed with a lipstick red sofa, twin black leather sling chairs, and framed photos of area talent. Many of the faces I recognized. On the glass table was a three-ring binder labeled "Our Talent Shines." I flipped it open to see various studio shots and descriptions of people of all ages, sizes, ethnicities, and genders.

"Hello," said a young woman in high heels. She extended her hand for a shake. "I'm Elise Gifford. May I help you? Did you have an appointment?"

"Uh, no," I said.

Elise's reddish hair was pulled back in a classic French twist. Taken with the simple long-sleeve sheath dress, she looked like Audrey Hepburn. I liked her immediately for the genuine smile she offered.

"I'm getting married, and I was thinking about booking a…" I stopped. I couldn't bring myself to lie to the woman. Instead, I started again with, "Could we go somewhere and talk? Do you have an office?"

"Certainly. I have ten minutes until a new talent is coming in. Is that enough time?" "Sure," I said.

She led me down a hall to a nicely appointed conference room. The soft gray walls contrasted with silver stars and photos of more talent. The table was clear glass, but the effect wasn't cold. Not with the softly padded gray chairs.

"May I offer you a beverage? Coffee? Tea? A cola? A bottle of water?"

I accepted a cup of mint tea eagerly. "This is hard, but I'm going to be perfectly honest with you. Yes, I do have a fiancé, but that's not why I'm here. I'm a friend of Laurel Wilkins."

"How is she? I couldn't believe what happened! I've been trying to find out if she's okay!" Elise leaned forward. "How do you…? Oh, you must be Kiki! She talks about you all the time. Kiki this and Kiki that. She's always going on and on about what you're creating or the cool idea you've had."

I blushed and struggled for words. "I think the world of Laurel, and I was there when she was stabbed. I mean, I was in the next room. She's going home today, but that's why I'm here. I'm worried. I'm scared that whoever tried to kill her will try again."

"Let me guess, the cops aren't doing much, are they?"

I clamped my mouth shut. Since I'm planning to marry a cop, I hated the change in attitude. But I wasn't here to defend the police or the law enforcement community. I was here to gather information to help Laurel. So I waited.

Elise jumped to her feet and started pacing. "I was afraid of that. See, there was another incident a month ago."

"You're kidding!"

"No, I wish I was. We got a package for Laurel. Inside was a threatening letter. I called the police. They couldn't do anything." Elise stopped walking and hugged herself. "I guess I can see it from their viewpoint. There really wasn't much to go on. The letter was pretty general."

"Do you still have it?"

"No. They took it and said they'd file it away. Evidence, I guess."

I got my hopes up and just as quickly, let them be dashed. This was yet another municipality. All Detweiler could do was ask to see the letter. That might take days, if the force here was willing to cooperate at all.

"Do you remember what it said?"

"I don't think I'll ever forget it. Someone had gotten a hold of a publicity shot of Laurel in her belly dancing costume. They'd stabbed a hole in the picture, right about where her heart was. In black marker they'd written something like, 'You led him into temptation.'" Elise shivered. "I have to tell you, it made me sick." She wasn't too worried about the other belly dancer. "Abby is hot tempered, but she gets over things quickly. Sure, she was put out that Laurel was hired and she wasn't, but that's the way this business goes. Abby knows that."

"Maybe there were bad feelings. It's possible, isn't it?"

Elise shrugged. "Abby and Laurel often appear together. Customers really dig that whole two women fantasy thing. Besides, Laurel's the one who helped Abby put together her costume. Believe it or not, authentic belly dancing garb is very expensive. Laurel paid a customer to bring back two outfits when he went to the Middle East. One was a gift for Abby."

That was how Laurel operated. You could hate her for her good looks, but you couldn't hate her for long, because once you got to know her, she was so sweet that you put aside your jealousy.

"I wonder if someone who saw Laurel dancing got hot and bothered. Maybe some wife somewhere. Do you have a list of her engagements?"

Elise stiffened. "I couldn't share that with you. Those customers are proprietary to our business. Even though Laurel trusts you, my boss would kill me."

"I understand." And I did. Their client list was the lifeblood of the agency, just as our customer list was ours.

Time to take another tack. Detweiler often asked the same question in different ways until he got a satisfactory answer. "Was there any function where wives attended? And did the nasty note arrive immediately after such a function?"

"Let me check," said Elise, getting up gracefully and leaving me at the table. She came back holding a folder with Laurel's name on it. Elise kept the folder open so she could read from it. "Right before the letter arrived, she danced at a birthday party for a ninety-nine-year-old man. I guess his lifelong fantasy was to see a belly dancer, but he was too feeble to fly to Egypt or wherever, so his sons bought an hour of Laurel's time. Once she got there, she was such a hit that she stuck around for three hours. You wouldn't believe how happy the sons were with her! I guess the geezer nearly died in ecstasy."

"Did Mr. Geezer have a wife or lover who might have gotten jealous?"

Elise grinned. "Yes, he and she have been married seventy-plus years."

I couldn't imagine a ninety-year-old woman having the

energy to stab Laurel repeatedly. In fact, I hadn't seen anyone that old at our crop or at the gathering in the haunted house.

"How about this. How about if I send you an email with our list of customers who attended the Halloween fundraiser? You can check those names against your client list. If someone appears on both, perhaps that person would be worth looking at more closely."

"You would do that for Laurel? That's pretty risky stuff. I could share your list with a competitor."

"You could, but why would you? Besides, if you attended one of our crops, you could write down the names of the other attendees and share them with a competitor. That still wouldn't give you access to their contact information."

"True."

I toyed with my tea bag. "Is it possible that there was someone else in the audience? A wife who got annoyed by her husband's attention to Laurel?"

"I doubt it. If so, she would definitely be a one-off. Most of the wives start out being jealous of Laurel and end up being her biggest fans. She does this thing where she encourages the other women to join her as she dances. They get the chance to feel special and sexy, too. It's such a smart trick that Abby has started doing the same."

54

*M*argit glared at me from her cats' eye glasses. Rotating her wrist and tapping her watch, she said, "You are late."

"You are right, and I owe you an apology. What's that I smell? Sauerbraten?"

Her frown eased as she said, "*Ja*. I made it for you and for Brawny. She said she'd never eaten German food. I told her that was a shame. I made extra for you to take home."

"Margit, you're the best," I said, as I threw my arms around her and gave her a hug. She smelled, as always, of peppermint and eucalyptus, the rub she used for her arthritis. Although she didn't offer affection, she did bask in it when it came her way. I gave her a kiss on the cheek as I let her go.

"*Ja*, but the time," she sniffed.

"Let me tell you and Clancy where I was and what I did. Then you can fuss at me."

I buzzed Clancy with the intercom function that I'd recently added to our phone system. She came back and took a seat next to mine at Margit's desk, a makeshift sort of affair my co-worker had carved for herself out of the back wall. The workspace perfectly reflected Margit. Whereas Clancy had a touch of OCD that made her germophobic and organized, Margit's OCD tendencies caused her to crave processes. When Clancy settled in, Margit sighed and put her forms back in the appropriate folder. I knew from experience that she would go through them one by one with me when she had my total attention.

"I made peace with Mert."

"Honestly? That's great!" Clancy whooped with joy. "I know it had been bothering you because you two weren't speaking to each other."

"This is good," said Margit. *"Zeige mir Deine Freunde und ich sage Dir wer Du bist."*

"Translation, please," I said.

"Show me who you are friends with, and I will tell you who you are."

I wasn't exactly sure what my friendship with my former cleaning lady said about me, but considering how much Margit valued neatness and Clancy craved clean, I suppose it was all good.

"More to the point, Mert and I brainstormed who might have stabbed Laurel. See, Detweiler and Hadcho can't investigate. It didn't happen in their jurisdiction, and no one called for the Major Case Squad to be put together. Worse news, because Johnny's had run-ins with the law, and because they know Johnny is Laurel's uncle, the local authorities near Laurel's apartment aren't inclined to make sure she's safe."

"Wait a minute," interjected Clancy. "How do they know that Johnny is her uncle? We didn't know that Mert was her mother until recently."

"Good question. I assume that just because we didn't know, it doesn't follow that they didn't know."

"Ja," said Margit, "that would make sense. They might even have looked up personal records that we don't have access to."

"That reminds me," I said to her, "when Hadcho was here, I realized I don't have adequate paperwork on any of us. None of the typical forms were in Laurel's file. I thought back to when she started, and I remember her coming in with a bunch of papers. Wasn't there a resume there?"

Margit gave me the sort of sour look that would make sauerkraut seem like cotton candy. Fortunately, I knew her well enough to realize she'd get over this affront to her organizational skills, so I waited.

"There are no papers for her now. I do not know if there ever were, but I have not seen any."

"Okay. Fair enough. I realize that this wasn't your responsibility, most of us were hired before you were put in charge of the paperwork, but would you see to it that all of us have filled in typical employment forms? Just in case there's ever a question again?"

"I will," said Margit.

"Back to Laurel," said Clancy. "So what did you learn? What do you know? Any good leads?"

She was really getting into this whole amateur snoop business.

"Sort of. I learned that Laurel and another dancer were up for the same job and Laurel got it. There were threats made against Laurel. Really ugly stuff. I also heard that she'd received an inappropriate email from someone at the community college. That's about it."

Because I wasn't sure whom I'd told what, or what Clancy had shared with Margit, I went over my visit to the church. "Father Joe wants to marry Laurel. Mert was surprised to hear that. Naturally she's worried about how Laurel will fit in as a priest's wife, but the Episcopal Church has a long history of believing that human sexuality is a gift, not a sin."

"Just because you think they'll be accepting and because the church hierarchy will be accepting, doesn't mean the congregation will be. I'm Episcopalian, and I can promise you that some of the members of my church would foam at the mouth if they heard our priest was marrying a belly dancer," said Clancy.

"She wasn't only worried about the dancing," I said. "She was also concerned that Laurel was illegitimate."

"Who cares about that in this day and age?" Clancy threw up her hands. "My mother used to say there are no illegitimate children, only illegitimate relationships."

"I agree that her worries are silly, but she is Laurel's mother. I imagine Mert's overly protective because she couldn't protect Laurel when she was young. When they were both young, actually," I amended.

Margit adjusted her glasses and tapped a pencil on the folder. "You were late because you were talking to Mert?"

I explained about visiting the Star Bright Talent Agency. "Margit, would you please email them a copy of our crop participants?"

Clancy opened her mouth to protest, but I waved her to silence. "I know, I know. But Elise promised to compare any attendees on our list with their clients. If you have a better idea, let me know."

She didn't.

"Then let's go over the crop forms and get that done. Because afterwards, I better get to work on a make-and-take for next week," I said.

THE REST of the work day passed quickly. Since Brawny was assigned carpool duties, I worked until five, texting her to say that I had our main dish covered. Detweiler messaged me that he'd be working late. At ten after five, we locked the doors on

Time in a Bottle, and my friends and I drove off in three different directions.

Gracie did her usual graceful leap from the car when I parked it in my gravel drive. How I'd miss this place! I loved the trees, the shrubbery, and the bounteous flowers that Leighton took so much pride in. He'd been nipping back the mums all summer, and now they exploded with spicy fragrance into huge pillows of autumnal colors, pink against maroon, yellow next to burnt orange.

Anya came out of the house to meet me. "Mom, I'm worried about Monroe."

"Why?" I asked, as I handed her Gracie's leash.

"Yesterday when I fed him an apple, he nearly took my fingers off. I noticed his feed pail was empty. Today it's still empty and his water was empty too. I would have fed him, but the grain bin doesn't have any feed in it. All the pellets are gone."

I walked slowly to our back door. A part of me wanted to shout, "That's not my problem!" I was so angry with Leighton, and Monroe is his pet. But I'd never willingly hurt an animal. Or leave one neglected.

"Have you seen Leighton?" I asked. "Nope."

"Okay. Take Gracie and my bag into the house. Be careful with it because Margit made dinner for us. I'll go knock on Leighton's door and tell him that Monroe is without food. You did give him water, didn't you?"

"Of course."

She and I went our separate ways. I took my time walking the paving stones that led to Leighton's door. Fussing at him wasn't likely to change our situation. I supposed that if I'd been a negligent father, and suddenly I had the opportunity to fix my relationship with my daughter, I'd do the same thing he was doing. Yes, it stunk for us. But I was gladder that we'd been allowed to live on this lovely piece of land than I was sad to be moving away from it.

With that attitude of gratitude uppermost in my mind, I knocked on his door.

Since his house is big, I always give Leighton a long time to answer. Today my wait seemed particularly lengthy. I could hear Petunia barking and carrying on. I knocked again, rang the doorbell, and waited. Since Leighton keeps his trash can next to the back door, waiting there is never very pleasant. This time there wasn't much of a smell. So far, so good.

A red-gold leaf drifted down from the sugar maple over-hanging Leighton's house. I tried to remember the last time I'd spoken to him. A week before he'd met with Detweiler? Usually if Leighton was going on tour, he'd ask me to watch Petunia. Maybe he'd gone touring and left Melissa in charge. I wondered. Maybe she didn't know how often Monroe needed to be fed.

Stepping away from the stoop, I cranked my neck to an unnatural degree and stared up at the third floor, the level on which Leighton had finally found his dream office space. The blinds were pinched together, top and bottom, to form a peep-hole. Was he afraid to face me?

I pulled out my cellphone and called him. "Look, Leighton, I just wanted to tell you that Monroe is out of—"

The back door opened. Melissa stood there, balanced on one leg with her arms crossed over her chest in a defensive posture. Her hair hung in greasy hanks around her face. She was wearing a man's muscle tee and a baggy pair of pants. "What do you want?"

Lovely.

"Monroe is out of food." She stared at me. "So?"

"May I speak to your father?"

"No."

"Does he know that Monroe is out of food? Does he plan to buy more? The donkey was also out of water. My daughter—"

"Keep your kids out of the shed, do you hear me? This isn't your property. You're squatting. You're lucky that Dad gave you a week to move out. Don't press your luck!" And she slammed the door in my face.

55

etweiler came home after the kids were in bed. "How're they doing?" he asked as he pulled up a chair at the kitchen table. Since Brawny now slept in our living room, he and I didn't have a place to hang out except for our bedroom or the kitchen. While she watched television, I often sat at the kitchen table with paperwork, crafts, or a book. That way I could greet Detweiler as he walked in the door.

"Erik brought home his work with two stars on it. Maggie sent me a message that he seems to be adjusting well. She and I are having lunch together next Monday at school. I've asked her for a list of names of other boys who might make good play buddies for Erik," I said. "Anya is hating French. She did get a good grade on her art project, and she's fine with going to the Moores' house Friday after school."

I asked him about his day, but he didn't feel like talking about the case at hand. Although I wanted to know what was bothering him, I had learned to give him his space. Especially when he first came home. Instead of pressing him for details, I told him about my meeting with Mert.

"I'm glad you two have made up," he said, taking my hand in

his and kissing my fingers. "You two have been friends for too long to let all that go to waste."

"I wouldn't exactly say that we've made up. I'd say she's willing to tolerate me if I can help find out something that will protect Laurel," and then I told him about my visit to Star Bright Talent Agency.

"Kiki, I wish you wouldn't do things like that. It's not safe and it's not wise."

"Being downtown in the West End in broad daylight isn't exactly risky behavior," I said, although I knew what he meant. I proceeded to tell him what I'd learned from Elise. "See? Nothing really. Nothing at all."

I neglected to mention that Margit had forwarded our customer list to Elise. *Oops.*

"Have you seen Leighton?" I asked, trying to change the subject. I explained what Anya had told me about Monroe being without food. Then I told him about knocking on the back door, and how charming Melissa wasn't.

"I can go feed him some of those carrots we have in the refrigerator," said Detweiler, "but we have to be careful. If we feed him too many raw veggies, he might get sick."

I nodded. "But how long can he go without grain? It's not like he can graze in his pen. There's not enough vegetation there to fill his tummy."

"I don't know," said Detweiler. "I'll call Dad and ask. Did Leighton respond to your text messages?"

"No." I shared with him what Jennifer Moore had told me about Melissa Haversham and then I added, "She didn't seem at all concerned about Monroe. She was too busy warning me that our kids shouldn't be in his shed."

"I guess maybe she doesn't care about him the way we do. We've known Monroe for a while," said Detweiler. He rubbed his hand across his mouth, a gesture that told me he was picking his words carefully. "Although I admit I'm not inclined to like the woman, it's possible she's right. Anya's old enough to handle herself around Monroe but Erik isn't."

"Spill it, buddy," I said, shaking his shoulder. "What aren't you saying that you're thinking?"

He laughed and leaned in for a kiss. "You know me too well. I was thinking that I wish I knew more about Melissa Haversham. Especially after that litany that Jennifer gave you. But I'm reminding myself that it doesn't matter. Even if I found out that she's an axe murderer, it's not like Leighton is going to change his mind. This is about feeling guilty, not about *being* guilty."

56

Wednesday morning...

*B*rawny promised to stop by and get more boxes for us from the U-Haul place on her way home from dropping Erik and Anya off at school. Since I didn't need to go into the store until noon, I opened a few closets and tried to sort items. Anya had outgrown a lot of her clothes. Many of them I could safely toss into a black garbage bag. I planned to take them to Plato's Closet and see if we could get credit against future gently worn merchandise. My daughter and I both were big fans of the chain. I'd found a few nice men's flannel shirts that I planned to wear as the weather got nippy. Anya liked the jeans and since she's so small, she often found a nice outfit or blouse.

After about an hour, my lower back started aching. I decided Gracie needed a potty break. Besides, I wanted to see if Monroe had been fed. Grabbing an apple from my cooler drawer, I snapped the leash on my dog and stepped outside.

The air promised a chill was coming. There was a cold undertone to the ground as I walked from our converted garage to the shed. Monroe saw me coming and brayed loudly. That's unusual. He's typically pretty quiet.

The apple disappeared in an eye-blink. His feed pail was empty. I checked the bin where Leighton kept a bag of horse kibble. That was empty, too. In fact, Monroe was out of water. I grabbed his bucket and took it to the faucet at the side of the shed, but when I turned on the tap, nothing came out.

"Must be a break in the water main," I told the donkey, as he watched me carefully. Since Webster Groves is an older area, this wasn't totally unexpected, but it was rare. Especially since I'd showered earlier and hadn't had any problems. I took the bucket to my house and turned on the tap. It ran clear and clean and crisp. After filling the bucket, I lugged it back to Monroe's shed and hung it on its hook. He drank thirstily.

I text-messaged Leighton again. I figured there must be some way to tell if he was getting my messages, but I wasn't sure how.

That got me thinking...

How on earth could I get Leighton's attention?

I remember that he had an author's website. Could I go through that? How about an author's Facebook page? He had once told me that was the best route for readers to "talk" with him.

"Not by going through your publisher?" I asked.

"Heavens no. It takes forever for mail to get through their system and back to me," he had explained.

Putting on my thinking cap, I came up with a plan. First I'd try once more to talk to him face-to-face. If that didn't work, I'd go online to contact him. He could run but he couldn't hide from me.

But he had been hiding. He'd been watching out his window and pretending to not be at home. Well, I knew how to foil that little trick. I decided to check to see if his car was in his garage. I walked around the back of his house to the detached garage that he'd added when he converted the original detached garage into what was now my living quarters.

Sure enough, his beautiful black antique Jaguar was there, snug as could be. Walking from one window to another and shading my eyes with my hand, I stared at it. Something wasn't quite right. But what?

Leighton was incredibly fussy about where he parked the Jag. He'd not only hung a tennis ball from a string to help him center the car, he'd also purchased small bumpers that sat on the floor of his garage. These helped him line up his tires.

But the Jag wasn't resting on the tire bumpers. It had been parked off center, missing them entirely. That's not anything he would have ever done! He was totally paranoid about banging his car doors on anything. Those floor bumpers were his salvation.

Why wasn't his car parked properly?

There could be only one answer: Melissa. She must have driven it.

Leighton never let anybody drive his Jag.

Once I was back inside my house, I turned on the computer in Anya's bedroom. I tried one social media site after the other. Leighton's website hadn't been updated in a while. That didn't surprise me. Websites are like kitchen remodeling projects. They go on and on and on. Leighton's Facebook page had seen activity as recently as ten days ago. That was when he made his last post. By my calculations, that would have been right around the time that he heard from Melissa, when he'd gotten her request to move in. I turned off the computer and grabbed my keys.

Was it possible that he was having so much fun with his daughter that he was letting everything go? Could it be that he'd given up his prissy ways? His self-discipline? That didn't seem like Leighton. He was incredibly focused on his writing. I heard him speak about his work at the Webster Groves Library. He told the crowd that he wrote every day without fail. "If a writer doesn't write, how can he call himself a writer?" he'd asked to the general merriment of all in attendance.

Even if Leighton was worried that I'd be angry with him, why go to such lengths to avoid me? It wasn't like I'd spoken to him since he had told Detweiler that he wanted us out of the little house. Leighton had no reason to think I'd yell at him. I'd never said a cross word to the man. Not ever. Was he really such a coward?

Wednesdays are trash days. Ours had been sitting by the curb when I backed my car out of the drive this morning. Usually, Leighton's bin sat right next to ours, looking like two soldiers at attention. But today, his bin remained beside his backdoor. Because he traveled so frequently, Leighton sometimes forgot Wednesday was the day.

Should I be a good neighbor or not?

With a sigh of disgust, I put my car into park and hopped out. I ran to Leighton's back door, grabbed the wheeled bin, and rolled it to the curb. The whole contraption was surprisingly lightweight. In fact, too lightweight. Maybe I was hauling a bin that didn't have any trash in it. Maybe that's why Leighton and Melissa hadn't bothered with taking it to the curb.

I plucked the lid off and stared deep inside. At the bottom was one small white bag. On top of it were four pill bottles. I tipped the bin over so I could reach inside.

All four were for OxyContin. None of them had Melissa's name on them. Or Leighton's. Instead, they'd been prescribed for another woman, Melinda P. Haviland.

After tossing the empty vials in my purse, I climbed back into the car and started toward the store. Ever since Brawny's arrival I've felt a delicious sense of freedom, simply because I don't have to rush from one place to another. Even though our living quarters have been more cramped since her arrival, Brawny was a godsend.

I called Detweiler from the road, as I was eager to tell him about my discovery. I don't know much about drugs, or drug addiction, but I did recall that Rush Limbaugh had a rough time shaking his dependency on OxyContin.

My sweetie didn't answer, so I left him a message to call me back. When I got to the junction of Highway 40 and Lindbergh, the steering wheel turned east as usual. But I passed my usual exit. Instead, I got off at the Big Bend and headed north toward Prairie Central Community College.

If I remembered correctly the notes Catherine had scribbled on Laurel's old homework, Brian Overmeyer would be teaching this morning. If I hustled, I could be there when his class let out. Even if I got the room number wrong, I could find him by asking the students where his class was held. Because I had Gracie in the car, I knew there'd be no shortage of eager people willing to help me. A dog can be a wonderful ice breaker!

Finding a space in the parking lots proved daunting. I didn't have a student sticker. The visitors' spaces were severely limited in number. I wished I had a handicapped tag, because most of those spaces were empty.

Isn't a big belly a handicap? I grumbled to myself.

Gracie eagerly tumbled out from the passenger side. Since I had no idea where we were going, I headed for the biggest cluster of buildings. She trotted alongside of me, wagging her tail as we went.

Of course, she caused quite a stir. Students begged to pat her. Others called out, "Cool dog!" It took four tries, asking about Brian Overmeyer, until a student was able to tell me where the man's class was held. By then I was worried that I would miss the teacher entirely. When I went to college, most of our professors vamoosed out of the classroom the minute the lecture was over. If you wanted to meet with a teacher, you had to make an appointment during office hours.

But I reminded myself, as I huffed and puffed along, that this was a community college. From what I'd heard, the teachers were here because they loved teaching or loved their subjects. Instead of being burdened with research, they often worked in their chosen fields. There was a different atmosphere on this campus. One that I picked up on right away. More of the students were adults. Most were dressed in business attire, as if they'd come from work to school without a break in between. Most seemed more serious than what I remembered from my days as an undergraduate.

It did occur to me that each college or university was probably different. Each probably had its own style, personality, and temperament. Jennifer told me that when they were looking at colleges with Stevie, she knew immediately which schools would be a good fit for her son. "It's like going on a blind date. You get this sense of whether there's a good fit or not immediately."

Finally, I found myself outside the double doors that supposedly led to Brian Overmeyer's classroom. With any luck, his room would be close to the outside doors, so I wouldn't have to parade Gracie through the hallway.

I stepped in, glanced at the room numbers, and knew that this was not my lucky day. If I calculated correctly, the door I wanted was in the middle of the building. Tugging at the leash, I urged Gracie to step lively. She did and immediately her four paws slid out from under her.

"Come on, girl," I said. Making a hoop with my arms, I pulled her to her feet.

Whomp! Down she went again.

So close and yet so far. I couldn't tie her to a bush and leave her outside. I didn't dare. She was too dear to me to risk it. I lifted her again with the same result as before.

There was no help for it. I got behind Gracie and pushed her locomotive style down the hallway. Fortunately, the doors all had little bitty windows up high, so no one gawked as we choo-chooed our way along. Blessedly, Gracie is a good sport. She put up with my maneuvers.

I was within two feet of my goal when the door I wanted flew open. A young man with thinning hair and a blotchy complexion came racing out. His eyes were on his watch, so he didn't even give me a second glance.

"Mr. Overmeyer?" I called to him.

"Huh?" he paused, turned on his heel, and studied me. Then he noticed Gracie. "What in the world?"

"Um, I'm a friend of Laurel Wilkins," I said, straightening up from behind Gracie. "I was wondering if we could talk."

"How is she? I heard she was hurt. There was an email in my box." A few wisps of hair waved from the top of his pink scalp.

"She's home now, but still recovering. Uh, could we go some-where and talk?"

"I have office hours in twenty minutes. Across campus. Perhaps we could talk and walk?" As he spoke, he checked his watch one more time.

"Sure thing," I said. "Just point us in the right direction."

He took a couple steps and then looked down. "Is there something wrong with your dog?"

"Nope," I grunted, as I pushed Gracie back the way we'd come.

"Then why isn't she walking?" "Because the floor's too slick."

"Excuse me if I sound rude, but are you pregnant?" "Yep." I paused long enough to suck wind.

"Do you think I could help?"

"With my pregnancy? I'm a little far gone for that."

"Pushing the dog. Here. You take my briefcase and these books." He stepped next to me. "Um, she won't bite me, will she?"

"I seriously doubt it."

He pushed poor Gracie down the hallway of the Social Sciences Building.

57

---

*L*ike most of us, Brian Overmeyer had been totally charmed by Laurel. He waxed ecstatic about her looks, her smarts, and her great personality. After hearing him go on and on, I suspected that he wasn't aware that Laurel was spoken for, or that she had her eyes on Father Joe. And I wasn't about to spill the pinto beans. No sirree. As long as Brian —as he suggested that I call him—wanted to talk, I was willing to listen.

"Can you think of anyone in the class who might have wanted to hurt Laurel?" I asked. "Or even anyone on campus who might have a grudge against her?"

"Absolutely not!" he protested. After a pause, he added, "I imagine that some of our female students might have felt, um, competitive. With good reason. But Laurel is always so nice, so thoroughly approachable, that I can't conceive of anyone wanting to harm her."

"Somebody did," I said. "I was there the night it happened."

"Did you see any of our students?"

That was a ridiculous assertion. How would I know if anyone I saw was a student at Prairie Central? Short of the person wearing a Prairie Central tee shirt, I wouldn't have been able to pick one out of the crowd. But rather than throw a damper on his freewheeling commentary, I said, "Not that I know of."

"So why are you here? Did the police send you?"

I fought the urge to roll my eyes. Clearly, this man was one of your absent-minded professors. "I'm here because I'm her friend. She's also my employee."

"She bellydances for you?" His face lit up.

"No!" I nearly shouted, and Gracie turned to see what upset me. "I own a scrapbook store. Laurel works part-time for me."

"Aha! Now I see. But aren't the police involved?"

"Sort of. However, we're not entirely sure that the local police where the crime occurred are giving the situation the attention it deserves."

"Ah," he said, thoughtfully.

I wasn't totally sure how to decipher that two-letter word, so I continued with, "Needless to say, I'm very worried about Laurel's safety. That's why I'm curious as to how the other students reacted toward her. Like most of them, I was intimidated by her looks at first, but now that I've gotten to know her, I see that she's every bit as lovely on the inside as she is on the outside!"

He nodded. "Yes, she is. I can't imagine anybody wanting to hurt her, much less to doing something so heinous."

"Would there be anything in her files? Anything they share with you teachers that might point to a motive?"

"Those would be highly confidential," he tut-tut-tutted.

"I know. I'm not asking to look at them. I'm just hoping that if there was anything, and if it did stick in your mind, you might share it with me, in the hopes that I could pass it along to the proper authorities."

"I understand, and the answer is that I know of nothing. You are aware that she attended another community college, as well as continuing her studies here at Prairie State?"

"Yes, I'd heard that." I needed to word my next question carefully. "I also heard that someone had sent her inappropriate text messages. Do you know if that was a student or a faculty member?"

"Are you accusing me?" he fairly screeched.

"Nope. I'm asking you. If I thought you were the one who'd sent them, I would have accused you, but I didn't."

"Again, you are trespassing on areas that I would never speak about, for fear of violating the responsibilities expected of me by this college."

Terrific. As we said in the Midwest, he had a corncob up his backside. I switched gears. "I would never ask you to betray a confidence. It's entirely possible you might know of the emails through casual conversation. After all, Laurel's also taken classes at Washington University."

"Right. Laurel is fascinated by the status of women, throughout history and in present times. She's curious about the social implications of a variety of factors, including but not limited to female beauty. As you are probably aware, different cultures have defined beauty differently at different times in their histories. When food is scarce a pleasingly plump woman is highly desirable."

I slowed my pace. After pushing my dog around on the floor, I was sweaty and cranky. Was he telling me something? Like maybe that I would have been desirable but I wasn't? I felt like saying, "See how desirable you feel when you're seven months pregnant," but instead I shook it off.

"Okay, well, I need to get back to my store. If you happen to think of someone who might have been involved in the attack on Laurel, I hope you'll let the authorities know. Better yet, call me. Here's one of my business cards. I'm engaged to a homicide detective. He'll handle your information in confidence."

58

"You missed Faye, so she said she'd come back by for her check tomorrow," said Clancy, as I walked onto the sales floor. "Why the grumpy face? Is Laurel worse?"

"I hope not." I explained about my visit to Prairie Central Community College. "I'm on the fast track to nowhere."

"That's one way to look at it. Another is to strike off the avenues you've pursued. Where's your list?"

"I'm not sure." With that I started digging in my purse. "I could have sworn I stuck it back in here after Mert and I talked about it."

"That's another reason to be happy. The two of you are on speaking terms again," Clancy said. In her hand was an order form and the sign-up sheet for the Zentangle session. We'd both pulled up stools at my work table, sitting companionably side by side.

"How's that going?" I gestured to the Zentangle session. "Those three women from the church? They've signed up. Said they wouldn't miss it for the world."

"Goody-goody." I could not keep the sarcasm out of my voice.

"Maybe when I talk about zen, one of them will volunteer that she's been meditating ever since she escaped from the looney bin. Then this case will crack wide open."

I'd no more than gotten those words out of my mouth than the door minder rang. Clancy and I both turned to see who our guest was.

"Joseph! Just look at you!" Clancy rushed to greet Father Joe. With her in trim black slacks and a black cashmere sweater and the priest in the same, they looked like twin penguins at a family reunion. Somehow that tickled me. When I told them why I was laughing, Father Joe chuckled, too.

"Ah, penguins," he said. "Remember when they first added those Humbolt penguins to the St. Louis Zoo, and they enjoyed the slide in their new home so much that they would swoop down and fly right over the safety railing? The crew members coming into the Penguin and Puffin Coast each morning were greeted by the penguins marching around all over the building. They had to do a daily round up."

"What I remember is that one of the penguins bit Newt Gingrich when he was campaigning for president," said Clancy with a giggle.

"Do you two always have to carry on like this?" I asked, as they reluctantly stepped away from each other.

"Of course, we do," said Clancy. "Even when he was my student, we were always cutting up and laughing. Joseph, Kiki told me that you're planning to propose to Laurel. That's just wonderful!"

Although she seems terribly straight-laced, Clancy is really a total romantic who has memorized every line in *Casablanca*. And if you think that's obsessive, just get her started about *The African Queen*. She knows everything about the movie, including the fact that Director John Huston found a black mamba snake in the bathroom of their set in Africa.

"I guess we strike Father Joe off our lists of suspects." I jammed my hand deep in my purse again, and this time I fished out the paper Clancy and I had started when we first noodled around whodunit.

"Was I a person of interest? Seriously?" He looked wounded.

"Kiki has a sick sense of humor." Clancy smirked at me. "Better than no sense of humor." I retorted. "Look, I'm having a bad day. Let's change the subject. Have you seen Laurel? How's she doing?"

"Yes. I dropped by her apartment. Mert was there, guarding her young," said the priest, as he pulled up a stool and sat down. "She isn't quite sure of me, I can tell."

I explained about Mert thinking the Pope would be involved, somehow.

At that, he and Clancy and I all started giggling. "Just think of it," said Father Joe. "After all the efforts that King Henry VIII went to, word still hasn't gotten around that the Anglican Church no longer bows low to the man at the Vatican."

"That's so odd because Mert's a highly educated woman! Really, she is!" I said.

"All of us have great gaps in our education," said Clancy. "I know better than most. I was a teacher remember? I had a student who wrote on a test that The Scarlet Letter was a movie starring Demi Moore. She refused to believe there was a book by the same title."

I smiled and said, "I'm sure that your church-goers will be warm and loving toward Laurel."

Father Joe's face turned grim. "I wish that were true." He held up a hand as if to erase his last comment. I stood there trying to wrap my head around what he might be thinking. Rather than speak, both Clancy and I waited until the young man mastered his emotions.

"Most of the members of St. James have been wonderful.

True Christians in every sense of the word," he said. The words came out with difficulty.

Clancy and I exchanged looks. Obviously, there was more to the story.

"Would you like a bottle of water? A cold Coke? A Pepsi? Or a Sprite?" I asked. We'd recently revised our offerings to include the lemon-lime flavored drinks and Pepsi products.

"How about a cup of coffee? Or tea?" asked Clancy.

"A cup of hot tea would be much appreciated," he said. As he spoke, his shoulders hunched over with defeat. Facing the subject at hand had clearly taken a lot of his moxie.

While Clancy ran to the back, I fiddled around with my Zentangle handout. Since we each took turns teaching a tangle, or pattern, I created a handout with a blank "step out" or empty boxes so that we could fill in the various steps that had to be taken to create the pattern. Before each class, these needed to be collated, so I did the work while Father Joe took his cup of tea from Clancy and doctored it with two heaping spoonsful of sugar. After he'd had a sip, he said, "Since I haven't formally proposed to Laurel, there hasn't been a specific announcement of our plans. However, she has been coming to church regularly, and you'd have to be blind not to notice that I reach for her hand as soon as I've completed the services, hung up my robes, and left the sacristy."

I sipped from a bottle of water and waited. Clancy's eyes were narrow with concern.

"A few weeks ago, a mimeographed letter was sent to all the members of the vestry. I won't bore you with the details, but the message suggested that I'd been hoodwinked. That during my outreach activities to those less fortunate, I'd been associating with people of low morals. The author of the letter didn't specifically name Laurel. The charges were vague. Most of the vestry members thought this amusing. One, in fact, noted that Jesus consorted with persons of low status."

He sighed. "In retrospect, ignoring it wasn't a good idea. Someone had actually mimeographed the letters using an old machine that we'd locked away because our new photocopier works so much better. That should have been a tip off to me that this person was too close for comfort."

"You mean the author had to be someone with keys to the office area of the church," surmised Clancy.

"Exactly. After the letters came, I took the old mimeograph machine to Goodwill. I figured that would be the end of it. But of course, it wasn't that easy. The next letter included a color photo of Laurel in her belly dancing gear. It wasn't one of the pictures used by her talent agency. It wasn't one taken from her website. The quality was poor, and the angle suggested the photographer had been at the back of a crowd. Probably in a restaurant."

"Then the photographer must have been at an event where Laurel was dancing," I said.

"Right. This letter was much more personal. The author uncovered Laurel's birth certificate! A copy of it was in the packet. So were a variety of scandalous accusations, just salacious enough to paint her as the proverbial bad seed."

"What did you do about that?" I asked. I couldn't imagine such a letter, so I wondered how the young priest would respond.

"I called an immediate meeting of the vestry—and I'll be the first to admit that I lost my cool. I babbled like an idiot. I asked them who among them was without sin and wanted to cast a stone. I pointed out that Laurel's lack of a father was not her fault. That Mert's situation was a terrible commentary on our broken social welfare system. I explained that belly-dancing had ethnic origins. I must have ranted and raved for nearly fifteen minutes until the president of the vestry took me by the arm and led me out of the room."

"Thank goodness," said Clancy, "I bet your reaction did more harm than good."

He nodded. "That's what Franklin Eaton said. Nearly word for word. He took me outside and told me to take a walk around the block while he repaired the damage. When I got back, he was sitting there by himself, having dismissed the vestry. He told me very gently that I needed to get a grip."

Franklin Eaton suggested that the letters were now a matter for the police.

"But when the detective from the local police form came, he admitted he couldn't do much to help," explained Father Joe. "I changed all the locks on the equipment cabinets, closet, and my office."

"Wow," I said. "That's just awful! It must feel like your home was invaded."

"I hate the fact that I'm now suspicious of everyone, especially those who work closely with me."

"Did you call the police after Laurel was stabbed? Did you mention the letters again? Maybe they can use them as a link back to the attacker," suggested Clancy.

"Yes, I did. They didn't hold out a lot of hope. Besides, they had bigger fish to fry. After the letters, someone soaped the windows on Laurel's car and spray-painted nasty suggestions on the church parking lot," he said.

"That's interesting," I said. "You'd think someone who was determined to be hurtful would have picked pranks with longer lasting results."

"I know," said Father Joe as he rubbed the back of his neck. "Wouldn't you? It's almost like the perpetrator was a reluctant vandal. Can you believe it?"

After asking him to wait, I packed up a "care package" for

Laurel, including a fresh box of Skinny Cow Heavenly Crisp peanut butter bars from my personal stash and a few "get well" cards that had arrived with her name on them.

"Please take this to her," I told the priest. "I assume you'll see her soon."

After Father Joe gave us both a hug and took off, Clancy and I discussed what we'd learned. "I bet one of our three women is involved with these hateful incidents, don't you?"

I agreed with her. "Mary Martha is Father Joe's personal assistant. Can you imagine the amount of personal information she's privy to?"

"Right, and she'd also have all the addresses of all the vestry members, plus access to the copier."

"If we're smart enough to figure this out, so is Father Joe," I said.

Clancy nodded. "You're right about that, too. He's either in denial or too upset to give her the boot."

"Or," I said, as I shuffled the Zentangle papers, "it's possible he has a plan. If she's the one with the history of mental illness, maybe he's planning an intervention. Or even talking to her family and suggesting that they step in."

Clancy sighed and closed her eyes. "Joseph was always a very thoughtful and meticulous young man. Calling in the police to investigate wasn't his idea, after all."

I thought about everything he'd said. "It sounds like Laurel's presence in the church was the catalyst for all the misbehavior. If she's out of the picture for a while, then the harassment should stop. Temporarily."

"That boy was one of my favorite students. Bar none. Just a terrific kid. I can imagine him considering every option. Like you said, now he has the time to move slowly."

Right then, my phone rang. Detweiler was returning my call.

I excused myself and went to the office so we could talk in private.

When I told him about the empty vials of OxyContin, he asked me to spell the name on the labels. I did, and I mentioned Leighton's car. "You know how picky he is about how it's parked. I can't help but think that she's been driving it."

"He never loans it out. In fact, he doesn't drive it for long trips. He always puts the mileage on a rental," said Detweiler.

"Exactly. That makes me think she's been driving it, which isn't really a big deal, I guess. She is his daughter," I said.

"Right," Detweiler dragged the word out. "But I haven't seen hide nor hair of Leighton since he intercepted me on my way to the gym. That's got me worried."

I thought about this. "Frankly, I've been happy to avoid him because I'm so angry, but now that you mention it, he's usually out puttering around in the yard. The lawn guys come this afternoon. I've got the store covered. Maybe I'll go home early. Surely, he'll show up out in the yard."

"Kiki, don't get into a fight with him. That won't make things better," warned Detweiler.

"I won't, but I do want to point out that poor Monroe is suffering from neglect."

"Let me see what I can find out on this end. You said there wasn't any water coming from the tap? That spigot we use to fill Monroe's bucket?"

"Right, but that could be a break in the water main."

"Except that we have water. If the main was broken, we'd be going without, too."

I thought about that. I wasn't sure we were on the same feeder, but Detweiler would probably know best. "Yup. Doesn't make any sense, does it? I've been sending Leighton text messages, but he doesn't respond. That's unusual. He told me he loves texting because it doesn't interrupt his work the way a phone call does."

"I suppose he might be so busy connecting with his daughter that he's not being as diligent about Monroe as usual," said Detweiler.

"Look, I've known Leighton longer than you have. He's always careful with his pets. That reminds me, I haven't seen Petunia running around in the yard at all. Usually Tunie gets walked a couple of times a day, and Leighton lets him race around while he does work on his flowers."

"I don't like this," said Detweiler. "There's something hinky going on. I'll get my work wrapped up here and get home as fast as possible. I think that you and I need to bang on Leighton's door until we can talk to him face to face."

"Pick up a bag of food for Monroe, would you? He likes that Purina feed. You know where the Purina Farms store is."

"Will do."

CLANCY WAS fine with closing the store by herself, so I left early. I enjoyed driving down the residential streets, gawking at the brilliant displays of fall foliage. Leaving Leighton's property wouldn't just bother Anya. It would also break my heart.

But I would heal.

Turning into the drive, I took pleasure in the thick profusion of mums leading up to my back door. "Come on, girl," I said to Gracie, helping her out of my car.

Since my dog didn't like Melissa Haversham, I left her in the house while I went to check on Monroe. He was nearly out of water, so I fed him another apple and filled his bucket. As he'd done before, he grabbed the apple and gobbled it down. Usually he's pretty dainty about taking food from my palm.

"You poor baby," I said, petting him. "You must really be hungry. I'd feed you more apples, Monroe, but I think they'd make you sick. Detweiler will be here soon with some kibble for you."

Since the spigot still didn't work, I carried the bucket to the side of our house and, after dumping what was left of the old water, refilled it. Once it was on the hook, Monroe lapped it up gratefully. While I watched I also noticed that his stall hadn't been mucked out. Usually Leighton makes this his morning exercise. When he's away, Anya mucks out the stall. But now poor Monroe's home was stinky with a layer of dirty straw.

Even if Leighton was enthralled with his daughter, I couldn't imagine him neglecting Monroe. And Petunia! Where was the little pug?

I grabbed the pitchfork and shoveled up the old straw. While I didn't do the sort of thorough job that Leighton or Anya typically did, I managed to move the old stuff off to one side and spread new, sweet-smelling strands on the floor. I planned to ask Detweiler or Anya to come haul out the gunk for me. Unfortunately, I just didn't have the physical power to lift it over my belly and into the composting bin.

While I worked, Monroe watched me carefully. Did he need something else? Something I didn't know how to provide? Leighton had taught Anya all about caring for the donkey. When she got home from school, I'd ask her to brush him down and check him over.

By the time I set the pitchfork aside, I was dusty and itchy from the decaying matter getting inside my shirt.

I was also angry. Really, really mad.

If Leighton no longer cared about me or my family, that was his business. But if he wasn't going to take care of Monroe, he needed to let someone know. Even though my budget was tight, we'd find a way to keep the donkey fed. And clean. And loved.

That spark of anger fueled me. My arms ached, my lower back spasmed, but I was on a roll now. I was hot under the collar and seriously ticked. I marched out of the shed and up the path to Leighton's back door. No one answered when I rang the bell repeatedly. I switched to beating on the door. Nada.

Frustrated, I returned to my kitchen.

Gracie turned sad brown eyes on me, pleading with me to make sure that her little friend, Petunia, was okay.

Fine. I'd leave Leighton a message. A note that he couldn't ignore. I grabbed paper and pen and scribbled: *Call me! Worried about your pets! This is imperative! Kiki*

Now I just needed to make sure the message would be found. I didn't trust Melissa to hand it over to her father. But if he was driving his Jaguar, or accompanying Melissa as she drove, a message stuck under the windshield wipers was sure to get his attention.

If that didn't work, I planned to message him through Facebook and text-message him. One way or the other, I'd make him pay attention.

"You can run but you can't hide, Leighton," I said, even though he wasn't around to hear me. Then I got an idea, a flash of brilliance.

A long time ago, Leighton had told me that he kept a spare key to the garage under a fake rock in the flower bed directly across from the side door to his garage. Since I was already covered in dirt from mucking out Monroe's stall, I walked around the house to the side lawn. Once there, I dropped to my knees and picked through the mulch in the flowerbed. At first, I couldn't find the plastic rock, so I shifted my weight and sat back on my heels, thinking. When people stick potted mums in their yard, as they often do for seasonal color, the result is a small circular cluster of blossoms. They show up like floral polka dots on a lawn. But because Leighton carefully tended his mums and treated them as perennials, and his mums were outrageous. These weren't your ordinary dots of color. Oh, no. These had spread out. As I rested on my knees, I faced a swath of brilliant magenta interrupted by pink. Red-orange and canary-yellow flowers had intermingled with the purple red shades. As the plants had grown, sharing the same space, they formed a riot of color.

Was it possible that the mums had grown over the fake rock? That the stone was deep in the tangle of stems? I reached my hand into the thick of the chrysanthemums and felt around. My fingers bumped a slick surface. I pulled up the fake rock.

With a bit of prying, I popped open the secret compartment.

Clutching the key in my hand, I headed toward the garage.

As I did, my face turned red with embarrassment. The engine of the Jaguar was humming loudly. Here, I'd gone through so much trouble to find that silly key, and all I needed to do was walk over and confront Leighton.

Except something was wrong. I couldn't quite figure out what.

After walking along the side of his garage, I made a right turn to face the rolling door. It was down. Sealed shut. That didn't make sense. I could hear the car engine. Why wasn't the door up?

"Leighton?" I banged on the garage door. "Open up!" No response.

The car engine continued to purr.

"Leighton!" I screamed louder. I slammed my fists into the section of the door at eye level. It echoed like a bass drum. The pounding sounded incredibly loud to my ears, but still I didn't get a response.

I ran around to the side, where I'd been earlier. Pressing my hands around my face, I looked in through the door window. I could see a shape in the driver's seat. Shifting my stance, I caught the glimmer of Leighton's white hair. It appeared to be resting against the seat.

Carbon monoxide poisoning. I had to get to him and get him out fast.

My hand shook as I stuck the key in the door lock. At first, it resisted turning. My palms perspired and I couldn't get a good grip. The lock wouldn't yield. I grabbed the handle and pulled the door toward me, thinking I could align the deadbolt better with the slot. Maybe that would help. Using all my weight as a counterbalance, I turned the key. I felt the deadbolt give, sliding, popping free.

With a shove, I put my shoulder into the door. It flew open.

I stumbled forward, into the dark garage—and then tripped over a box. I rolled to my knees and then my feet. My throat began to close. My asthma kicked in, and the coughing began. Fighting against the spasms, I looked around. The path to the car was blocked by a ladder, boxes, a plastic storage bin, a rake, and the plastic bin I'd fallen over. Wriggling like a snake, I moved under the ladder, over the boxes, stepping on the bin, and around the rake. No way could I drag Leighton through this mess!

What could I do?

Exhaust fumes took my breath away.

Even though the side door was open, the garage was thick with exhaust. I pressed my face against the passenger window of the Jag. Leighton wasn't moving.

Had I arrived in time?

59

$\mathcal{M}$y coughing doubled me over. I hacked so badly that I couldn't walk. My first instinct was to grab the car door and yank Leighton out onto the concrete floor. But then what? One step at a time, I reminded myself.

I coughed my way to the driver's door. Giving it a mighty yank, I pulled it open. Reaching under Leighton's chest and feeling around on the dash, I turned off the car engine.

Pressing my fingers against Leighton's throat, I tried to find a pulse.

Nada.

Who was I kidding? I couldn't find my own pulse on a good day!

I tried to lift him. The coughing jarred me so badly that I couldn't control my own body, much less his. Slipping both arms under his chest, I only managed to move Leighton an inch before I had to give up.

Think, Kiki, think!

Without fresh air, it wouldn't matter whether he was in the car or out of it. I calculated the distance between the driver's door and the door I'd come through.

Even if I could handle Leighton's weight, the ladder was blocking the door. I couldn't haul him over it and over all the junk. There wasn't any way I could move all the stuff and then drag him out the door fast enough. In addition, I was wheezing like an antique church organ. I couldn't handle much of this. How could I help Leighton?

I had to open the big door.

Pawing my way through the fumes, I stumbled to the side wall and punched the garage door button. Nothing happened. By touch alone, I moved along the side wall until I reached the folding door itself. I remembered a red pull rope. If it functioned like the one we'd had at our house in Ladue that cord was an emergency opener. Used in case of loss of power. Like right now. Since I'm short, I wasn't sure I could reach the toggle. All I could do was wave my hand over my head and hope my fingers would brush the cord. My hand bumped the cord and sent it flying in circles over my head. I raised my hand again, fishing around in the air. But I was coughing so hard that I could barely keep myself from doubling over. I fought to suppress the coughs.

I had to calm down or I'd never get a purchase on the rope.

My second interception was more fruitful. I grasped the plastic plug that dangled from the end of the rope. I began walking and pulling the cord backwards. I got so far and then, nothing happened. I couldn't go any farther.

Then it hit me. First you needed to unlock the overhead mechanism. To do that, I needed to pull straight down. My coughs were so intense that my head was pounding. I could barely think, much less control my motions.

I can do this, I told myself. Slow up, be deliberate.

I tugged the cord straight down, at a sharp right angle to the roof of the garage. A shift told me that I'd succeeded in unlocking the mechanism. Now I began my trek backwards once again, pitting as much of my weight against the cord as I dared.

If it popped, I'd be back to square one. But it didn't. A loud creaking sound and a rumble suggested I was making headway.

A stripe of light appeared down along the floor. I forced myself to keep pulling. If I quit, the whole door would probably tumble back down.

A few more steps, and I was even with the side door where I'd entered. The fresh air flowing through it revitalized me. Delicious, but the contrast made the heavy taste of the exhaust fumes more obvious and obnoxious. Had I really breathed in so much gasoline vapor?

I kept marching backwards. At some point, the weight of the door would shift. When it did, the door should roll up of its own accord.

Although this process seemed to be taking forever, in reality, it took seconds.

Come on, nearly there.

As the door rose, the fumes should be leaving. In theory at least.

My muscles protested. My head felt like someone was poking hot daggers through my brain. My ribs ached from coughing. My throat was raw.

I didn't care. Only a few more steps to go.

Bumpitty-bumpitty-bump-bump.

Gravity and motion tipped in my favor. The tension on the garage door changed. It began rolling upwards of its own accord. I hesitated, fearful that if I let go too soon, the door would crash down. I followed the cord, on tiptoe, until momentum jerked it out of my grip.

A glorious scene emerged—the outside! Fresh air! I could see the fence around Leighton's next door neighbor's property! I coughed and coughed, blinking in the light, as I turned and raced around to the other side of the Jaguar, where the driver's side door was slightly open.

Now to rescue Leighton.

His head was lolling to one side. Wrapping my hands around his torso, I pulled and pulled on him. My coughing continued, and now my stomach roiled. I thought I'd puke at any second. I braced my foot against the floorboard for leverage. Leighton seemed to be wedged between the seat and the steering wheel. I changed my grip. Grasping his belt with my left hand and his shirt collar with my right, I managed to pull him towards me.

Now his head rested again my chest and his arms dangled.

If I could pop him free of the car, moving him wouldn't be so hard.

Going back to my original grip, I locked my arms around his upper torso and threw myself backwards. My back rammed something curved and hard. His wheelbarrow was on a hook on the garage wall. I must be up against the front wheel. That meant I didn't have any more room on that side.

I ducked low and braced my feet against the concrete floor.

One more try, I promised myself. If this doesn't work, I'll break the windows.

I braced myself again. "One-two-three," and put all my weight in opposition to his limp form. With effort, I managed to pull Leighton out of the car. I tugged him backwards until he was lying on the floor.

"Leighton? Leighton?" But he didn't respond.

60

*H*ow I managed to drag him out of the garage and onto the grass I'll never know. But I did. They say that your adrenaline kicks in and gives you super-powers. I guess that's what happened.

I remember how heavy he was. How he flopped like a big rag doll. How his feet fought me as the heels of his shoes scraped the floor. How loose his arms were. How I had to stop twice and renew my grip around his chest.

By the time I dumped him onto the grass, I was crying and screaming his name.

His color was gray. I turned him face up, on his back on the ground.

"Scoot out of the way." Detweiler's hand touched my shoulder.

Because he was there to take over, I threw myself onto the grass and dialed nine-one-one. Between sobs, I told the dispatcher that we needed an ambulance and police response. Had Leighton tried to commit suicide? I wasn't sure. As I ended the call, I wondered. I couldn't believe that. It wasn't in his nature.

Yes, I was more than ready to pin this on Melissa. Call me judgmental, call me nasty, call me mean. I had a hunch she was behind all this. It was simply too convenient. While Detweiler labored over my landlord, I sat on the grass and cried big gulping sobs.

"You okay?" asked Detweiler between breaths.

"Yes," I said quickly. I didn't want him to stop helping Leighton, and the truth was that I was okay. Sort of. Daggers of pain stabbed through my skull. My thinking was foggy. I couldn't concentrate, and saliva filled my mouth as a prelude to heaving.

Rolling to my knees I vomited in the grass. Detweiler stopped to check on me.

"Go back, help him," I said. "Please!"

As he continued to pump Leighton's chest, I kept puking. Tears streamed from my eyes. The force of my stomach's contractions knocked me onto my elbows. I couldn't see for the blur and I couldn't get myself to quit heaving. I upchucked until nothing came out but bile.

When the EMTs arrived, they saw me first. I waved them away. A second ambulance arrived in short order. A medic ran to me, and since I knew that Leighton and Detweiler were now receiving assistance, I didn't push him away.

"Are you...?" he paused and stared down at my belly. "How far along are you?"

When I told him, he screamed for a gurney. "No, no, really I'm okay," I protested.

Detweiler was talking to the first set of EMTs, telling them what he knew about Leighton. He glanced over and saw that they were bringing a gurney for me.

"Kiki? What—"

"Out of the way, sir," said a tech, as they slid the gurney under me.

Before I could protest, they clamped an oxygen mask over my face.

"This woman is pregnant. We need to get her to the hospital and continue her oxygen treatment. Her baby might be at risk," said the tech, as he pushed Detweiler away from me.

My baby? At risk? Oh, Lord, what have I done?

I heard Detweiler's voice go up a notch. Out of the corner of my eyes I saw him and the EMT get into a shoving match.

My baby!

I hadn't thought about my baby when I plunged into the garage. Now it came to me. My baby was breathing via my red blood cells. The carbon monoxide would have crowded out the oxygen in my blood stream.

I sank back onto the stretcher and wailed in fear. Was it possible? Could I have hurt my unborn child?

Why hadn't I waited for help? What had I done?

61

"*H*ey," said Detweiler, as he kissed my fingers a couple of hours later. "How are you feeling?"

I woke up to a flickering fluorescent bulb that buzzed like a bumblebee. My head hurt. My throat was raw from puking. The sheets felt scratchy and I had an IV stuck in my forearm.

Hospitals, you gotta love them. While I'd never recommend a visit for the fun of it, they sure had their act together when it came to patching people up.

"My baby?" I asked, touching my belly and trying not to cry. "Our baby is fine. You weren't in the garage long enough to

do any lasting harm." Detweiler's green eyes looked more golden than usual, probably because they were moist. The tip of his nose was pink. I could tell he was seriously upset. That vein along his temple throbbed, a sign that his blood pressure is high.

"Leighton?"

"Will be fine. Or so they think. They'll be doing tests on him.

He's dehydrated, malnourished, and sick as a dog." "Dog! What about Petunia?"

"Also fine. I found him at the pound. I sprung him just in

274

time. He was due to be, uh, euthanized." Detweiler's eyes darkened, a sign that he was seriously not happy. I could see by the set of his jaw that this cruelty had really gotten under his skin. He's accustomed to criminal behavior, and he deals with it in a dispassionate way, but when an animal is involved, his control slips.

"What? Why was Petunia there?"

"I guess Melissa didn't like him. She signed the papers."

"What a monster! I hate her!" I pushed myself to an upright position.

"Join the club." Detweiler helped me. "Your doctor is finishing the paperwork right now. I'll be springing you from this joint in just a while."

At my gesture, he handed me a glass of water. Once I'd had some, I asked, "Are our kids okay?" How easy it had been to move from "Is Anya okay?" to the plural of "Are our kids okay?"

"Everyone is fine. Brawny, too. In fact, she pulled up with Erik and Anya right as the police were taking Melissa away in handcuffs. I'm not sure what she said in Gaelic, but it was some version of 'Good riddance to bad rubbish,' I'm sure."

"Tell me what happened. How did Leighton wind up in the garage? With the car motor running?" I twined my fingers through his. After I moved over on the bed, he sat next to me, half on the bed half off, with his long legs touching the floor.

"Melissa used the OxyContin on Leighton. At first, she gave him just enough to keep him loopy. While he was out of it, she managed to empty all of his bank accounts. She maxed out his credit cards. But she'd already raided his online accounts. He'd given her a password even before she moved here. That's why we couldn't get any water. It had been turned off. Also why we didn't see him. He was zonked out."

"But why? If she'd been smart, he would have given her anything she asked!"

"She wasn't smart, and she was greedy. I think he might have caught her writing checks on his account. That must have been the last straw. When he confronted her, I bet she made some excuse, and then she increased the amount she was drugging him. After she'd emptied out all his accounts, and maxed out his credit cards, she decided he was worth more to her dead than alive. After all, she was his sole heir."

"Gosh, it happened so fast." I shook my head.

"That was her goal. She wanted to suck him dry, take the money, and leave the country. She had her passport and an airline ticket in her handbag. Even had her suitcase packed and ready to go. A cab pulled up as the squad car drove away. She was his fare. In some ways, she was a pro. She had all her moves planned in advance. That's why we didn't see him after she moved in. Melissa started drugging him from the minute she arrived. That whole song and dance about wanting to move into the little house was a ruse to get him distracted. And to get under his roof. When we offered her resistance, I think she decided to speed things up. Leighton has bruises on his body. I wouldn't doubt that she slapped him around to get him to do as she wanted."

"My gosh!"

"Listen, elder abuse is much, much more common than you might guess. The elderly are particularly easy to dupe, because they are often lonely. Actually the bruises were helpful. That gave us a reason to take her in right away while we sort everything out. Our instincts were right: Melissa was bad news. Petunia knew it, as did Gracie. I guess Tunie bit her twice."

"A dog with great taste. I can't believe Tunie was almost put down." I paused. He was stroking my head and I felt drowsy. "What happens next?"

"You go back to sleep. I'll come get you as soon as the paperwork is finished."

62

Thursday morning...

I slept late the next day. Not surprisingly, Anya had been worried, and by extension Erik was, too. He wasn't old enough to understand all that had happened. His connection to his new sister was strong enough that her worries were his. The children had worked together to craft a huge "Get Well" card for me. I opened my eyes to see it standing up on the bedside table. The two signatures put a lump in my throat.

Petunia has always been a scaredy-cat, but his stint in the pound really undermined his fragile sense of security. He had been whimpering non-stop until Detweiler put him on the bed so he could cuddle with me. Gracie lowered herself to the rag rug beside our bed with a loud *whomp.* I suspect she was a bit put out that Tunie was snuggling on the bed and she was on the floor, but there wasn't really enough room for both dogs.

"Petunia has been through a trying experience," I told Gracie as I rolled onto my side and rubbed her ears. "Try to be patient with him."

The little pug smelled good. Detweiler explained that when he'd brought the dog back from the pound, he'd been so filthy that Brawny immediately gave him a bath.

More and more, Brawny thought of everything and did everything to make our lives more enjoyable. She was a real blessing. I had a lot to be thankful for, especially given my close call in the garage.

"You should have just broken all the windows to the garage first," said the cop.

"Probably."

"And dialed nine-one-one and waited." "Probably."

"That might not have saved Leighton's life."

"Indubitably," I said, remembering the word from *Mary Poppins.*

"I still can't figure out how you managed to haul Leighton out of the car. Melissa had moved the driver's seat up so he was basically pinned inside."

"I'll never know either," I admitted.

Although Detweiler had thought it a bad idea, I decided I wanted to attend the crop I'd scheduled. I really do love Zentangle, and I badly needed the mental break it would provide. Besides, I felt antsy. I needed to get up and move around.

The IV had also done me a world of good. I guess with everything on my mind, I hadn't been drinking as many fluids as I should have. Of course, my throat was still raw from vomiting, but Brawny made me a soothing concoction of tea and honey. She also produced a package of Fisherman's Friend, lozenges of slippery elm, a plant that coats the throat wonderfully well. That helped, too.

Knowing that we wouldn't have to move was a huge relief. At least, Detweiler and I assumed we wouldn't need to move right away. With Melissa in jail and Leighton in the hospital, there wasn't a good reason to pack up. Detweiler cancelled the moving van we'd rented. If Leighton still wanted us out, we vowed to consider our experience a trial run.

Clancy stopped by on her way to the store. She brought a bouquet of flowers and some pastries from the Muffin Man, a bakery we both loved.

"Was the Muffin Man nice to you today?" I teased her. She and the owner of the bakery seem determined to butt heads. Even so, he makes the best pastries in the metro St. Louis area, so Clancy gets mad, gets over it, goes back, repeat, rinse, and repeat.

Brawny put the blossoms in a vase and added them to my bedside table. Detweiler extracted a promise from me that I would sleep as long as possible before going to the store. Brawny was assigned to come with me. Detweiler would pick up the kids after school and feed them dinner.

For lunch, Brawny fed me a soothing soup. "Cock-a-leekie," she explained. "The national soup of Scotland."

"I suppose that every culture has its own variation on chicken soup," I said, eagerly spooning it into my mouth.

"That would make sense, wouldn't it?" she said. "My mother told me that the leeks should always be cut into half-moons, to remind us that God is smiling down on us."

She hesitated and then added, "I left out the sliced prunes.

For some folks, they cause, um, problems."

In the early afternoon, the doorbell rang with another bouquet of flowers. This was from Leighton. On the card were two words: *Thank you.*

I couldn't imagine what he might be feeling. First he thinks he has a chance at redemption for not being a good dad. Then he thinks that Melissa has forgiven him. When did he realize she'd gone totally off the tracks and ride a crazy train? At what point did it become clear to him that she planned to hurt him? How did you cope with the fact that your own child wanted you dead?

The thought of it made me want to start heaving all over again.

63

I was getting dressed for the crop when Sheila called. I recognized her phone number on the caller ID. A part of me didn't want to answer the phone. I really didn't have the energy to deal with her. But another part was pleased. I knew she cared about me. She might not say that, but the fact that she called proved it.

"I can't believe you risked your life like that," she said, without the preamble of a greeting. "That old codger owes you big time. It's all over the news. He was in his own car in the garage and nearly dead when you hauled him out. Good thing Detweiler knows CPR."

"Yes, it sure came in handy." I'd been thinking I needed to take a refresher course. The old way had you doing more breaths, while the newly revised protocol involved more compressions of the chest and fewer breaths.

"Your baby is okay?"

"Yes," I said. There was the slightest of possibilities that our baby was not okay, but I wouldn't let myself go there. The doctor had assured me that the chance was miniscule. Infinitesimal. But that was enough for me to worry over. However, I didn't see any reason to share my concern with Sheila. She would use it to beat me up. She can be like that.

"Well, it's all over the news. I bet the reporters are banging down the door at your store."

I groaned. That was all I needed. I probably should have cancelled the Zentangle session, but I had been looking forward to the evening. I could use a little zen in my life right now. Actually, I needed a *lot* of zen.

"Do you know that his daughter managed to grab the rights to his books?" Sheila kept prattling on.

"Pardon?" I sank back down on the bed. My head was still achy, and I was having trouble concentrating. "Could you repeat that?"

"Melissa Haversham was in cahoots with her father's literary agent. The agent wanted to go off and start his own firm, so he made a deal with Melissa. If she could get the rights, the agent would have his first big client. The two of them ganged up on Leighton and convinced him to sign over his rights for The Overland Trilogy. Can you believe that? So she will be getting his royalty checks. Of course, you know that she emptied out his bank accounts. He's ruined. Busted. Even though attorneys say he might be able to retrieve his rights, the outcome is uncertain. I mean, everyone is speculating that Melissa is going to jail for a long, long time. But who knows? These situations can be tricky, and they generally take a while to get resolved. The upshot is that right now Leighton's out of funds. No cash. No revenue stream. No income."

I scrunched the pillow up under me. I didn't really know what to say. A part of me felt incredibly sorry for Leighton. The idea of two people he trusted conspiring against him made me weary with sadness.

"Kiki? Are you there?" Sheila demanded. After I answered, she continued, "He'll have to put that house up for sale."

"Rats," I said. "We just cancelled the moving van."

"It'll take a while to move a behemoth of a house like that," said Sheila. Her diction was slightly slurred.

Was it the result of only one Bloody Mary?

"Of course," she continued, "Leighton's place is worth a mint, being on that big lot and all."

I closed my eyes and wondered, Where would Monroe go? I knew we could move into the house in U City, but what about the donkey? Where would he live? And Leighton? What about him? His heart was probably broken, and now he would lose his house, too.

"They'll probably tear down his family house and your small one and put three houses on the lot," continued Sheila.

"Double rats," I said. "This lot is gorgeous. If they do that, they'd have to knock down a lot of trees."

"Absolutely. Who cares about trees when you can put up three brand-spanking-new houses and make a lot of dough?" she cackled.

"Look, I need to go," I said. Truth to tell, I was feeling sick again. Brawny must have sensed what was happening. She appeared in the doorway with a cup of tea doctored with ginger root. I could smell the spicy concoction from my spot in my bed.

As I struggled to sit up, Brawny handed over the mug. "You ought to avoid stressful situations for a while."

"Do you really think that'll happen?"

She laughed, sending that gray knob of a ponytail bobbed. "I suppose that's as likely as seeing Nessie, the Loch Ness monster, starring in a feature film. You do remember that Miss Lori is coming in tonight, don't you?"

I'd forgotten.

"Not to worry. She asked me to book her a nice room at the Ritz. I'll pick her up from the airport and get her settled," said

Brawny. "They allow dogs there, so her new pup will be welcome."

"My gosh," I said. "You told me to avoid stressful situations."

"Trust me, Miss Kiki, the two of you will get along famously.

Like two peas in a pod."

She walked me into the store and stayed long enough to see me settled at my work table. Our Zentangle guests were due to arrive in half an hour, so I was comfortably early. It felt good to be back in the saddle. Brawny changed out my stool for an adjustable office chair with a back and arm supports.

"Now, don't let her get flustered," Brawny lectured Clancy. "She's to stay off her feet as much as possible."

"I think I can manage." An annoyed look flickered over Clancy's face.

I put my hand over my mouth so I wouldn't giggle. "I'll treat her like visiting royalty."

"*Aye,* you better," said Brawny. I sensed a friction between them. Clancy didn't like being bossed around. Brawny thought of Clancy as a staff member and treated her accordingly. Of course, from what Brawny had told me and what I had read, people in the UK accepted the idea of class distinctions and their resultant hierarchy. After all, the Royal Family was simply born into their good fortune, and for the most part, that was unquestioned.

Once Brawny left, Clancy pulled a stool up next to mine and got right in my face. "What on earth got into you? You could have died! There could have been serious repercussions for the baby. Kiki, you have to promise me to be more cautious. You have to put yourself first!"

To my surprise, her eyes filled with tears.

"Clancy, how could I have lived with myself if I didn't help Leighton? I didn't have a choice. I'm all right. Really I am. The chance that my baby has been harmed is tiny. Too tiny to worry about, according to the doc. I was in and out of that garage pretty fast."

"But you could have succumbed. You could have died!" and she threw her arms around my neck and started crying.

Clancy only cries when she watches romantic movies. Not in real life. I held her and soothed her. "It's okay. Honest. See? I'm okay."

Margit toddled up from the back room. "You scared us half to death, Kiki."

Pretty soon, she was crying, too. That got me started.

"Look, guys, we can't do this right now," I said, as I wiped my eyes. "We have customers coming in. Margit? Let's schedule a time to cry, okay? You're in charge."

"*Ja,* but what are you crying about?" she asked in a huffy tone. "We almost lost you. You knew what you were doing!"

"Yes, and either of you would have done the same. You know it. So don't fuss at me, please." I sniffed and sat up straight. "As for what I have to cry about, well, plenty. Sheila just told me that Leighton will probably have to sell his house."

"Yes," said Clancy, dabbing her eyes. "I heard that. It's all over the news. First he escapes with his life. Then he learns he's flat busted, and he no longer has control over his own books."

"*Allein ist besser als mit Schlechten in Verein: mit Guten in Verein, ist besser als allein,*" said Margit. "It is better to be alone than in bad company. I understand how he wanted his daughter close by, but he was asking too much. At least, too much from her. She was not worthy and not able to return his affection."

"Right, well, here I was all yippee-skippee happy that we didn't have to move. Now I wish we were moving, and he wasn't because I'm not sure what will happen to Monroe—and I hate the fact that lot will be divided up." I stopped and added, "Plus I feel awful for Leighton. I can't imagine the sense of betrayal he must be dealing with."

"Speaking of disappointments on a minor scale, Faye Edorra came in for her check," said Clancy. "She was none too pleased that you hadn't signed it."

"Argh," I said. "She has a right to be ticked off with me. I'll do it before I leave tonight, if you'll remind me. Any news about Laurel?"

"Ja," said Margit. "She called to say that she was home and that she was thinking of all of us. I talked with her on the phone for a few minutes. She also told me to tell you that when she comes back she wants you to do a crop featuring a skinny cow?"

Clancy and I busted out laughing.

"You know," I said. "That's a great idea. We could all do pages of food that we love or our favorite snacks."

"This is funny how?" Margit glared at us. She hates not being in on anything, so Clancy reached under my work table for the box of Skinny Cow bars that I keep as my personal stash.

"Here," she said as she tossed a bar toward Margit. "You're going to love this. I guarantee it. I bought two boxes."

"Ach! A skinny cow!" marveled Margit. When she bit into the treat, she grinned at us. "Moo, moo, moo!"

64

I'm not sure whether it's absolutely correct to call a Zentangle gathering a "crop." After all, we don't cut around photos. So I'm hereby coining a new term. From now on a Zentangle gathering will be a tangle-ation. See, it's a combination of tangle and celebration. Pretty cool, huh? The name fits what we were doing. It was Amy Goodyear's week to teach us a new tangle pattern called Scalez. Amy not only showed us a new tangle that she and I had worked up, but she also gave us a mini-tutorial on watercolor painting with salt lifts.

"Salt absorbs the water," she explained. "When you sprinkle rock salt over the watercolor, it acts like a blotter. The crystals suck up some of the color. You get this lovely mottled look to your paper."

She also showed us the tangle she'd done, using the watercolor background. Since our own watercolors would take time to dry, she'd very thoughtfully made sheets of watercolored paper for all of us to use as backgrounds to our tangles.

"I am so glad I came," I said. "Just looking at this beautiful paper makes me feel calmer."

"I agree," said Jennifer Moore. "This afternoon, I was

thinking that I didn't have the time to come and play, but now I'm realizing how much I needed this."

At the opposite end of the table, the not-so-gleesome three-some—Mary Martha, Patricia, and Dolores—sat like human gargoyles, glaring at us.

"This," said Mary Martha, "is nothing more than doodling!

"No, it's not," said Amy Gill, the other Amy in this session.

"When you doodle, you make aimless, random marks on the paper. Zentangle has specific patterns that are reproducible. Think of the tangles like vocabulary words. Here's another difference: I can't teach you to doodle, but I can teach you to draw a tangle. Furthermore, once you learn the patterns, with their repetitive, deliberate strokes, you'll feel a tiny click happening in your head. Your body will shift from one mode of brain function to another. It's a lot like meditating."

"Is that Christian?" Dolores sneered.

"I can answer that," said a deep male voice. We all turned to see Father Joe. "I'm late, but I did call ahead and reserve my spot with Mrs. Whitehead."

I tried to stand to welcome him, but he waved me back to my seat. "I've heard you've had a rough day."

"Yes, but it's better already. Glad you could make it." As I spoke, I glanced toward the end of the table. The three women from his church preened, touching their hair and fluttering their lashes. Mary Martha's cheeks pinked up, while a slow red stain began at Dolores's throat and moved north. Patricia looked as though she was on the brink of ecstasy.

"Regarding your question, Dolores, the word 'meditate' appears fourteen times in the *King James Version of the Bible*. In Matthew, Jesus tells his followers to close the door and pray, while cautioning them not to babble words," Father Joe explained. "Meditation prepares for the trials and tribulations ahead."

The attendees sat with jaws open and eyes wide as the young man spoke. As mesmerizing as his beauty was, his words were even more compelling. You read about charisma, and how certain people have it, but rarely do you see it in action. There was an aspect of divinity about Father Joe that kept all of us riveted.

"Well," he clapped his hands. "I came here to learn a new skill. I apologize for being late. Where do I sit?"

A few minutes before the break, Theresa George hopped up to heat the casserole she'd brought. The fragrance of her Chicken Tetrazzini caused our mouths to water."

"Wait until you see what we have for dessert," I told Father Joe. "Victoria Hrabe brought her Better Than Sex Cake."

"There's something better than sex?" asked the priest. "I wouldn't have missed this for the world!"

"I also brought a pan of my Cheesy Chicken and Dressing Casserole," said Victoria. "We always send Kiki home with left-overs. If we don't, she'd never get any dinner!"

"Not since Brawny came to live with me," I said. "But she doesn't fix my lunches, so bring it on!"

BY THE TIME Brawny picked me up at the end of the evening, I was exhausted. I asked her if Lorraine Lauber had made it in and how the older woman was doing after her travels.

"Miss Lorraine was very tired when I got her from the airport," said Brawny. "She asked that I take her straight to her hotel. I know Detective Detweiler was looking forward to greeting her, and she wanted to see Erik, but you can understand that she has to be careful with her energy. She was very pleased with her accommodations, especially because she has her new canine security companion with her. A Giant Schnauzer named Paolo."

"Good," I said. "I'm glad she has the guard dog. We can all breathe a little easier about her safety, right?"

"Aye," said Brawny. "Although he's still young and she'll need to work with him. They'll send a trainer to her home to help her learn how to shape his behavior. He's already very, very well-trained, as you might imagine. A handsome lad."

"Why is there more training involved?"

"They need to work together as a team. But he's whip smart. Doesn't shed either, which is a blessing because I think Miss Lorraine might just wear black the rest of her life."

"She really loved her brother, didn't she?"

"Aye, she did. They got along so well. That's why she was so accepting of Miss Gina. Whatever made Mr. Lauber happy was fine by Miss Lorraine. The three of them enjoyed their times together. They liked each other's company. Sort of like the Three Musketeers."

I smiled, thinking how my sisters and I also appreciated that iconic reference.

Brawny continued, "It was a near thing that Miss Lorraine wasn't in the car when Mr. Lauber went off the road."

"Do you think he was murdered?" I said. This was the first chance the two of us had had to discuss the matter privately.

"I think it's very possible," she said, that soft burr turning "very" into "vera." "We all have a sixth sense, a gift from our Maker, and it warns us when a person's a *bajin.*"

"A *bajin*?"

"A bad one." She sighed. "Mr. Thornton saved Mr. Lauber's life when they was young. The mister was always one to be thankful, but I think he went too far. Mr. Thornton has a black heart. He's a *bajin.* I wouldna put nothing past him."

By the time we got home, the kids were already asleep since

this was a school night. I felt bad that I hadn't spent time with them, especially since they probably needed reassurance that I was okay. Detweiler insisted that I, "Go straight to Bed, do not pass Go, and do not Collect $200."

"Why would Miss Kiki need to collect money for going to bed?" Brawny raised her eyebrows.

Detweiler and I laughed about that. We said we'd show her how to play Monopoly come Sunday.

After Detweiler closed the bedroom door, and we were alone, I sat down on the bed and asked, "What about Sunday? Can we continue to live here? And for how long?"

"I don't know," he said, while rubbing his chin. "I plan to talk to Leighton tomorrow. He's due to be released from the hospital, but we need to take his statement at the station. The social worker has already filled out the forms alleging Elder Abuse, and we have more than enough for that. I'm worried he won't help us prosecute Melissa. Of course we have your testimony and mine, plus what the EMTs discovered when they arrived, but Leighton might back down and refuse to testify against her."

"I'm not sure I could testify against one of my own kids," I said. "Of course, I can't imagine one of ours trying to hurt me."

"That's true," said Detweiler, as he sank down onto the bed beside me. "Much less deprive us of the money we rightly earned."

"You heard about him losing the rights to his books?" I was so tired I could barely hold my head up.

"Yes. That really stinks, doesn't it?"

"Sheila called me to tell me." I was slurring my words. "She thinks he'll have to sell this house and the big one. Where will Monroe go?"

Detweiler pulled me close. He kissed me gently. "Trust you to worry about the donkey."

"The donkey is the only one of us who's flat out of options."

"Don't worry. My parents will take Monroe if it comes to that."

"I hadn't thought of that." Relief flooded through me.

"No, I bet you didn't. You were too busy worrying to think about the family farm." Detweiler nuzzled me, roughing up my skin with that beard of his. "Next to scrapbooking and doing your tangles, worrying is your favorite hobby."

"Nope," I said, looking at him and smiling. "I have another favorite hobby. Want to see what it is?"

65

The next morning both kids were full of themselves. Erik hugged me and said, "You're okay? Right?"

I told him I was. I gave him a big hug and patted his back, marveling at how small those shoulder blades were. My little man. He would grow up so quickly. We walked, hand-in-hand, out to the car.

While Brawny buckled him into his car seat, Anya leaned close and whispered, "Erik was scared, Mom. He climbed into my bed last night. I guess after what happened to his mother, he has a right to be. I told him it would be okay."

Putting one hand on each side of her face, I directed her gaze. "You are being such a wonderful big sister. I'm so proud of you. Thank you, sweetheart."

She smiled and said, "So I get to keep my job as oldest sibling?"

"You betcha, Anya-Banana."

Detweiler protested loud and long when I said that I wanted to drive myself to work. Finally, I agreed to let him do the driving.

"Let's see," I said, putting a finger to my lips. "First I get a nanny, and now I have a chauffeur. Who owns a uniform, no less. I'm well on my way to becoming a lady of leisure."

Detweiler laughed at that, causing Gracie to stick her head between the seats. After giving the cop a loving look, she licked his shoulder.

Since we both had a little time before our work days started, and so little alone time, he drove to the nearest Kaldi's. The weather was mild enough for me to sit outside with the dog while Detweiler went in to get our orders. As I sat there, soaking up the last of the autumn sun, my cell phone buzzed. Gracie rested her head on my knee and stared at me as I checked my messages.

Will you PLEASE sign my check? This is ridiculous! was the text message from Faye Edorra.

Yes, sorry. I sent the message back, clicking on her email address. When I did, I noticed the suffix. The three unusual letters puzzled me.

As Detweiler handed me my decaf coffee and a sugar cookie, I asked, "What does 'edu' mean as a suffix on an email address?"

"That the address is processed by a server at an educational institution," he said. "Why?"

I shrugged and gave myself over to the joys of coffee, butter, and sugar. "Just wondering. Faye just sent me an email and that was on the tail end of it."

"Who is Faye Edorra?"

I explained that she had been our ghostly guide during the Halloween party. I finished by turning the conversation back on him. "Any word on the situation with Laurel? I figured you'd keep your ear to the ground."

"When I talked with Father Joe, I suggested that he visit the local police and remind them of the many acts of vandalism directed against Laurel."

"And?"

"He called me last night on his way to your event to tell me that he'd done exactly that. They promised to look into the matter. Unfortunately, that's the best he can do, and my hands are tied as well."

After swallowing a mouthful of cookie, I changed the subject. "When are you going to interview Leighton?"

"He and an attorney are coming in this afternoon."

I had nibbled the edges off of my treat. I was trying to show restraint. Not that I have much of that. I dove into our Better Than Sex dessert last night as if I were personally gearing up for the Last Supper. Oh, boy, was that ever good! "Does the presence of an attorney mean that he won't answer any of your questions?"

"It might," Detweiler said. "But don't go getting your hopes up about staying in the house, okay? I talked with Hadcho and Robbie last night. Melissa really took her father to the cleaners. Leighton will be lucky if he gets to keep the shirt on his back. Of course, there are limits to what can be put on your charge card without a proper signature, and all that, but situations like this take a while to untangle."

"Did you feed and water Monroe this morning?" I asked. "What do you take me for? A farmhand?" He gave me a light punch in the bicep. "Of course I did. I told Anya that she has to take over on the weekends."

"Good," I said. "That reminds me. She was supposed to go to the Moores' house tonight for a sleepover. A night with her friend Nicci will be good for Anya. That might mean that you'll be mucking out the stall tomorrow morning. "

"Anya asked me to cancel her sleepover," said Detweiler. "She is worried about Erik. He's been pretty clingy."

"Wow," I said. "Do you think she'll always be this loving of an older sister?"

"Are you asking if they'll never fight?" He raised an eyebrow at me. "Because that would be abnormal, wouldn't it? I think I'd choose normal sibling spats over abnormal any day."

I told him what Brawny told me about the Laubers.

"That confirms everything I've seen and heard from Lorraine," said Detweiler. "I can't imagine losing one of my sisters. I'm glad for you that Catherine has come home. How's she working out at the store?"

"Really well. I have to admit that I was sort of looking forward to living in the same house with her once again. Mom is really mean to her, and she deserves better."

"Maybe we should send Brawny over to do another therapy session."

"Maybe."

As DELIGHTFUL AS the morning was, the time had come for us to get to work. The drive was pleasant. It seemed as though the landscape was on fire with color. We enjoyed pointing out the turning trees along the way. The red maples stood out like huge bonfires tickling the blue sky. All too soon, we arrived at Time in a Bottle. My honey opened the car door for me and helped me to my feet.

"Come on, Gracie," said the cop, as he tugged on her leash. "You're got to go inside the store, like always."

The black-and-white Great Dane was not happy about saying goodbye to the love of her life. She adores Detweiler, and I'm a distant second in her affections.

Gracie stubbornly planted her feet, pitching her weight against the cop's strength.

I watched him struggle with her. "She seems to have a firm opinion about leaving your car, and the answer is no."

The harlequin monster finally gave in to Detweiler's urgings.

Ignoring me completely, she walked happily alongside the cop. Margit must have heard the car doors slam, because she greeted us at the back door. She reminds me of Gracie, because my co-worker also gets a wistful smile on her face when Detweiler's around. He's taken to giving Margit a welcoming peck on the cheek, and, by golly, she turns red as a tomato.

But for me, Detweiler had a real kiss, not a peck on the cheek. Handing me the leash, he said, "I'll let you know what I learn when I talk to Leighton. About the house, that is."

"About our living accom-accommo-accommodations?" I asked as I held up a pair of crossed fingers.

He looked at me curiously. "You okay?"

I promised him that I was fine, but I was lying. My head was foggy. I'd noticed it on the drive to the store. Even as I thought about the day again, I found myself forgetting things. A panic was rising inside me, but I pushed it down. The ER doctor had warned me that this was to be expected after a dose of carbon monoxide. Even bouts of dizziness and nausea could re-occur.

Had I endangered my baby? Would I recover from saving Leighton? Would this get worse instead of better?

I didn't want to worry Detweiler. "You okay?" he asked again.

"Sure," I said brightly. "You know me, I'm not an early morning person. I'm still waking up. I owe, I owe, it's off to work I go! Now shoo. Get to work, sweetheart." I gave him a little push toward the door.

After he left, Margit shook a finger at me. "There is much to do. We owe this woman money." Clancy had told her about Faye Edorra's calls. My partner handed me the check, watched me sign it, and tucked it into a security envelope.

"Go put this up at your work table," Margit directed me. "Okay." I was too befuddled to think for myself, so I took the envelope from her and did as she suggested. Under my table were shelves, and on those were various woven baskets. I slipped the money for Faye into one of them and went back to Margit's work area so we could sit down with the figures from the Zentangle tangle-ation.

"Very profitable/" Margit pointed to a column of numbers. "This brought us five new customers over the past month and a half. Only one problem."

"What's that?"

"The materials for tonight's crop did not arrive. We have twenty people signed up."

"How many people?" I was still having trouble processing information.

"Twenty," she repeated.

Dodie had kept a large amount of stuff in inventory. Too much, actually. Margit, Clancy, and I agreed to keep our inventory as low as possible. With high inventory, too many items got lost, the trends changed too quickly, and worst of all, paper got funky when it sat in storage.

Most of the time our inventory needs were spot on. We came up with exactly what we needed before we needed it. But once in a while, things didn't work as planned. On occasion, suppliers didn't ship items as they promised. When that happened, all my creative talents were taxed to the max.

"We are so close to Halloween," I said, "and we announced in our email blast that this would be a Halloween décor crop."

"*Ja,* the premade Halloween houses were in that shipment. That's what you planned to use."

"I can't go back on my word. I have to come up with something."

"*Ja,*" she said, "and you will. You always do."

A walk always got my creative juices flowing. "Come on, Gracie."

As we started our trek, I put on my thinking cap. *What to do, what to do?* I was at the corner, watching Gracie water the grass at the end of the sidewalk when I glanced up at an elderly man standing in the window of one of the few remaining houses on our block. Since this patch of real estate has slowly become commercial, but still primarily residential, a few houses are still occupied by their original owners.

"Hiya, Mr. Hastlehorst," I said. I'm not sure whether he heard me through the glass or not, but he waved. Mr. Hastlehorst was probably in his eighties, a scarecrow of a man, with no hair on the top of his head, just owl-like tufts over his ears. He stared at my dog and me through foggy glasses.

What was his life like? Was he lonely like Leighton had been? Who visited him? I'd never seen a car in his drive. Nor had I seen anyone coming and going. The paper cat in his window was tattered, with neon green eyes. Was that his idea of decorating for the season? I decided right then and there that my store would be a better neighbor. We could go from door to door, introduce ourselves, and hand out goody bags. A sort of reverse trick or treat. Since I knew that most of the residents were older, we could also check on them frequently and make sure they were doing all right. It was the least we could do, and something well within our means.

Gracie and I made our last turn and headed toward the store.

As it often happened, an idea popped into my head.

"Come on, Gracie!" I said, and I started running for Time in a Bottle. I couldn't wait to give my new idea a whirl!

MARGIT WAS IMPRESSED by my makeshift make-and-take idea. She shook her head in amazement. "*Schwarze Katze* with eyes that glow!"

"A black cat?" I guessed at the German translation.

"*Ja!* You will learn my language one phrase at a time."

I sent Margit out for battery-operated tea lights, the one item we needed and didn't have. Once she left, I hurried to my work table so I could start sketching and cutting paper.

"Miss Kiki?" said Brawny.

She startled me so much that I dropped my pencil as I jumped into the air.

"Sorry to have frightened you. I'd like for you to meet Miss Lorraine Lauber. She couldn't wait to see you."

I turned to face a woman who was hunched over a metal-framed walker. Her sweet face immediately broke into a warm smile. Without a word, I reached for her and gave her a hug. "Thank you," I whispered in her ear. "We love Erik so much. You handled everything with Detweiler just right."

"My pleasure," she said, as we broke apart. "I couldn't wait another day to meet you."

"I told her it was all right for her to bring her new companion. Is it all right that the dog's here?" asked Brawny. "His name is Paolo."

I followed her gaze to a spot by the front door. There rested a large black dog covered in wiry, curling hair. His eyes alert, his ears perked up, but his body in the "down" position, waiting patiently for his next instruction. When Lorraine patted her leg, Paolo trotted over. At her command, the dog sat down beside her walker.

"Of course, he's welcome here! We're all lovers. I mean, animal-lovers, of course."

Drat. I still wasn't one hundred percent. Thankfully, both women ignored my *faux pas.*

Brawny pulled up a chair with arms for Lorraine.

"May I pet him?" I asked to cover my embarrassment. "I realize he's a working dog."

"Yes, yes. He's still young so he needs socialization. Please do pat him." Lorraine backed carefully into her seat and looked around. "This is fascinating. So this is where you do your work. I loved the album that you made for Erik."

"Brawny, show her the album you're doing of St. Louis sights," I suggested. "Miss Lauber have you had lunch? We have tons of food left over from last night."

She asked that I call her Lorraine, and no, she hadn't had lunch, so Brawny offered to fix plates for us after she handed over the album. I sat next to Lorraine and turned the pages. Since Brawny hadn't been scrapbooking for long, she hadn't done the journaling, the verbiage that accompanies the photos. Instead, I acted as narrator.

"That's, um, that's the house..." and I paused because I couldn't remember where the house was.

I started again. "The house that my mother and sisters rent in U City. The one we might be moving to," I finished inelegantly. Rats. I could tell that as the day went on, and I was getting tired, my focus was slipping.

The carbon monoxide had really done a number on my brain.

What number?

I didn't know...

"Moving? But I thought that Anya loves where you are living now, even though it is small." Lorraine's eyes were laser sharp. Whatever her problems with her body, her mind was obviously keen.

"Yes, well," and I told her about Leighton and Melissa. My discourse rambled. I babbled. Brawny observed me with her head tilted. She was assessing me, and I had a hunch she was finding me wanting. I hoped she wouldn't tell Detweiler. I didn't know who would lead the crop tonight if I couldn't.

"I heard that you rescued your neighbor, but Brawny didn't explain what that meant in terms of your living arrangements,"

Lorraine said. Either she didn't think anything was wrong with me, or she was too tired to care.

I tried to keep it light. "We're not homeless, but Detweiler has warned me not to get my heart set on staying in the little house. He'll be talking to Leighton later today. The poor man lost everything, or so I've heard. Even if his attorney can get everything untangled, that might take time. He might not have any choice but to sell the house so he can pay the attorney when it's all said and done."

"Are you familiar with *To Kill a Mockingbird*?" "Yes, of course. One of my favorites."

"Harper Lee also lost her rights to the book. As I understand it, there are negotiations for her to get them back, but she's in poor health," said Lorraine, letting her voice trail off.

"I can't imagine what Leighton is going through," I said. "I'm trying not to focus on the problems this might cause us. Instead, I keep counting my blessings that he's alive."

The expression on Lorraine's face changed. There was a narrowing of her eyes, a thoughtfulness. "Yes, I can see how lucky you both are," she said. "Have you considered buying a house?"

"Sure, uh, sure thing," I said, losing focus again. "In fact, that's what we want to do. I have a little money coming from my late husband's business. That might be enough for a down payment, but not for a house in Webster Groves where we live now. Detweiler and I told Anya that we'll start looking. She can have input. The problem is that the houses in our price range will be quite a drive from CALA. Since you've been so kind to help with Brawny, she can do the carpool duty, although I sort of hate having the kids in a car for too much of the day."

Lorraine nodded. "I wouldn't want them on the highway either."

"That too. Although since they remodeled Highway 40, it's not as bad as it once was, but with Anya getting older, she'll want to do after-school activities. Webster Groves is closer to the store, too, so it's more convenient all the way around. But there are other options. We could try South County." I paused. "I guess we'll just have to see what we can do. Before, uh, the holidays."

"Ah, but you'll be heading into bad weather, won't you?"
"Yes," I said. "The worst will be in January when the baby's

due, because we always get an ice storm. But I remind myself that even if the weather is frightful, I love having holidays, the changing of the seasons, and all the trimmings. You'll be here for Thanksgiving?"

"I knew I was invited for Christmas and Hanukkah, but Thanksgiving, too?" she truly looked surprised.

"Of course. You're family. We're thankful for you. Why? Do you have other plans? If so, may I remind you that Paolo is welcome at our house? Not every hostess can boast of that!"

Brawny came out of the back room with a serving tray. On it were two paper plates piled high with the yummy leftovers from the night before. She excused herself to get her own food and then came back to join us.

"Do you eat like this every time you have a cut?" asked Lorraine.

"A cut?" I was mystified.

"Yes, isn't that what you call it when you get together and scrapbook?"

"A crop!" I said, and all three of us got the giggles.

After we calmed down, Brawny asked me to tell Lorraine about our crops and what they were like. I did, and of course, the conversation turned to the horrible stabbing at the Halloween event. "It was just ugly," I said, as I explained the complicated dynamics behind the situation. Lorraine listened to

Johnny's saga, the story of Mert's childhood, and to the events that led Laurel to hide her diabetes.

"A new American tragedy," she said. "May I have another helping of this dessert?"

"Better Than Sex?" asked Brawny.

"Beg pardon?" Lorraine's eyebrows shot up.

"That's what they call the dessert. Better Than Sex," I explained. "Although I've also heard that it's called Robert Redford."

"Robert Redford?" asked Brawny. "The actor? Why?"

"Because it's so yummy you want to lick it off your spoon."

Again we burst into gales of laughter. I had a hunch that my giggles were part of my not-so-keen mental function. But what the heck? If you can't laugh with friends, who can you laugh with?

"I don't think I've laughed like this in ages," said Lorraine, using a paper napkin to dab at her eyes. "I'm so glad I came!"

"So'm I," I said, sloppily. "I mean, I am glad that you're here. Brawny, could you do me a great big favor? Gracie hasn't been outside for a while. Would you take her for a walk? How about Paolo?"

"He's fine. He did his business on the way in, but I'd be delighted to take Gracie outside."

Just as Brawny headed toward the back room, Faye Edorra marched through the front door. She looked mildly unhappy in her lavender pants suit, a white blouse, and a men's tie. I wondered if she was actually channeling the Lavender Lady. I hoped not. Faye's arms were crossed over her chest as she held a black leather notebook up, the way you would a shield.

"Faye, I am so sorry it's taken me this long to write your check." I stood to greet her. "My only excuse is that I've been pre-occupied. I have it right here."

She responded by glaring at me.

"Um, right here. The check's right here, under the work table," I said, sliding off my stool. I misjudged the movement. My legs went soft and collapsed out from under me. Instead of going into a squat, I actually landed on my knees with a *thunk* that hurt.

Next thing, I knew I was staring at the underneath of my work table. I couldn't remember why I was on the floor. I had the vague impression that I was forgetting something. While down there, it occurred to me that I should have introduced Faye to Lorraine. However, Faye was obviously steaming mad, so I didn't see a reason to encourage her to hang around. It wasn't like I'd purposely tried to stiff her.

By now I'd sunk into a kneeling position. Despite being eye level with the shelves under my work table, I didn't see the security envelope. I rummaged around in the baskets while Lorraine asked Faye about the weather.

Good, I thought. My little lapse in manners was being overcome.

"I don't have all day," Faye said. Or her legs did. I couldn't see anything but the seams in her lavender pants.

"I know the check's down here somewhere," I sang out. But I sure couldn't put my hands on it. I looked inside one basket and then the other, all while staring at Faye's knees.

After a bit, I forgot what I was doing. Why was I down here? What was I searching for? I was totally lost and feeling dizzier by the second.

I stuck my head out and looked at Faye in an attention to pull myself together. She glared at me, so I tried to focus anywhere but her eyes. My attention was caught by her necktie. "That's a nifty tie, Faye. Really goes with the suit. Beautiful colors. Must be fine silk."

"It belonged to my late husband," she said. "He died a few months ago."

"Sorry to hear that. Was it sudden?" I asked as I shifted my weight so I was resting my butt on my heels.

"He was fired from his job. Stabbed in the back by his colleagues. Fell into a depression. Very, very deep depression. It killed him."

"Oh, my!" said Lorraine. "That's just tragic. I lost my brother and sister-in-law a short while back. It broke my heart."

"Yes. I...I miss my husband terribly." Faye uncrossed her arms and brought a trembling hand to her face. With a quick decisive action, she brushed away fresh tears.

"I've lost a husband. George's death turned my world upside down. Please accept my deepest sympathies."

"I'd rather accept my money," Faye snapped, but even so, she seemed to relax. The mutual losses the three of us had accumulated worked as a bonding agent. Before my eyes, Faye's posture seemed less rigid. The notebook dangled in her right hand. The logo was at my eye level. On the leather casing was the emblem for Charbonneau Community College.

My head spun. I felt a tingle, like a breeze of cold air had traveled over my neck. Simultaneously, I heard a soft growl. Paolo was standing at attention with his ears pricked. I followed his gaze, sweeping my eyes upward, and realized he was watching Faye with the sort of coiled attention that precedes action.

I struggled to think. What was happening here? Why was Paolo so intense? What was I forgetting? Something important. Something about schools? Or teachers?

"My check?" Faye's voice reverted to a menacing tone.

"Right. Just had a brain hiccup. Sorry. Hormones, I guess." I made one more foray under the worktable, pulling out baskets, and this time I managed to find the security envelope.

"Here you go," I said, struggling to my feet. I flashed the envelope at Faye, but I didn't hand over the check. "I couldn't help but notice your notebook binder. Did you attend Char-bonneau?"

"My husband taught there." She spoke stiffly, and with a quick movement, she tried to pluck the check out of my hand.

I danced away, my feet moving clumsily. My mind was whirling. Someone else I knew went there. Someone else. Someone who'd been stabbed.

"Laurel! It was Laurel!" I blurted.

Faye shoved me backwards, pushing me hard enough that I bumped into the table. Using her energy, I propelled myself off the surface and grabbed her by the lapels. My goal was to buy time and protect Lorraine.

"Run, Lorraine! Get out of here!" I screamed, but I couldn't turn around to make sure Lorraine escaped.

Faye twisted in my grasp. Her fingers clamped down on mine. Gosh but she was strong. I wouldn't be able to hold her for long.

While I fought Faye, I managed a quick glance over my shoulder. Lorraine was trying to get away, but the legs of her walker had gotten tangled in Paolo's leash. The obedient animal was glued to his spot, acting like an anchor. I couldn't believe it. What crummy luck!

From his seated position, Paolo growled at Faye. His recognition of the gravity of the problem gave me renewed strength. I gripped Faye's suit lapels even harder. In response, she grabbed me by the shoulders and shook me, causing my teeth to rattle in my head. Faye reached for my hands. We wrestled, slapping each other's arms down. I gave up on that and again gripped her jacket. I stayed stuck to her lapel like a cocklebur sticks to your socks.

I could not turn loose. If I did, she would get away! She might hurt Lorraine. Or she might take another stab at Laurel.

Stab? Oh, golly, I was so messed up.

I concentrated on holding Faye. I told myself that Brawny would be back. A customer might walk in. Lorraine might get away.

We were at a stalemate. Faye lifted one hand to my face and pressed down on my nose. It hurt and made it hard to breathe. I tried to bite her, twisting my face this way and that. I actually did give her a nip. She yelped in surprise and slapped me. My head was already spinning, and now the room went twirling, too. I threw up my hands and then grabbed at Faye again, latching on to her sleeves.

I almost let her go. The cops could catch up with her sooner or later. I couldn't hold her much longer. But each time I was tempted to give up images came to mind. Laurel with blood running down her neck. Laurel nearly dead on the gurney. No way was I going to let Faye go free!

"You tried to murder her!" I yelled. "You aren't getting away with this!"

"Yes, I am!" Faye's face turned red with anger. She kicked at me.

"Ow!" I cried out as she connected with my shins, but I still didn't turn loose. In fact, I'd lost all feeling in my fingers. I couldn't have turned loose if I wanted to!

We'd all missed it how she'd done it. Faye had blood on her from the start. I'd thought it was part of her costume. It had been fake at first, but later it was mingled with fresh blood, Laurel's blood.

"How could you have done that to her? To Laurel? She never hurt a fly!" I screamed at Faye.

I heard a scraping sound once more. Lorraine was struggling with her walker. I had to keep Faye off balance until Lorraine was out of harm's way.

"She tempted him! With her twitchy little butt and her

perfect boobs! That gorgeous blonde hair. She sent him emails! All he did was respond!"

"Inappropriately!" I yelled. "He was her teacher!"

"He was only being a man! She was a Jezebel! That job was his whole life! They fired him because of her! And he died of a broken heart!"

I lowered my body and tried to head butt Faye, but she was too quick for me. She knew exactly what I was doing.

"Laurel is a slut! You are too!" Faye shoved her palm into my face once again. This time she forced me down to my knees. I couldn't fight any longer. I was too tired, too worn out. When I was almost in a kneeling position again, she lifted the notebook and slammed it into my head. That smack sent my head spinning and I fell over on my side.

"Fassen!" Lorraine yelled. *"Fassen!"*

Paolo sailed over me. I caught a glimpse of his tummy as he flew by. From my prone position, I watched as he knocked Faye to the floor.

EPILOGUE

Two days later...

*L*orraine and Anya sat on the sofa, shoulder to shoulder, looking through old albums I'd made. I curled up in the overstuffed armchair, reading a book on my Kindle. Brawny was out running errands. Erik was in the shed with Detweiler, helping his father muck out Monroe's stall. His Aunt Lori had found a miniature gardening set for him online and ordered it, so Erik was equipped with his own shovel. From time to time, the message function on my phone dinged to announce that Detweiler had taken yet another picture of our little big guy working hard. A few of the shots showed Paolo and Gracie romping in the yard with Petunia bringing up the rear.

The doorbell rang. "I'll get it. I need to stretch my legs," I said.

I opened my front door to Mert, Johnny, Laurel, and Father Joe.

"What a nice surprise. Come on in." I didn't know whether to try to hug Mert or not, so I settled for hugging Laurel and Johnny. I figured I'd give my old friend a lot of space.

"No hugs for me?" asked Father Joe. Of course, I gave him one.

"This is for you," Mert said stiffly, handing over a big plate covered with foil. A slightly crumpled pre-made holiday bow was perched on top. After introducing everyone to Lorraine and inviting them to sit down, I opened the foil covering to see what was inside.

"I don't know what these are but they smell divine."

"Nutella brownies," announced Johnny. "I even wrote up the recipe for you because I know you'll want to make more."

"You're onto my secrets," I said. "Thanks so much."

"It's our way of showing our appreciation for corralling Faye," said Laurel. "I'd like to think that I could have gone about my life without worrying about her, but that's not exactly true. If you hadn't figured out that she was my assailant, I'd be looking over my shoulder all the time."

"This is the person to thank," I said, gesturing toward Lorraine. "She sicced her guard dog on Faye."

Lorraine colored and smiled. "I would have done so sooner, if I could have remembered the German word for attack. When I got flustered, everything flew out of my head. And I was concerned that Paolo would attack Kiki, not that awful woman. Since I wasn't the person being physically assaulted, I wasn't confident that he'd figure out which person to bring down."

"Ah, but he performed admirably under pressure," I said. "Thank goodness. Now that you're here, Laurel, how did Faye know to slip you the Glucose? I didn't even know you were diabetic until that night."

Laurel reached for Father Joe's hand and squeezed it. "My

blood sugar spiked during one of the tests I took in her husband's class. One minute I was fine and the next I was light-headed, so I got up and ran out of the room. As you can imagine, letting a student leave a test and come back is frowned upon. The assumption would be that I was cheating. Dr. Edorra didn't believe I had a valid excuse. Finally the dean explained to Dr. Edorra that I was diabetic. I guess Dr. Edorra shared what happened with his wife."

"And the inappropriate emails?" I asked. "He sent them?"

"Yes," said Laurel slowly. "Anya, I'm glad that you're here so

you'll know about this, too. Of course, Dr. Edorra had my email address because students were required to share them with their professors. At first, he was a bit jokey. Just little comments. Nothing too bad. They didn't really cross a line so I ignored them. As the semester went on, his remarks definitely became more suggestive. I sent him an email and said that I felt uncomfortable. Then I flat-out asked him to stop, because the messages had nothing to do with homework. Finally, I took my cell phone into the dean's office."

"But she weren't the one who got him in trouble," said Johnny. "He'd also been sending stuff to another student."

"At least two other students," Mert corrected her brother. "That's right," said Laurel. "They had complained, too.

Unfortunately, Dr. Edorra saw me coming out of the dean's office, so he blamed me for losing his job. So did his wife, I guess. I didn't realize that they blamed me, especially because I'd been the last student to complain, not the first."

"Is that why you didn't worry when you saw Faye at the crop?"

"I'd met Faye years ago," said Laurel. "We were actually class-mates in a women's studies program. So I didn't think anything of her when we were at the crop. I'd sent her a sympathy card when her husband died, and I considered the matter closed. It never occurred to me that she was so off-kilter or that she blamed me."

"What about the women from your church? Were they responsible for the vandalism and nasty letters?" I directed my question to Father Joe.

"Yes, they were. I sat down with the president of the vestry, Franklin Eaton, and told him everything that had happening. Of course, he knew some of it, but not everything. Lucky for me, he had endured instances of corporate espionage against his business, so he had the number of a private detective who could help us. Once the man gathered the evidence, Franklin and an attorney for the church called a meeting. The women were presented with proof of the mischief they'd caused. We suggested that they consider another place to worship, since they weren't happy with St. James."

"But they acted like the injured parties. They had the nerve to ask what prompted the suggestion that they leave," said Mert. "Can you believe it?"

"That's when the private detective's efforts came in so handy," said Father Joe. "He had caught them, almost in the act, of sending yet another round of nasty letters."

"Wow," said Anya.

"Yes," Father Joe said. "When we confronted the three culprits, they began hurling accusations at Laurel. Mary Martha even had the gall to suggest that she was doing the church a favor and protecting my virtue by running Laurel off. I explained that harassing someone and defacing property is never appropriate."

"How did you leave it?" I asked.

"We suggested that they apologize," said Father Joe. "However, none of the three were willing to say they were sorry. When their attitudes suggested that they might actually continue their campaign, I told them that I'd recommend that Laurel file for a restraining order. Franklin told them that he intended to do the same on behalf of the church."

"Can a church do that?" I wondered. "Keep someone from attending services?"

"Yes," said Father Joe. "There's a criterion called 'irreparable injury,' and their vandalism met that standard. Other churches have had similar problems. Leadership has the right to protect the church and its members from harassment and injury."

"That's good to know," I said. "

"I heard you're going to move into Clancy's house. In U City," said Mert. "That'll be hard, won't it? I can help you with the boxing up if you want."

This was a huge concession from her, and it caught me by surprise. Just as quickly, I smiled at Lorraine, and she smiled back at me. "We will be moving, but not into Clancy's house. Lorraine has come up with an alternative for us."

"Leighton's lost all his money," said Anya. "His daughter cleaned him out!"

"Anya!" I warned. "That's not for sharing."

"I heard all about it," said Mert, and she winked at my daughter. "I guess it's too late for spanking her, huh?"

"Yeah," said Anya. "It's way past that!"

My cell phone rang. Usually I'd ignore it, but the call was from Robbie Holmes. Since they were still processing the charges against Faye Edorra, I excused myself to answer it. I sure didn't want her to slip away because of me.

"I don't know who else to call!" he said. There was raw panic to his tone.

"Is Sheila okay?" That was my first thought. Nothing else on earth would put such a quiver in his voice.

"She's been picked up for drunk driving."

***

KIKI'S STORY CONTINUES WITH...
*Handmade, Holiday, Homicide: Book #10 in the Kiki Lowenstein
Mystery Series*

EXCERPT FROM HANDMADE, HOLIDAY, HOMICIDE

CHAPTER 1

*P*eople think that being pregnant is all about your growing belly, but the truth is, it also messes with your head. For every inch my waistband expands, I lose ten points of my IQ. Maybe it's because I don't get much sleep anymore. My skin itches, the baby pokes me with his feet, and indigestion causes a burning in my throat. Don't even get me started on the hormones. Whatever the scientific reason for my brain fog, I'm just not as sharp as usual.

My fiancé Detective Chad Detweiler and I were lying in bed talking one night before Christmas, when he said, "I've been thinking about baby names."

"Oh, you have?"

"Yes, in fact, I've been giving it a lot of thought. I think we ought to name our son Helmut Detweiler."

Thank goodness it was dark. I could feel my mouth flop open. I couldn't believe what he was saying. "Name our son what?"

"Helmut Englebert Detweiler. That's a good, strong German name."

I couldn't even respond; I was that stunned.

Detweiler continued, "We could call him Mutt for short."

I gasped.

"Mutt Detweiler. It has a certain ring to it," he said.

The bed started shaking.

Detweiler was laughing.

"You!" I pummeled him with my fists. "You had me going."

"Yeah," he said, chuckling. "You believed me!"

I sighed. "Wow. For a minute there, I was really worried."

Detweiler rolled over and raised himself on his elbows so he could stare down at me. "You shouldn't have been. You know I can't name our kid without your approval."

"And you guessed I wouldn't be in favor of Mutt?"

"I guessed."

I raised my head to meet his lips and kissed him. "Well, you guessed right."

Kiki's story continues in **Handmade, Holiday, Homicide,** available here https://amzn.to/2S8rBib.

A SPECIAL GIFT FOR YOU

I am deeply appreciative of all my readers, and so I have a special gift for you. It's a full-length digital book called *Bad, Memory, Album.* Just go here and tell me where to send your digital book https://dl.bookfunnel.com/jwu6iipe1g.
All best always,
Joanna

For any book to succeed, reviews are essential. If you enjoyed this book please leave a review on Amazon. A sentence or two can make all the difference! Please leave a review of *Killer, Paper, Cut* here – http://www.Amazon.com/review/create-review?& asin=B07Z8HJBMM

THE KIKI LOWENSTEIN MYSTERY SERIES

BY JOANNA CAMPBELL SLAN

Every scrapbook tells a story. Memories of friends, family and ... murder? You'll want to read the Kiki Lowenstein books in order: Kiki Lowenstein Mystery Series - https://amzn.to/38VkBjW

Looking for more enjoyable reads? Joanna has a series just for you!

Cara Mia Delgatto Mystery Series, a traditional cozy mystery series with witty heroines, and former flames reconnecting, set in Florida's beautiful Treasure Coast - https://amzn.to/3oz9urN

The Jane Eyre Chronicles, Charlotte Bronte's Classic Strong-Willed Heroine Lives On. – **https://amzn.to/3r3Ybmd**

The Confidential Files of John H. Watson, a new series featuring Sherlock Holmes and John Watson. - https://amzn.to/3bDnSWo

About the author...
Joanna Campbell Slan

Joanna is a *New York Times* and a *USA Today* bestselling author who has written more than 40 books, including both fiction and non-fiction works. She was one of the early Chicken Soup for the Soul authors, and her stories appear in five of those *New York Times* bestselling books. Her first non-fiction book, **Using Stories and Humor: Grab Your Audience** (Simon & Schuster/Pearson), was endorsed by Toastmasters International, and lauded by Benjamin Netanyahu's speechwriter. She's the author of four mystery series. Her first novel—**Paper, Scissors, Death: Book #1 in the Kiki Lowenstein Mystery Series**—was shortlisted for the Agatha Award. Her first historical mystery—**Death of a Schoolgirl: Book #1 in the Jane Eyre Chronicles**—won the Daphne du Maurier Award of Excellence. Her contemporary series set in Florida continues this year with **Ruff Justice Book #5 in the Cara Mia Delgatto Mystery Series**. Her fantasy thriller series starts with **Sherlock Holmes and the Giant Sumatran Rat**.

In addition to writing fiction, Joanna edits the Happy Homicides Anthologies and has begun the Dollhouse Décor & More series of "how to" books for dollhouse miniaturists.

Joanna independently published **I'm Too Blessed to be Depressed** back in 2004 when she was working as a motivational speaker. She sold more than 34,000 copies of that title. Since then she's gone on to independently publish a full-color book, **The Best of British Scrapbooking,** numerous digital books, and coloring books. Her book **Scrapbook Storytelling** sold 120,000 copies.

She's been an Amazon Bestselling Author too many times to count and has been included in the ranks of Amazon's Top 100 Mystery Authors.

A former talk show host and sought-after motivational speaker, Joanna has spoken to small and large (1000+) groups on four continents. *Sharing Ideas Magazines* named her "one of the top 25 speakers in the world."

When she isn't banging away at the keyboard, Joanna keeps busy walking her Havanese puppy Jax. An award-winning miniaturist, Joanna builds dollhouses, dolls, and furniture from scratch. She's also an accredited teacher of Zentangle®. Her husband, David, owns Steinway Piano Gallery-DC and five other Steinway piano showrooms.

Contact Joanna at <u>JCSlan@JoannaSlan.com</u>.

∽

Follow her on social media by going here
<u>https://www.linktr.ee/JCSlan</u>

Made in United States
Troutdale, OR
07/28/2024

21578876R10186